When solar-cell batteries were invented in 1954, a *New York Times* article predicted that solar cells would someday bring "the realization of one of mankind's most cherished dreams — the harnessing of the almost limitless energy of the sun." While solar power has become widely used in the 21st century, solar batteries for consumers are still little more than novelties, partly because of the expense of making them.

But that cost keeps dropping. Meanwhile the cost of mining and manufacturing fossil and nuclear fuels keeps rising, while the damage they do to the world and to people grows more and more savage.

When will solar-cell batteries become the world's principal energy source?

Janis and Douglas,
you are the best! Will
you bring your spirits &
energies to Chicago later
this month? John Litweiler
8-8-13

Also by John Litweiler

FICTION
Mojo Snake Minuet: A Novel
(published by Goodbait Books)

ABOUT JAZZ
The Freedom Principle: Jazz After 1958
Ornette Coleman: A Harmolodic Life
See www.goodbaitbooks.com

Sundidos

A NOVEL

John Litweiler

A Goodbait Book ✷

Thanks to and many blessings upon Terry Martin for suggestions, to Rachel Kerwin for the cover, and to Cameron Poulter for immense help with the interior design. Long may they thrive. This book is not their fault.

All the characters and events in this story are fiction.

www.goodbaitbooks.com

First edition 2013

ISBN: 978-0-9798745-2-9

Printed in the United States of America

Chapter 1

ON MONDAY EVENING, five nights before she was murdered, Nora Heatley told her husband Joe, "Shut up. I'm sick and tired, all your arguing."

They were in the kitchen of their small home in Franklin, the home they'd recently moved into. Joe was chopping tomatoes and onions, fixing supper. Naturally, he didn't shut up: "You talk like your boss has one of those messiah complexes. Like God sent him on a mission to save the world from our sins. Like TV preachers. Like Hitler and Chairman Mao and Osama bin Laden. They were gonna save the world, too. That's what's wrong."

"What's wrong is, you're jealous of him. Because he has a vision. And you wouldn't even know what a vision is."

Joe was hurt at the way Nora was talking to him lately, but he thought the subject was more important than his feelings. He chopped some more and said, "So what is his vision? That he's the one gonna save us from the internal combustion engine? Just Herman and you and your solar-cell batteries?"

Nora blew up at that. Hands on hips, three feet in front of Joe, glaring in his face: "Is something wrong with that? Something untrue? Who else is going to do it? You act like we moved here so I could work for a crazy man. You act like I'm a mad scientist. I suppose you think sundidos are crazy, too."

He'd been afraid that harping on the subject of her employer Herman Sorg might push her too far. Now her fury shook him up. He said, "Naw, naw, not crazy. That's not what — Lookit, back in Ohio, didn't I help you hook the electric up to your batteries? The ones that replace fuses?..."

"Get it right. They don't replace fuses. They disable the electric line inputs and make electricity instead."

"Yeah. And I rewired the house for electric heat, everything, hooked them up to your solar-cell batteries..."

"They're sundidos. That's their name now. I've got to get used to it, so you have to too."

"And didn't I get you an electric stove, heat, everything, and put in solar, sundidos the weekend you moved here? So you know I got lots of faith in you, I know your solar-cell, your sundidos work. It's not them, it's you I worry about. From what you say, Herman acts like a con man. One day you're gonna show up for work and he's gonna be gone and you're gonna be left with nothing."

She was pleased at her power to make Joe try to appease her. Joe had finally left his old job in Ohio and moved in with her only three days previously. She had been almost alone in Franklin, most of the time just her and Herman, for a month and a half by now. That meant she'd gotten used to his vision of a world that runs on safe renewable energy — on sundidos, the sundidos that she and two partners had invented.

Main thing was, now she was working closely with Herman, she could appreciate his vision, his wisdom, his need for her expertise. He even insisted on a new name for her invention: "sundidos." Even though she hated that name, she knew he was right. Sundidos are as revolutionary as the steam engine was, over 200 years ago. His vision completed hers. Herman was going to be a giant, another Bill Gates or a Google, not a Mao or an ayatollah. And she intended to rise to the top with him.

Later, after supper, they were in their living room. Joe was reading a newspaper article about another failed attempt to stop an oil spill from a tanker in the Atlantic Ocean off the coast of western Africa, in the same week as the oil spilled in the Gulf of Mexico, off the southern U.S., was being carried up through the Gulf Stream across the north Atlantic. A cruel Bruckner symphony was on the radio — classical music was Nora's choice, Joe preferred pop music — and she was working with some sundidos, the little ones that look almost like fuses.

She was taking them from a sack, counting them, and putting them into small cardboard boxes, ten sundidos to a box. Without looking up she said, "Something else went wrong today. A city inspector this time. He said we have to take down the solar panels on the roof because we didn't have a building permit. So Herman showed him the permit. The jerk said it was the wrong kind of permit. It's just one dumb thing after another. At this rate we'll never get sundidos into production."

It was awful what she and Herman had to put up with lately, new obstacles every day, Nora thought. By then she knew she wanted to have an affair with him. More importantly, she deserved to have an affair with him. Of course, he must be having sexual thoughts about her already, she figured, since he worked so closely with her for long hours each day, the way he joked with her, the times they stood or sat or leaned closely, with nobody else in his office or her lab, not yet.

The next night, four nights before Nora was murdered, she worked late as usual. It had been a day when Herman had hardly even smiled and didn't respond to stimuli even though they were occasionally in close proximity. He had been in and out of his office, busy on the phone, then talking with a newspaper reporter named Ted Sicinski, a black-bearded friend of his who had invented the name "sundidos" for her photovoltaic batteries. She would never forgive Sicinski for that word. But she now was determined to form the habit of thinking of them as "sundidos" instead of "our solar-cell batteries."

At home that evening dreary old Joe said to her, "I called Liz today."

"You would. I suppose you already told her our new address, didn't you."

"Sure. I love her, you know. I didn't tell anybody else."

Nora said, "Of all the stupid things to do. She's a blabbermouth like you. Now your whole stupid family will find out where we are."

"They won't. Lay off my sister. You know she doesn't talk to the rest of them."

That night Joe was silent, moody, resenting the way Nora snapped at him. Silence was okay with Nora, who was moody, too. Joe made pork steak and fried potatoes for supper, which they ate mostly silently. After they ate, Joe softened. He brought her another cup of tea and said, "So how was your day at work?"

Nora thought it over before she said, "Garbage." She didn't want to say any more to her boob of a husband, but after a bit of silence she relented: "The company in Pennsylvania that's supposed to make our battery casings. The workers are still on strike. There's no end in sight. They told Herman that the union is still refusing arbitration."

Joe said lightly, "Course. I bet you that whole thing's a plot. That union's in cahoots with the car companies and the oil companies and electric companies. They don't want you and Herman to build sundidos."

"That's ridiculous. You just think that because everybody's plotting against you." That was an unusually potent shot from Nora,

3

she was seldom good at sarcasm. It hurt Joe because he was not paranoid and his own wife, of all people, should know that.

They watched the late news on TV. It showed demonstrators protesting a federal government plan to build an oil pipeline over vulnerable aquifers in the Great Plains. Meanwhile the heat wave in the south and east was in its second full month of 100-degree-plus temperatures and the cost of living in the U.S. had risen because the price of fuel, for the trucks and trains that transported goods, had risen. When the couple were getting ready for bed Joe said, "I had to tell Liz. I'm all she's got any more. And she's all the family I got. She and me don't have anything to do with the rest of the family."

"She and I. Don't talk ignorantly. I can't stand it when you do that."

A minute later when Joe was in bed and Nora was getting out clean clothes to wear the next day, he said, "Aw, Nora. Smile. We survived."

Nora knew what he meant, what obstacles they'd overcome to get this far in life. She thought about it and then softened, even did smile a little bit. Later that night when they made love she thought, I should push him away, I really shouldn't be doing this, before she lost herself in the urge and the surge. Afterwards, still tingling and barely aware of what she was murmuring, she breathed "Dear..." then realized that she was about to say "Dear Joe." She caught herself in time and whispered, "Dear Albert" before she drifted asleep. She didn't know anybody named Albert, she'd just happened to see Albert Einstein's name in a magazine that day, but Joe fell asleep wondering who Albert was.

Wednesday at home, after Nora worked late again, three nights before she was murdered, she said, "Alice called me today. She learned why our paper hadn't been published yet."

"Your solar-cell battery paper?"

"Of course. What else? She said *The North American Journal* went out of business. So now we have to find another publisher. If that isn't maddening." Nora and her fellow sundido inventors Alice Kim and Bert Dryden had written a paper titled "The Construction and Uses of a New Generation of Solar-Cell Storage Batteries" and had sent it to a scientific journal, *The North American Journal of Applied Photovoltaics*, for publication. The editors and their reviewers had taken an unusually long time, over a year, to approve the paper for publication. At last it was scheduled to appear on the journal's web site and in print — until, as Nora had just learned, that journal disappeared.

Joe: "Does Dr. Dryden know?"

Nora: "She tried to phone him. She left messages. And Herman found out the reason the new dyes are being delayed. There was a breakdown at that company's lab, before they could ship packages to him."

Joe: "How bad do you need it?"

"Oh, good grief, don't be so obtuse. You know we can't do without it."

"You're up a tree," Joe said. "You can't hire anybody if you don't have anything for them to work with."

"They told Herman he can't use another supplier because his contract with them is exclusive. Even if we do find one who'll make the dyes to my specs, it'll take weeks before we get enough to work with. Herman thinks there's a conspiracy to prevent sundido production. That all these things that keep happening add up to a conspiracy."

"Do you?"

"I'm just telling you what he says. He says it like he actually believes it." She knew Herman was persuasive. If things kept going wrong, she knew he could make her believe in that conspiracy too

After they ate Joe's salad and Joe's toasted cheese sandwiches for supper, he said, "I got a question. Don't hit me." That last sentence guaranteed Nora would get mad at him. She said nothing. This was one of those nights when Joe had a calm, quiet way of talking that was infuriating. Joe said, "Okay, Herman's joint has been in a mess ever since you started working for him."

Nora glared across the kitchen table at him: "It's not a joint and it's not a mess. Herman and I can deal with our business problems. Have you been telling people that Herman's sundido business is a mess?"

Joe blundered on: "Kemtrola Oil Company one time offered you a fortune for your patent on your solar batteries. Why not call them back and offer to make a deal?"

"Kemtrola Oil!" She rolled here eyes, then said, "Oh, good grief, I've explained it, when are you going to get it through your head? If Kemtrola Oil owned my share of the patent, they wouldn't build sundidos. The only reason they want to buy it is just to make sure nobody builds them."

"How do you know that?"

"Oh, you make me want to scream. Don't you remember that an oil company bought the patent on nickel metal-hydride batteries? The forever batteries? Remember what they did with it? Nothing. Not a thing. That's why you can't buy those batteries now. And in case you forgot, sundidos last a long time too and you can recycle them." She stood up. "I want everyone in America to get their energy from sundidos. And I'm glad that's what Herman wants, too. He's been starting this company from scratch. Of course we've got problems. That's not the same as a mess." She turned her back on Joe and went into the living room.

Joe had planned to spend that evening at home, at his own computer. Instead, since the atmosphere in the house was so unhappy, he went out into the evening heat. He found where a university-student film society was showing *Singing in the Rain* in an air-conditioned theater on the campus, and went to see it alone.

As usual while he was alone lately, he tried to think of some ways to please Nora, to appease her. He thought, are all these new problems at work getting her down? She didn't used to be so crabby. It's true she's a genius and, yes, her solar-, no, her sundidos probably are going to change the world. She thinks I'm dragging her down. His eyes grew wet, a tear even came down his cheek as he thought how he had to be so careful talking to her lately, like he was a steamroller and she was an egg. He also remembered how she used to be so sweet to him. Thinking how at least she still enjoyed making love to him made him feel better.

The movie got his mind off Nora, off his problems, off the news of oil spills and global warming. After the movie it was still hot as he wandered down by the nearby lakefront. There were lights across the lake and because of the city lights' pollution he could just barely make out a few of the brightest stars — Vega, the Northern Cross, Altair, Antares.

Nora stayed home because she was still feeling insulted by his question about that Kemtrola Oil offer she had turned down. It's like he has no foresight, he doesn't respect my life's work, she told herself. He won't accept that Herman and I are about to change the world. She thought these things while she tested an adapter that she'd invented. It looked like a fat surge protector and it had two size A sundido batteries inside. On the adapter were sockets, to plug in appliance cords. With these adapters, including the sundido batteries that would last for years, nobody would need to buy electricity from electric companies.

6

She thought about Herman. Today wasn't the first time he'd mentioned a conspiracy against sundidos. When Joe had said something about a conspiracy the day before, she had dismissed it as small talk. But hearing Herman talk like that again was starting to worry her. Was he getting paranoid?

She thought about her impending affair with him. He must be sexually inhibited, because all he does is flirt. He probably thinks if he propositions me I'd be offended because I'm married, or something. It's up to me to make a move on him. I'd better do it soon, too, while there's just two of us in his shop. Pretty soon when we begin production we'll have to expand.

After all, she figured, she'd worked hard, she'd overcome more than her share of obstacles to arrive at the beginning of success in life. Obstacles that had begun in girlhood. Since Nora's mother had always been afraid of her husband, she'd taken her ample unhappiness out on her daughter. Even now sometimes, after years of separation, Mom's vicious, relentless nagging could still stab her: What did I do to deserve you?, stop crying, I'll thrash you again, I'm sorry you were ever born, I'll slap your silly face again, you're a disgrace, ignorant, stupid, loser, tramp, failure, worthless, useless slut, you're going to get pregnant and have to quit school and raise your brats all alone — day in, day out, all day long, year after year.

The cruelest of all, Nora thought now, were, what makes you think you're so smart?, you're too dumb to go to a university, don't expect any help from your father and me, don't come crawling back here when you flunk out. Nora hadn't invited her parents to any of her graduation ceremonies or to her wedding. She did wish her mother was still alive, if only to weep bitter tears — of remorse? shame, surely — whatever, just so long as she'd cry her heart out over her daughter's current success.

As Nora thought about all that, she remembered what Joe sometimes said to her: "Smile, we survived." They sure did. Sometimes she admitted to herself that his life had been even harder than hers — their difficulties as kids were why he'd understood her ever since they were teenagers. He was a good provider. She'd married him when she'd needed him, he'd worked and made their home in Ohio while she'd studied for her advanced degrees and developed sundidos in Dr. Dryden's laboratory. Now it was her turn to work and support Joe while he finished his university education. Thinking this way made her soften toward him.

Would she have to give him up when she became Herman's lover? She thought, am I being selfish because I want an affair with Herman? She quickly decided that she was not being selfish. There are levels in life and now she was moving on to the next level. She used to live a narrow life before her sundido research, she had fallen for Joe because she had known so little of the world around her. Now she could see that Herman was dynamic, like her. They gave each other impetus, energy, they had szygy and synergy and all those vigorous things. She had outgrown Joe. She hoped that if Joe found out about their affair, and he surely would, he would understand.

On Thursday, two evenings before Nora Heatley was murdered, she told Joe, "I tried to call Dryden three times today. He didn't answer at his office and I couldn't leave a message on his cell phone, his voice-mail was full. I wonder what's the matter with him."

That night her boss Herman Sorg took her and Joe to a restaurant by a pretty riverside in a small town near Franklin. There he bought them steak suppers and explained to Joe his plan to save the world: "It's up to us people who understand the depth of the problem to lead the masses who don't understand." Joe had heard most of it from Nora already. Solar-cell batteries have been around since the 1950s. She had been part of a physics department group at her university that had researched ways to make inexpensive batteries using solar cells that absorbed more sunlight — photovoltaic batteries that lasted years, that held a charge for months and recharged in no longer time than it took to fill a car's gas tank. The batteries they'd invented were now named sundidos.

Herman wanted to make those batteries, those sundidos, in his shop, so he had hired her to design the batteries and chargers and adapters and begin to mass-produce them. They had already begun scouting for a place to build a factory to mass-produce sundidos.

This was Herman's plan. Since the internal combustion engine — the infernal combustion engine, he called it — was the root source of most pollution, wars, and international corruption, it should be eliminated. Where, then, would the human race get its energy? Sundidos, of course. They don't blow up, make radioactivity, cause global warming, or otherwise pollute the earth, air, or water. Nor do they depend on using energy from a source that pollutes. The sun is a renewable resource that won't run out, so there's no need for wars or corruption over petroleum, no need for nuclear fuel processing, storage, or nuclear radiation fear.

The reason these batteries were not already widely used was because of the cost and the low electrical charge — until now. By contrast sundidos would cost less than two dollars each and would stay charged for thousands of hours. Sundido adapters were almost as cheap. So sundidos would work in fuse boxes and with furnaces and stoves to eliminate the need for electricity, natural gas, coal. It time a few sundidos would power entire cities, even entire states. The shop where Herman and Nora were working this week would soon grow into a great factory. "And our sundidos will get the world out of the messes we're all in," Herman said.

He told it much better than she could have told it. As he talked she could appreciate the difference between tall, rugged Herman, with his little pot belly — it was kind of cute, really — and thick, black hair and moustache, in contrast to dull, bland Joe. Leave it to Joe to say the wrong thing, too, when he butted in: "You don't have to give me that sales pitch. I know it all from Nora. She's who invented sundidos."

Herman, she thought, covered nicely. He said, "I suppose I'm obsessed, so I talk that way to everybody without realizing it. You know that Detroit's going to make electric cars again?"

"Yeah. Sounds good, at least. And some Japanese car companies are doing it in the U.S.," Joe said. "And Israel is subsidizing electric cars that run on batteries."

"I've talked to Ford," Herman said. "And I've been in touch with some makers in Europe and India, too. But we've seen what happened before, haven't we?" Joe and Nora knew all about the quick appearance and disappearance of electric cars at the turn of the 21st century. "But you know about all the outfits that build custom cars. I've hired a little one in Indiana. Just a skilled man and a few employees. They've made old cars to order for collectors — Model Ts, Packards, Studebakers, some others. They've made cars from original designs, too. They designed and built an electric car to run on the solar-cell storage battery Nora designed. It's at least a ton lighter than any other four-door car. I'm taking one of our sundido prototypes down to Indiana tomorrow."

Nora, big eyes, big smile, shot up in her seat: "Oh! You didn't tell me. Is it just for the day? Or will we stay overnight?"

Herman was surprised at that. "I'm going alone. I won't be back until Sunday. I need you here. The accountant is coming over and my lawyer is supposed to report."

"Hey, those car batteries are the sundidos I made. I should be there with them." She was so obviously disappointed that Herman said, "A few weeks from now, after we hire some help, you and Joe can watch other demonstrations of sundido cars."

Afterwards, when they were home, Joe said, "Didn't you tell me you shipped one of your solar-cell car batteries to Alice in Colorado last week?"

"I did. The difference is, she's using it in a hybrid car and she's working on the car to bypass the fuel system that's already there." Nora was distracted. She was upset at Herman.

"He's quite a salesman. Really impressive. And he owes it all to you." Joe said that because for Nora's sake he wanted to accept Herman. He actually thought Herman was arrogant, the way he insisted on dominating the evening's conversations. That stuff about how powerful people were trying to stop him from making solar-cell storage batteries — sundidos — that was just his way of bragging.

Nora didn't say anything. Now she was upset at Herman. Up to then that day had been promising. She had bumped into him two or three times, he had kidded her, and she'd taken a mildly sexy joke he'd told as a special signal that he had feelings of intimacy toward her ("This man said to this lady, 'Do you smoke after sex?' And she said, 'Why, I don't know. I've never looked.'"). They had talked about how they would work together after she hired new people. Now she was hurt that he was leaving for two days without her. Later that night she lay awake in bed thinking, Herman doesn't appreciate me enough yet. Maybe I should renegotiate. Maybe I should take back my sundidos, withhold them until he makes me an equal partner.

Friday night was Nora Heatley's last night alive. That day Joe had gone downtown to the state university, had picked up class schedules and a catalogue, studied them. He planned to enroll the next week. That day Nora worked late again, bugged that she had to work alone this time. "What a lousy, stinking day," she told Joe when she got home. "Herman's accountant never showed up. The lawyer phoned. He said the city now claims that the block the shop is on isn't zoned for a business and the Sundidos sign in the window is illegal and they're trying to get an order to close us down. Of all the days for Herman to be in South Bend, Indiana." She almost spat out her words.

"Your old man called today," Joe said.

"Was he drunk?"

"He said he was gonna drive up and visit us this weekend. I told him we won't be here."

Nora said, "Does he want to come and beg my forgiveness?"

Joe laughed, said, "He wants you to loan him three thousand dollars."

Nora said, "The idiot. Tomorrow he won't remember what he said. He's probably forgotten already." Nora's father had once been a barber and her mother had been a part-time waitress. Over the years, as his sarcasm toward his wife and his general irritability had driven away friends and customers, his business had dwindled. He had retired early. He'd wanted sons instead of his only daughter and he'd always had little to do with her. Nora had made sure her parents knew how much they both disgusted her before she escaped home and went off to the university. Now her mother was dead and her father spent his days drinking beer and resenting how cruelly the world treated him.

That final evening Nora and Joe ate a carry-out pizza silently while they watched a baseball game on TV. Except she wasn't paying much attention to the game. While a Cubs batter was hitting into an exciting double play with the bases loaded and one out, Joe took the pizza carton and dishes and glasses and silverware to the kitchen. So Nora switched the TV to the day's news, which included the current drought in the midwest and south, ending the Iraq war, a protest demonstration against depositing nuclear waste in Nevada, the pipeline still leaking oil in Arkansas, deaths from air pollution in China's cities, and deaths in Siberia from methane gas that escaped from the earth as permafrost melted from global warming.

As the news announcer was talking about the new record-high price of gasoline, her cell phone rang. The call went on while Joe was returning. When she hung up she was pleased:

"That was Herman. The sundido car works. The guy there put it in his electric car and they drove for four hours this afternoon. Since it's not an internal-combustion engine, it doesn't have as many moving parts."

Joe: "So they can make it for a lot less than the cheapest Detroit car — "

Nora: "Less than half the price."

Joe: " — and sell it a lot cheaper than anybody else."

Nora: "Then they'll expand as much as we expand — "

Joe: "So Detroit'll have to make cars that run on sundidos just to compete."

Nora: "I should've been there. He said for me to Fed Ex him some papers to him there in Indiana. I'm not going to do any more work tonight. I'll do it in the morning tomorrow."

It was a major triumph for sundidos. Thinking about the successful car test put Nora in a much better mood, which was a relief to Joe. They stayed up late. While she read, in a news magazine, articles about rebels attacking a natural gas pipeline in a former Soviet republic and about ethanol production driving up the price of corn, they listened to a Beethoven piano concerto on the radio. Later that night they made love again and she again thought, damn it, no, damn it, I shouldn't do this, oh, damn, oh, yes. Her problem was, it was one of the few things she liked to do with Joe any more. Afterwards she stayed awake and thought, I hope I don't have to divorce him.

But damn it, I should be there with my sundidos. I shouldn't have said Herman wants me to Fed Ex those papers. I should have said Herman wants me to deliver those papers myself. Then I could meet him there in South Bend — it's just a few hours from here — I could be there with him. As she went to sleep she still was trying to think of ways to seduce Herman.

On Saturday morning Joe wanted to drive east of the city to a state park he'd discovered on an internet search and spend the day hiking the hills with Nora. He wanted her to go with him, they hadn't done much together lately during her heavy work load and bad moods and since they used to like to explore new places, Joe hoped a day together would bring them closer.

About six o'clock that morning she woke up Joe, said, "I have to go over to the shop and find those papers for Herman." She was in high spirits and had no intention of going with Joe that day. Just the opposite, a night's sleep made her decide to go to Herman in Indiana. As she drove over to the office she thought, what I'll do, phone Joe, tell him Herman called me and wants the papers in a hurry and he says Fed Ex isn't fast enough and faxes aren't good enough. So I have to bring them myself. But what if Joe offers to drive me there? Then I'll tell him Herman can't wait. I won't even call Joe till I'm somewhere down the road. Thinking this made her smile, perked her up like the cup of coffee she hadn't yet had time to brew or buy or drink today. She was going to spend the day and then the night with Herman there.

While she was driving over to the shop, Joe pulled himself out of bed, got a bagel out of a sack, and picked up the weekend newspaper from the front door. The newspaper had articles about Chicago politicians protesting pollution in Lake Michigan from an oil refinery in East Chicago, Indiana, about poor gas mileage in S.U.V.s, and about an electricity brownout in the Southwest, the result of heavy air-conditioner use during the current record high temperatures. He was starting to read the paper and munch the dry bagel when he got a call on his cell phone.

It was Nora. "Joe, something's wrong here. There's a green Ford parked next to the shop, it was there when I pulled up. But Herman's gone and anyway he doesn't have a Ford and I'm the only other one who has a key. Now I'm inside, and look at this."

She showed the scene on her cell phone. On Joe's own cell phone screen he saw an open file cabinet and open desk drawers and some papers strewn around on the desks. He said sleepily, "Somebody broke in?"

"It looks like it. We didn't leave those drawers open when we left yesterday. Whoever got in didn't take any equipment. The computers and the fax machine are still here. This is just the office. I'm going to call the police right now and then look in the shop — Hey! Who are you?" She started to scream. Joe heard a quiet thud, and her scream turned into a gasp. He heard her cell phone hit the floor. Silence. She was the only person he saw on the screen before it went dark.

He was suddenly wide awake. He called 911 on his own cell phone while he ran to his own car and opened the door. The drive to Herman Sorg's shop, a zigzag route, ordinarily took at least fifteen minutes. Joe made it in ten. Two cops were already getting out of their car when he pulled into the lot next to the building. Her car was there. No Ford was there.

The door to Herman's office was open. Nora was lying on the office floor.

Chapter 2

JOE PHONED NORA'S FATHER about her death. Her father tried to get Joe to loan him five thousand dollars this time and said he knew Nora would have loaned it to him if she were alive. Joe also phoned his sister Liz and a few of Nora's friends, the ones he knew. Some of them said they'd call or e-mail her other friends. Two newspaper reporters and two television reporters interviewed him briefly, though he had nothing to say.

Dahlmann was the name of the cop who came to Joe's house to question him about Nora's murder. He wanted to know all about Joe's activities the day she was killed, and during the week preceding, too. He seemed to believe Joe was somehow guilty of murdering his own wife. He didn't say that, but after the way Dahlmann looked him over, kept his eyes on Joe's face, snapped out questions, Joe expected to hear "You're under arrest."

The next week, after Joe wasn't completely numb any more, he held a little memorial in his little back yard and planted an oak tree where he had buried Nora's ashes. Her father didn't come, but Herman was there with two women whom Joe didn't know, along with Joe's sister Liz and eight of Nora's friends, three men and five women who'd traveled long distances, who'd worked with her back at the university physics lab. One of the women was Alice Kim, who had invented the new generation of solar-cell storage batteries along with Nora and the physics department's Dr. Dryden. She was slender, long-armed, long-legged, she'd played softball, Nora hadn't, also unlike Nora she was a violinist, a good one, played in school orchestras, amateur groups, churches. She seemed worried, she often looked, eyebrows up, at Joe. In the moment he had to speak with her she said that it was urgent that she and he had a serious talk, just the two. He was hurt that Dr. Dryden wasn't at the memorial too.

One of the men told a story about what a hard worker Nora had been, working at the lab on Thanksgiving and Christmas days. One night when a tornado had been knocking out electricity all over the city Nora, unaware of all the havoc around her, had worked all alone in the physics building, in a room lit by her solar-cell battery lights. Two days and nights passed before electric lines were working again and Nora who was the only one who had gone on working, because she had lighting from her invention: "That's when I saw her solar batteries were here to stay," he said. One of the women remembered how Nora had struggled in her studies at the university until she began taking math and physics courses, when she had suddenly blossomed into a top student.

A woman reminisced about how competitive Nora had been, how she'd more than once stayed up at night to look up information, for no other reason than to win arguments. Once she'd suckered someone into betting her $100 that Dave DeBusschere had only played professionally for the New York Knicks basketball team. Easy money — Nora had won by showing him DeBusschere's American League pitching record on a baseball statistics web site.

The night after the memorial Liz stayed with Joe. Liz was now divorced for the second time and taking a few days off from the bank where she worked, so they drank coffee and she smoked cigarettes and they talked till birds were chirping in the morning twilight. Usually when they were together they wound up arguing. This time they just talked, and they cried, too. They had been each other's only hope ever since they were kids, they'd taken turns cooking for each other because their parents were usually out drinking or else working at their father's dingy tavern.

One day when his mother had been drunk she'd even attacked him with a portable radio because she'd suspected he'd been conspiring with Liz over something or other. No serious harm but a lot of blood on his head. His father had taken him to a hospital emergency room. Their two older brothers had been their parents' favorites and now refused to have anything to do with Liz or Joe. Mercifully, both parents were long since dead.

Liz knew the story of Nora and Joe. They were all from the same place, Zaine Heights, Ohio, had gone to the same high school. It was a town without enough to keep two bright kids stimulated. They had their curiosities about the world and their sympathies for each other's savaged youth in common. Mainly because Joe had loved Nora so much, Liz had tried to tolerate Nora, though she had always been eager to point out to him what was wrong with his previous girlfriends. When Joe and Liz talked that night she held her tongue and didn't point out Nora's flaws. "Damn," Liz said. "It seems like everything started to go wrong for her since she came here to Franklin. And then she got killed."

"She was just like us," he said. "Her old man and her old lady didn't beat her like we got beat. But they treated her like she was dirt and they were pure gold."

"I remember. Like she was nothing but shit," Liz said and toked on her long cigarette. "S'no wonder she was such a quiet girl. Living with two old bags like that."

"She'd talk to me. Maybe other people thought she was quiet. But she knew me and I knew her. That old man of hers wouldn't give her money to go to the university, oh, no. Got mad and wouldn't let her get a student loan. He told the bank not to loan her the money. Said it would teach her a lesson. A genius like her. She was a genius in science, you know. But he wouldn't let her go to the university, oh, no. And now he wants her money." Just thinking about how Nora's parents had treated her made him bitter all over again.

"When did you and Nora start going together?" Liz knew most of the answer, but tonight she thought it would do Joe good to tell the story anyway.

"The first time was when we were in high school. We didn't get serious till after I got out of the army." Joe had joined the army with the vague hope of traveling and learning a trade. Instead his dismal military career consisted of sitting around a storeroom on a base in Texas and doing almost nothing at all day after monotonous day. He was alone much of the time, so he filled his hours reading magazines, newspapers, books, literature, science, history, actually most anything to try to keep from getting bored witless. It sometimes worked. The good parts about Joe's army service were that his unsystematic reading kept his curiosity about the world active and that sitting around provided more than a year's rest from the rest of his hectic life.

Liz stubbed out the cigarette in the ashtray and Joe continued, "When we got together again, Nora was going to the university part-time and working. She had that room in that house next to the river and she drove that old car that kept breaking down. Always at night it broke down, never when a garage was open. Remember that time I drove halfway to Akron to get her? It was on Easter Sunday."

Liz lit another long gasper and said, "I remember. And after you got married you worked three jobs and put her through graduate school."

Joe: "It was worth it. She was happy there, Nora was. Studying and working all the time, that's what she liked. Cause she was a ge-

16

nius." Joe had dropped out of the university to marry Nora. They'd agreed he'd work and put her through graduate school, then when she got a job she'd work and send him to finish his undergraduate degree. Joe said, "When she wasn't working we'd go to movies, she liked all the George Clooney movies. Comedies. Dr. Dryden saw how smart she was. He's a real good guy. He liked her, taught her good, let her work in his photovoltaics lab. Sure enough, that's where she invented her new kind of solar-cell storage batteries."

"Yeah, I could see she really loved you." Liz toked, exhaled, stubbed out the cigarette.

"Seven billion people in the world," Joe said, looking at her, "and all my life only you and Nora ever loved me. And now she's dead."

Meanwhile, the two women who had joined Herman in attending Joe's little memorial for Nora rode to his shop right afterwards. "Without Nora Heatley," sighed Mrs. Mildred Baugh as they rode, "Herman's sundido empire now seems about to expire. Not quite yet defunct, but fated to perish soon. To become only a memory. Then after that, to become history. And after history, to become forgotten." She was wearing a black dress, black nylon stockings, black shoes.

"Not necessarily," said her employee Barbara Fleming, who was used to hearing her boss talking like a nineteenth-century author. "There are alternatives. Even though Herman now thinks somebody's plotting against sundidos." Barbara was dressed in black jeans, black blouse, black shoes out of respect to Nora's memory.

"Oh, dear," said Mrs. Baugh. "He's right, there's a plot."

Barbara said, "Are you sure he's not just getting paranoid?"

"I'm afraid it's a conspiracy," murmured Mrs. Baugh sorrowfully. "Remind me to explain it to you later." Mrs. Baugh had a peculiar sense of humor that often amused only herself. She was very wealthy, was also Herman's mentor, the financier of his venture. She was of an advanced age when she was often aware of the rapid approach of her release from this vale of tears. Of innate natural causes, or sooner if from natural or other disasters. Like Monty Python's Flying Circus, she now found pleasure in thinking of gloom, demise, and death, at least the deaths of herself and of strangers, though not of some friends. She hoped her own dying would be at least amusing.

Barbara was driving Mrs. Baugh' s new hybrid car, instead of her own new hybrid car. This one still smelled new, and as she twisted down streets, accelerated, stopped suddenly, the car was absolutely silent — except for its silver color, it would make a perfect nighttime attack vehicle. Barbara's car would too. She remembered, "Nora was so much more than his only employee. Almost all he had when he started was his ambition. He knew so little about photovoltaics — "

"He had his vision," said Mrs. Baugh. "His vision of a world without internal combustion engines. A world without the wars and death and disease and misery that combustion causes. A world where the only sorrows are those we cause each other by our own pride and selfishness and callousness and ignorance. And the rest of our vanities."

"You," said Barbara, eyes forward, looking serious behind big, black-rimmed glasses, concentrating on her driving, "are now waxing sentimental. Which is a mentality less than monumental yet more than detrimental." She had a deadpan way of talking, so listeners sometimes did not know if she was serious.

Mrs. Baugh decided her employee's observation was a modest jest and said, "No, dear, I'm now waning. I keep trying to tell you." Mrs. Baugh was obviously in a good mood today. Funerals often cheered her. At her age she got to frequently attend funerals of her contemporaries, so she was often in good moods.

"Whatever. It's up to us to try to console him now," Barbara said. "To suggest some alternative possibilities. To bring him hope."

"However faint a mirage such hope may be," said Mrs. Baugh.

Now it was Barbara's turn to sigh. "It's immoral of you to enjoy despair so much," she pointed out. "True despair belongs to the young, the lonely, and the destitute. That's at least half the human race. But not to you, with all your money and privileges."

Mrs Baugh thought that over before she said, "Say no more. I'll cease adding further unhappiness to your burdens."

"No, you won't," said Barbara without a smile. "I hope I'll reciprocate."

At Herman's office they saw most vividly how the murder of Nora had devastated him. "I depended on her," he said. "She built the shop in back and set up this office. She developed sundidos, she was going to get sundido manufacture off the ground. She figured out how to expand, to begin mass production."

"She knew how to bring your moribund ideas to life," Mrs. Baugh observed.

"We understood each other," said Herman. "She had compassion for her fellow creatures. She wanted to lead them into a future that nobody could have even dreamed of before she and I met. A utopia. Peace and prosperity. She was one of the enlightened elite. Like you and Barbara. I knew they didn't want me to make sundidos. But I had no idea they'd go this far."

"So ruthless," sighed Mrs. Baugh and Barbara said, "Who? Who doesn't want you to make them?"

"The energy establishment. The power structure," Herman said. "I could have solved all my other problems. But now I'm sunk. My whole business is sunk. Without Nora I can't make sundidos."

"That's not true. You can," Barbara said. Today, hearing Mrs. Baugh's preoccupation with her own impending demise left the black-clad minion little tolerance for others' self-pity. "Nora was one of three people who invented sundidos. Others worked with them. So you just need to get in touch with those people and learn how from them."

"You know about the physicist who taught her. Something like Doctor Dryden, if my few remaining memory cells still function," Mrs. Baugh said.

"Doctor Bert Dryden was his name," Barbara said to Herman. "He's in Ohio. I'll e-mail you his phone number. I already tried to call him for you, but he doesn't have an answering machine or else it wasn't turned on."

"Ah, yes, Bert Dryden," said Mrs. Baugh. "I should remember that name. He'd know who else conducted sundido research. He can recommend someone for you to hire."

Barbara: "Nora's husband is another one. He knows who her associates were. Eight of them were at the service today, you saw him talking with them. He'll probably be glad to help you." She and Mrs. Baugh had only met the aggrieved Joe that day, had only spoken with him long enough to express condolences. She felt sorry for him.

As Barbara was driving back to Mrs. Baugh's mansion she said, "We seem to have lightened his gloom a little."

"Too bad," Mrs. Baugh said.

Barbara was not amused. She said, "Tell me about this conspiracy against Herman and his sundidos." Mrs. Baugh explained it to her at length. Barbara listened and now she took her boss seriously. In fact, the two of them really did manage to introduce a glimmer of hope into Herman's unhappiness. Later that day he got an email from Barbara, which simply gave Dr. Dryden's phone number. He tried to phone Dryden. No answer.

As for Barbara's other idea, Herman did not like it as much. Nora's henpecked husband, Joe Heatley, was probably not as enlightened as himself or Nora or Mrs. Baugh or Barbara. In fact, if anything, Heatley seemed to be a bit of a dumbbell today at the memorial, and also last Thursday when they'd met. But he knew things that Herman needed to know and, since he grieved for Nora, he could surely be willing to further the work that she'd started. And to find her killers, which would lead to whoever was responsible for sabotaging sundidos. The next day, after another failed try to phone Dr. Dryden, he liked the idea of enlisting Joe's help somewhat better.

Liz drove back to her Chicago-suburb home the next morning. By then the ashtray was full of two-thirds-unsmoked cigarette butts. After she was gone Joe had a long cry alone again, for the second time. He cried for the emptiness in him now, for all the things he and Nora had done together, for how they'd gotten along perfectly, she'd never argued with him or spoke harshly to him. Except, well, maybe a little bit lately. But he believed that had all been his fault, which made him unhappier. How could he have been so mean to poor Nora?

Two hours or so after Liz left, while Joe was still feeling terribly alone in his little house, he had two phone calls. The first was from Herman, who wanted to show him something that very morning. Even though Joe didn't much like Herman, he needed something to take his mind off Nora, so he said he'd come over to the shop right away. As he was about to lock his front door, his phone rang. This call was from a woman who had been at the memorial: Alice Kim, Nora's best friend, a co-inventor of the new generation of solar-cell batteries. "I'm still in Franklin," Alice said. "I stayed over because you and I have to talk. I'm going to come over to your house now."

"Not now, I'm not gonna be here. I don't know how long it's gonna take me, either."

"Oh. Whatever it is, can't you call it off? I can't wait. I'm supposed to be back in Colorado today," she said. Joe would have been willing to tell Herman to wait, but then Alice said almost without a pause, "Well, now I can't get to the office today anyway. All right, I'll meet you there this afternoon."

"I don't know when I'll be back..."

"Okay, okay. But we absolutely have to meet today. I'll stay in Franklin another night. This is too important, you really have to talk with me. Did Nora know Doctor Dryden is missing? Nobody's seen or heard from him in over two weeks."

"Missing? Why, what's — ? She must not've heard, cause she never told me," Joe said. Back in Ohio Doctor Bert Dryden had been Nora's and Alice's faculty advisor in the physics department while they were getting their degrees. They had worked on solar-cell storage battery research in his lab, with his help. Although all three had invented the new generation of solar-cell storage batteries, only the two women, for no reason Joe knew, shared the patent. Alice had graduated first and gone to work in Colorado. Nora had graduated six months later and gotten the job with Herman. Joe promised to call Alice when he was free later that day.

Herman Sorg did not consider himself a curmudgeon, would have gotten bummed out if any boob ever called him that. Maybe when he grew old he might decide to become one, but not yet. Curmudgeonly behavior, curmudgeonly thoughts, he believed, did not fit with his compassion for all the ignorant fools and nitwits and dolts and drudges and dunces and perverts and psychopaths who comprised the vast majority of his fellow human beings, all over the world.

But living his life in a hick city, really an overgrown hick village, like Franklin was turning Herman into a curmudgeon before his time. He'd grown up with an airhead sister, a doting mother, and a mushy lawyer father, and he'd been determined to escape to civilization as soon as he was old enough. Instead, most of the time he'd lived no farther away than West Boring, Wisconsin and Tedium Center, Michigan, though for a couple years he'd also actually lived away down south in Misery, Florida. Circumstances somehow always drove him back to the gooey shelter of his all-forgiving family.

This shop of his, for example, where he was that morning. This one-story building used to house a neighborhood grocery store before new Bland-Foods chain supermarkets ("Fatten Up! On Our Delicious Hormones, Chemicals, And Artificial Flavorings") and Sudden-Serv convenience stores ("Why Wait For Your Overpriced Artery Blockers and Cancer Cells?") drove it out of business. Except for the solar panel installed on the roof it hardly looked like a place that was going to change the world. But everything has to start somewhere. Even the universe was infinitesimally tiny before it began to expand.

The shop where Nora had worked on sundidos was in the back. In the front was the office, with three tall, second-hand file cabinets (two and three-fourths empty), each painted in three colors, a total of seven colors, and four scarred, battered metal desks: Nora's, Herman's, and two recently acquired and equally shabby others, already cluttered with cardboard boxes and papers, for the employees she'd intended to hire that week. Along two walls were wooden shelves left over from grocery-store years, shelves mostly empty apart from a few still-packed cardboard boxes that he'd moved in weeks ago. Today, Herman was convinced, the smug yokels of Franklin looked down on his dingy shop and made fun of the solar panel on top. But in the future, after sundidos changed their lives, after he received his Nobel Prize, they would go on to resent his wealth and fame, they'd tell each other that he was too high class for them.

Joe and Herman, in blue jeans and a blue R. Kelly t-shirt, were in that room. Joe was seated at Nora's desk, which was bare on top except for a tidy row of sundidos on display — fuselike little ones, sundido batteries of various sizes, sundido adapters, but not her car-battery sundidos. Herman had cleaned up the office after the police had left and it was now almost as clean and tidy as it could possibly be. Thanks to a sundido that Nora had installed, an air conditioner was keeping the room cool. Herman said, "There were a man and a woman in here that morning. The police are saying they were probably drug addicts looking for something to steal, and they killed Nora because she just happened to walk in on them. They haven't caught anyone yet."

Joe was solemn, his forehead was lined today. He looked as miserable as he'd looked at Nora's memorial. To Herman he naturally looked miserable anyway. How did this dreary guy ever marry someone as dynamic as Nora? Joe said quietly, "A man and a woman? How do they know?"

"They're on DVD. I have a hidden system here. See there?" Herman pointed to the ceiling over the front door. Joe just saw water stains and cobwebs where Herman was pointing, so Herman went over to the door and pointed. "It's right there. A recorder in the ceiling. You can't see it up there, it's opaque to us. Just looks like the

22

ceiling from here. It's glass, transparent from the other side. It's a camera that's action-activated. Every time someone comes in the office and makes a movement, even a little tiny one, it turns on. I gave the DVD to the police. They show the man and woman murdering Nora. But I made a copy. I'll show you."

Joe shot out, "No! No, oh, no! Good Lord, don't do that! Don't show me them killing my wife." What kind of insensitive person was Herman? He was immediately sorry he'd put off Alice Kim to come over to this place instead, the place where Nora had died.

"Take it easy," Herman said. It was a choice of words guaranteed to make the listener take it hard. Herman said those cold words because he was faintly annoyed with Joe. He was expecting a compliment on his cleverness in the way he'd had that DVD recorder installed, and Joe had made no such compliment. "I won't show you that part. But you have to see what they look like. I want you to see who did it. See if you recognize them."

A TV set was on one of the new desks. Herman started the DVD then stood to one side of Joe, patting himself on his thigh, looking alternately at Joe and at the TV. Joe watched the TV with fascination and alarm, curiosity mingled with horror, ready to walk out of the place if it showed the murder of Nora. What he saw on the monstrosity was a man and woman entering the office — the man had a little metal something in his hands that must have been a lockpick — and turning on the light switch by the door.

Just seeing the two made Joe shudder. The woman was rather short and thin, square-faced with a long jaw, black eyes, and straight dyed-yellow hair combed back, cut rather short. Those deep-set, black eyes were upsetting, penetrating, to Joe's imagination they suggested cold determination. The man was barrel-chested, more than a head taller, with a stupid, vertical face, long, thick nose, and darker hair in a widow's peak. She was wearing blue jeans and a gray shirt. He was in brown bermuda shorts and a dark blue shirt, a large canvas bag hung from a shoulder, and he was video recording everything in the room.

Her voice was rather low, she was apparently describing the office to someone who wasn't there, but Joe couldn't see a cell phone or a walkie-talkie on her. He could hear most of what she and the man said, though. "No security at all. Go figure. With all this fucker's equipment?" She said that as she was looking around the walls and ceiling. Then Joe could see she had a mobile phone attached to her left ear. The two desks in the office faced each other. Her partner was climbing on the first desk, Nora's desk. Herman, intrigued by seeing all that on the TV, was patting his thigh faster now.

The woman talked on to the unseen listener as her partner unscrewed the light bulb in the ceiling, attached something to the bulb, fitted it back into the socket. "Their own recorder," Herman said. "It broadcasts. I found it as soon as I got back to town and gave it to the police." He was then disappointed that Joe did not comment on his ingenuity in finding the gizmo.

A minute later the blond woman on the video said, "The workshop is in the next room. Veli's going in there."

The man was going through the opposite door as she said that. Herman stopped patting his thigh, said, "I've got another hidden DVD recorder in the lab, there, too. He looks in the refrigerator and on the tables and the shelves. He sees all the batteries Nora finished this week and some others she was working on. Then he opens his bag and reaches into the refrigerator like he's going to take something. But he doesn't have time to take anything. Look."

The video showed the woman pawing through the filing cabinet by then and saying, "...just bullshit. Correspondence with auto companies. And here's letters from custom car makers. Here's some from MacGregor in Indiana. Another one, check out Lucius O. Bryan Automobiles in Ontario, Canada, Hamilton it is. Here's one looks like an agreement or a contract wi — oh, fuck! Shit!" She looked startled at the front door as she said that, and then tried to close the file cabinet. But the drawer was stuck open.

"She hears Nora driving up," Herman said. Now he was patting his thigh fast again.

The video showed the blond woman dashing into the lab. Joe was on his feet, said, "Stop it now. Don't show me any more." He was about to walk out if Herman didn't stop the show. He would remember the fake-blond, sunken-eyed woman and the big-nosed, stupid, balding man for the rest of his life.

"Cool it," Herman said, another annoying thing to say, as he shut off the TV. "But do you see what I mean? That's not just a random break-in. They knew what they were doing. They know what Nora and I were doing here and they want to stop it. Did you ever see those two before?"

"Never saw them." Joe was thinking Herman was a jerk, he was glad Herman's TV show was over. He was on his feet now, ready to get out of Herman's place. But first he said, "If the police saw this, how come they think it was drug addicts breaking in?"

"They don't think so at all. They had to tell the TV stations and the newspapers something, so that's the story they came up with. Now that they know what those two look like, they're looking for them and they've got the state police hunting, too. They won't find them, though. Those two are at least a thousand miles away by now."

"How do you know?"

Herman said slowly, as if he was carefully considering every sentence, "They're working for the oil companies. I know they are. They and the electric companies and the natural gas and coal companies are trying to stop me. They don't want me to make sundidos. Look at this dinky little office and this dinky little shop. They're afraid of me, afraid of the competition they're going to have with sundidos. They're afraid of how big this is going to grow." Herman was now sitting at his desk as he talked, watching Joe for his reaction.

Joe said, "You think there's a conspiracy against you?" Was Herman paranoid? Did he watch too much Fox News or something?

"Of course. I know. It's obvious." Herman, tilting back in his chair, didn't look like a crazed conspiracy theorist as he talked: "Look at what happened just this last week. A strike at the factory that builds the battery casings. A breakdown at the factory that makes our dyes. Franklin claims this shop is breaking some zoning laws — they bought off the city of Franklin. And now Nora got murdered. Do you think all this happened by accident?"

Joe was now interested enough in Herman's conspiracy theory to venture, "Doctor Bert Dryden is missing, too. Did you know him?"

"Dryden! I know all about him. Nora told me. Now he's missing, too?" Herman shook his head. "The dirty little bastards." He was silent for a moment, coming to a decision about how much he needed Joe, how much to open up to this mopey guy. Ordinarily he wouldn't confide in such a sad sack, but this was not an ordinary time. When he spoke again it was quietly: "I need Nora so bad. I was depending on her. I can't build these sundidos. She was the one who was going to build them and start the factory, do whatever it takes to mass produce sundidos and adapters. She and Dryden were the ones with the knowledge. I don't know what to do without her.

Or without him, if I can't get to him. So you've got to help me."

Help Herman? That startled Joe. Time to go. I've been standing here listening to this talk too long. "Not me. No way. I'm not a physicist. I've got Nora's papers, her instructions, the formulas, the whole thing, complete. I can give you all that stuff. But I can't make her solar-cell batteries for you." Did Herman have an idea Nora had taught Joe all she knew?

"I don't expect you to mass produce sundidos yourself," Herman said. "What you need to do is tell me who else can make them. Some people Nora knew. People who worked with her and Dryden. I'll hire them."

Joe said slowly, "I could help you hunt for somebody, whoever. I could try." There was something about Herman — his slickness? his presumptuousness? definitely his paranoia — that Joe didn't trust. So he didn't tell Herman who Alice Kim was or that she was still in Franklin and he was going to see her later that day.

Herman usually didn't want to confide in anybody unless he respected that person, or at least knew that person well. Most boobs had a tendency to misunderstand him, so he wanted to keep a comfortable personal distance apart. Up to today what he'd known about Joe was mostly based on what Nora had told him: A plodder, a guy who worked dreary jobs to support her while she was getting her advanced degrees and inventing sundidos. Right now Herman was thinking what he needed to get done was drudge work. So he said to the drudge, "Something else for you to do. This is just as important. Find out who killed Nora. Not just those two who broke in here. Work for me and we'll find out who put them up to it. Find out who or what's behind all this."

He looked expectantly at Joe, who was suddenly interested in what Herman wanted. Joe said, "Talk to me. What can I do that the police can't find out?"

"What's behind the conspiracy. Murdering your wife is the climax of all the other things that went wrong last week. I didn't even tell the police about this conspiracy. They'd think I'm crazy." Joe was also now thinking Herman might be crazy. True, he remembered he himself had whimsically ventured the conspiracy possibility to Nora — and Nora had said Joe was crazy. Herman continued, "I want to find out who's behind all this and break up their scheme. So I need to hire you to work on this, all right?"

Joe didn't like Herman's preemptive ways, didn't like his conspiracy theory. But two of his uncles had been cops, he knew them too well to have any faith in a police investigation. He didn't have to think twice about his reply: "Sure, yeah, I'll turn over rocks for you. I want to get whoever killed Nora."

As Joe was leaving, Herman handed him a stick about three-fourths as wide as a computer flash drive, as long, and no thicker — it could have been a magic wand, for all Joe knew. "I use this everywhere. It's how I found that bug in the light bulb even before I went to my hidden camcorder. Here, I'll show you." He took a another stick-like thing out of his desk, turned it on. A magic wand, Joe thought, because a red light inside it blinked, grew bright and steady as Herman moved it next to the recorder. "It works on all kinds of bugs. On GPS bugs too. You take it. I've got another one for myself. Use it whenever you get in your car or in your house or your garage or anything."

After Joe left Herman was surprised at himself for hiring Joe to find Nora's killers. Following Barbara's advice, he'd actually hoped to get Dr. Dryden to instruct him in mass-producing sundidos. Now with the disappearance of the professor, this pathetic guy was his only connection to sundido research. I need Joe Heatley, that's how helpless I am, Herman thought. Luckily he has enough intelligence to understand how crucial my mission is. Herman was more surprised that he'd admitted his conspiracy theory to Joe, especially since he hadn't needed to. After all, Joe just wanted to find his wife's murderers. Just what I need, Herman thought, a guy who thinks I'm the paranoid one. I'm just too trusting. But after all, isn't being misunderstood the fate of all enlightened people?

Joe thought as he went to his car, the one good part about this is, he just hired me to get who killed Nora. This crazy guy wants to know. Now, I'm not important. Why would anyone bug me? He pointed the magic wand at the car, thinking, am I gonna get paranoid like Herman? The red light in the wand didn't light.

Chapter 3

"DOCTOR DRYDEN just left his home one day like he usually did. Like he was, you know, going to work. He didn't show up. He'd cancelled his, you know, appointments for that day and nobody at his lab knew where he was. One of his assistants phoned me the next day, she wondered if he flew out to Colorado to see me. Nobody's seen him or heard of him since then."

Alice Kim was talking. She and Joe were drinking thick, sweet coffee at a twilit restaurant near the university. Faint Middle Eastern music in the background, dimly lit Turkey travel posters and photos of Turkish mountains, seashores, people on the walls, young people at most of the tables. Quiet, though, the kind of setting that encouraged conversation. The two had finished dinner and were conversing seriously.

She continued, carefully: "I was afraid something like this would happen. He always worked too hard, as long as I knew him. He was, like, compensating for all the, you know, tragedies in his life. I tried to help him, you know, I mean in a nice way, of course. I suggested to him that he see a therapist. Not mine, though. I had to fire her. She couldn't accept me, she wanted me to change. She didn't back me up, you know, she couldn't, you know — well, anyway, he never saw a therapist."

Alice had been born in America after her parents had immigrated here. Her father and mother were both retired mathematics teachers, both parents were in poor health and expected to move in with her because she was alone, unmarried, and their oldest offspring, whereas her younger sister and brother had their own families to care for. So now that she was living in Boulder, Colorado, she had to find a place big enough for the three of them to live in. That on top of her own problems at work and now the death of Nora and the disappearance of Dryden. As recently as last year Alice and Nora had been together almost daily at the university in Ohio, Joe had even met some of the guys Alice had dated in those days. She and the Heatleys had been so close that she was surprised to hear Joe say, "What does Dryden's family say? He ever call them?"

"Joe, don't you remember? He almost has no family any more. He's a widower. His only son is in a hospital in Germany. The Army took him there after he was wounded in Afghanistan. He hasn't heard from Dryden either. Did Nora tell you he had computers stolen at his office?" No. "Well, at least she told you he was losing his laboratory, didn't she?"

Bright-eyed Alice wasn't aware of it, but to Joe the problem was that her talk jumped back and forth. She had a way of saying so much, so fast, that she was often a few sentences ahead of Joe's absorbing what she was saying. She was making him nervous tonight, too, or maybe it was the strong coffee. He said, "Yeah, he didn't get another federal grant, another NSF grant. But he got the Photovoltaic Institute to keep him and his lab working. She said all that."

"The Institute gave him something this year, as much as they could afford. Didn't she tell you it wasn't as much money as the NSF gave him last year? He had to lay off most of his people. And then the physics department at the university, you know, told him they're eliminating sundido research entirely. Effective this fall already. That sucks like a black hole."

So Alice is now calling them "sundidos" too, Joe thought. The waitress brought them baclava, but they hardly noticed. He said, "Can he move to another university, do his research there?"

"This is another reason I'm so upset. The solar programs at the other institutions he went to were either underfunded or else they were losing their NSF grants too. Other sources like the Institute can't afford to take its place. So there's going to be less research everywhere, beginning this fall — just two months from now. I mean, it's sucky all over the country, just suck, suck, suck, everywhere. Did you ever meet Ira Mavety? He was on the physics faculty when we were at the university."

"Don't remember him."

"I e-mailed him about Nora — Nora's death." She'd just caught herself about to say, Nora getting murdered, but she wanted to spare Joe's feelings, she couldn't handle an outburst of emotion from him just now. "Ira's at Stanford now. He was on the National Science Foundation physics panel this year. Last spring Ira told me who some of the, you know, black holes were that were doing the sucking. He said the NSF was getting pressure from Congress to cut funding for a lot of research. He'd even had letters from Senator Glenwright and Senator Whitlock that insisted the government stop wasting money specifically on solar energy."

Joe tried to remember what he'd read or seen on TV about the two senators. "Well, that's sure dumb," he said. "Which political party are they?"

Alice took a nibble of her baclava, so Joe began eating his. She swallowed and said, "They're opposites. Glenwright is a strict conservative and Whitlock is a liberal who voted against the Iraq war. I told Nora about this. Didn't she tell you?" No. "I can't believe it. My god, she treated you like a mushroom. She kept you in the dark and fed you shit. Didn't she talk to you at all? Were you and she having problems?"

"She had her hands full working for Herman Sorg. Things went wrong there all the time. They couldn't get supplies they ordered, someone claims Herman's violating a city zoning law — one thing after another. And then she got killed."

While Joe was saying that Alice was thinking, oh, my big mouth, think before you talk, stupid, their marriage is none of my business, I just put her down in front of him. Poor Joe, no wonder he's defensive, how can I apologize? She looked Joe in the face, he didn't look upset, so she changed the subject: "Do you know about our patent for the batteries?"

"Sure. Is somebody making you trouble again?" That wasn't the answer she was expecting, she was surprised. He explained, "I remember some lawyer claimed he worked for some energy industry bunch and threatened to sue Dryden and you and Nora last winter. Claimed your research was infringing on somebody's patent. Dryden told him their solar-cell battery patent wasn't on the same process as our batteries. Same guy again?"

"That's not what I mean. You know that now Nora — I mean, since she's gone, you know, her share of the sundido patent is yours, now."

Joe: "You call them 'sundidos' too, now?"

"I don't like that word very much. But you know Nora started me calling them 'sundidos.' It's easy to say, it'll do unless we think up a better word. But I mean, you realize you now own half the sundido patent?"

This was a downright grim conversation. All evening Joe looked, to Alice, like he was seriously upset, on the verge of tears, like someone who was making himself play a violin and concentrate on getting the notes right. She knew that he didn't play the violin, of course, and she also realized that she must look pretty serious too. His mood was lending ominous shades of darkness to her own unhappiness. He said, "You want Nora's half? I'll sign it over to you. It oughta be yours. You and her and Dryden invented sundidos, not me."

"No, no, my god, no." Alice shook her head, frowned, looked down at her coffee cup awhile: Should I remind him that Dryden was mostly an advisor, that Nora and I did most of the actual work on the new solar-cell batteries? She wasn't handling this conversation right. After some thought she said, "We've got to have an agreement about this. I don't know where to turn any more. Nora's gone, nobody knows where Dr. Dryden is, I've got a new, you know, therapist now that I'm living in Boulder, but she's no help."

Alice seemed to be struggling to articulate what she wanted to say. What she came up with was, "Joe, it's better if you and I went on holding the patent jointly. I don't like all the, you know, things that are going on at Sonnestrahl Systems. I came to work there cause I thought we were going to make our solar-cell batteries. So far we haven't even started. Did Nora tell you I had to have her ship me a car-battery sundido last week? It was because Sonnestrahl still isn't set up yet for me to make one myself."

"She told me you're fixing a hybrid car to bypass the gas engine altogether and just run on sundidios."

"Yes, I am. Something else, Kemtrola Oil has their own solar-cell battery process and this month they filed a lawsuit against us. It's another patent infringement suit. They can't win it but, you know, they don't have to. If we don't settle out of court, the court costs will probably put us out of business."

"What's that got to do with you and me sharing the patent?"

She sat up straight, looked in Joe's face: "Somebody has to make sundidos. It might not be my company. Right now you're working for Herman Sorg, right?" Right. "Then he needs your, you know, patent to manufacture sundidos. You know, our patent. But you should keep your eye on him. Let me know if Kemtrola Oil tries to sue him too. Or if he stops trying to make sundidos for some other reason. I don't trust him."

"Why not?"

Alice thought, should I tell him the truth, that Herman tried to hire me and I didn't think he was competent, so I turned him down? And that Nora was his second choice? Instead she said, and she hoped Joe couldn't tell she wasn't telling the entire truth, "Oh, just some things Nora said to me over the phone, you know. She

31

told me how she was starting his business from scratch. It looked to her like he was completely lost without her."

Joe just cut another piece of baclava with his fork, put it in his mouth, chewed. Did that mean he agreed with Alice or not? She returned to that thought while they ate the rest of their desserts in silence. When they finished, Joe licked syrup off his fingers, said, "I don't like all this stuff that's going on with sundidos. Herman thinks it's a conspiracy."

Alice gaped at Joe, almost drooled saliva and baclava. She swallowed, said, mushmouthed, "My god! A conspiracy!"

"He won't say so publicly cause people already think he's gone nuts."

She swallowed again, said, "He has. I mean, a conspiracy! You know, a lot of things are going wrong, but don't forget the American economy's gone to hell these last few years. To have a conspiracy, people have to conspire."

Joe said, "Yeah, I know. But so much crazy things've been happening. Today he hired me to make sense out of it."

"Hired you!" Something has to be done about Herman, Alice thought. Or, to be kind, for him.

Joe's own thoughts had been mostly jumpy, scattered, ever since Nora's death, but that day's talks with Herman and Alice made him want to try to get himself together. He took a restaurant carry-out menu and a ballpoint pen out of his pocket. "This is all the stuff that's happened. One. Nora got murdered," he said as he wrote it down in small letters on the white space on the front of the menu.

"Two. Doctor Dryden disappeared."

While he wrote it down, Alice said, "Go on."

"Three. Car companies won't make electric cars that run on sundidos."

Alice said, "Of course they won't, not yet. Wait till we show them how they can do it. And sell inexpensive sundido-powered cars even in this recession, or depression, or whatever we've got."

Joe continued: "Four. Breakdown at the dye plant.

"Five. Strike at the factory where they make Herman's battery casings.

"Six. The city says Herman's breaking zoning laws.

"Seven. *The North American Journal of Applied Photovoltaics* goes out of business before they can publish your paper about sundidos."

Alice said, "I'm sending it to another journal. Until we publish that paper, almost nobody's going to even know that sundidos exist. Let alone know what they do. Or, you know, their implications for improving the quality of everybody's lives all over the world. Nobody outside of a few experts will take sundidos seriously."

"Eight. The government cuts funds for solar-cell storage battery research."

Alice: "Not just solar-battery research. They're cutting off all solar-power research."

"Well, who were those senators that were fighting it?"

"Glenwright and Whitlock," Alice said. "There are other suckers who agree with them, but those are the suckers who pressured the NSF."

Joe wrote down the two names, then said, "Nine. The university cancels Dryden's solar research. And Kemtrola Oil sues your company over the patent. That's ten things that go together."

"That doesn't add up to a conspiracy, though. It's crazy. Herman has a severe ego problem, he needs to get some help," Alice said. "Surely he doesn't believe all those Fox News conspiracies, does he?"

"That's the same thing I wondered about."

"My god, he's got to be realistic. This country is in a terrible recession or depression, that's what's making a lot of this bad stuff happen. So of course, you know, there are a lot of coincidences. It's just insane to say that somebody, you know, some conspiracy is trying to prevent solar-cell storage batteries and electric cars that use them. If he gets any worse, you should try to do an intervention on him. You surely don't agree with him, do you?"

"Well, he's sure these incidents he knows about aren't just coincidental," said Joe. Right them he was thinking about the video he'd seen of the purposeful black-eyed woman and barrel-chested man breaking into the office before murdering Nora. But instead of telling her about that he said, "Talk about coincidences. See that guy at the table in front, next to the corner? Sitting all alone, glasses, light hair. Do you recognize him?"

"That one in the dark suit, I see. I don't recognize him. But I'll bet I can remember that look on his face. He looks bitter with that long chin of his. Like he lives on a diet of lemons. What about him?"

"Not lemons. He looks like that cause he's sick from too much coffee and doughnuts. There's a doughnut joint across the street from Herman's shop. He was there when I went to see Herman this morning. I remember cause he was leaving there in a black van when I pulled out of Herman's lot. And then this evening I saw him again in a van. It was black colored and he was driving by as we were walking to this restaurant."

Alice frowned before she said, "Are you sure it's the same guy? Even if it is, it's surely just a coincidence." When Joe didn't answer right away she said, "Do you really think he's keeping an eye on you? Why? If he's part of Herman's conspiracy, shouldn't he be watching Herman instead of you?"

"Yeah, shouldn't he? Let's see if Sourpuss goes when we go," Joe said as he waved at the waitress. All the day's talk about a conspiracy made him think, against his better judgment, just maybe that guy really was following him.

As they left the restaurant they both passed within four feet of the sour-faced man. He didn't look at them because he was intently staring at a newspaper article about how nuclear fuel, fuel to build atomic bombs, was stolen by terrorists from a Russian electric-power-er plant. Neither of them looked at his face for more than a glance.

It was still twilight, about half an hour after sunset that midsummer evening. The commercial street was only moderately crowded, mainly with university students. The blocks were short, each one had restaurants, most had bars. As they were walking toward Joe's car and were waiting at a stoplight, Alice said, "Joe, you're starting to worry me. I'm beginning to think you believe in this conspiracy theory too. Have you talked your problems out with a counselor since Nora died? You know, grief can be very hard on people. It can distort their thinking and — "

Joe, glancing back, interrupted: "Look back there — it's true! He's really following us. He's a block back and coming toward us."

Alice: "My god, I really believe you think that man's spying on you. All right, let's find out. We're in luck, there's a taxi over there." She started waving at a cab that was cruising the cross street in front of them.

"Hey, what're you doing?"

She ignored him, continued to wave until the taxi pulled up at the corner in front of her. Then she said to Joe, "We'll see whether he really follows you. You go to your car. I'll have the taxi circle around and follow Sourpuss when he pulls out. If he has a car, I mean. We'll find out if your conspiracy theory is true or not. If he follows you, I'll follow him and, you know, see what he does and where he goes after you get home. We'll stay in touch on our cell phones. If he doesn't follow you I'll go back to my motel and go home tomorrow morning and you should go get some help." And she got in the taxi before Joe could voice an opinion.

As the taxi drove off, Joe realized what a good idea Alice just had. Joe's car was on a side street just a short block away, by then. When he got there, he scanned it with the wand that Herman had given him that morning. Doggoned if his car didn't have a GPS bug on it. The winking red light on the wand grew bright and steady as Joe moved it around the back. Under the fender, near the license plate, was the bug: a metal button about the size of a beer-bottle cap, attached apparently by a magnet.

Joe's first impulse was to remove the bug, throw it in the nearest trash can. But if someone was following him, ditching the bug would make no difference right now. It would only show them that he knew it was there, so they'd go on to find sneakier places to hide bugs on him next time. So he left it.

Joe called Alice on his cell phone and turned on his ignition. He told her, "I'm leaving now. Can you see Sourpuss?" He started to pull out of his parking space.

"He's running now. He's going across the street over here." A few seconds later: "A black van, like you said. I think he's parked illegally." A moment later: "He's pulling out. Driver, that's the one to follow."

After living in Franklin for most of two weeks, Joe knew enough about the city's complicated layout of streets to get to his home fastest. He took a long boulevard that ran miles from downtown to the north. "My god, he's really doing it! He's going the same way you're going. We're about a block behind him," Alice said. "I can't see you, you're too far ahead."

"I see his van in the mirror. I'm gonna turn left on highway 64 up here. I'll tell you when, so you can be ready."

"Okay, Joe. This is interesting. I'll bet you he doesn't turn."

It was twilight, the road was six lanes wide, traffic was heavy, blurs of headlights whizzed by in the opposite direction. They moved from the old part of the city to the newer, with larger shopping centers, fast-food spots, and auto parts stores, the farther they went. They didn't say much more to each other for a long time until Joe said, "I'm in the left-turn lane at highway 64. The stoplight is still red."

"He's not following you at all. We're three cars behind him and he's in no hurry. We're still pretty far from a stoplight."

Joe didn't feel like explaining to her just now that Sourpuss was probably following the GPS bug's signal, so he said, "Never mind. He knows where I'm going. Just keep following him."

A minute later Alice said, "We're coming up on 64 — oh, no! He's turning now!" And then, "We lost him. He was three cars ahead of us, and he turned left on the yellow light. It's red now, and we have to wait."

"You're still all right," Joe said. "Come on to my house. He's come this far, he's following me home. You can probably find him there in a few minutes."

"If he's really following you, that is. Okay, I remember how to get to your house. And we'll see whether your conspirator is after you or not. But I can't stay long, I need to go back to my motel and get some sleep because I'm leaving early — " Alice said. At that point her cab driver said something that Joe couldn't hear. She said something to the driver, then over the phone she gasped, "Joe! Somebody's following me!"

Chapter 4

THE TROUBLE WITH A CHASE LIKE THIS ONE, if "chase" is the correct word, is that the movements get complicated:

B is skulking behind A.

C slinks behind B.

D slithers behind C.

In this chase A and C don't want B and D to know they know B and D are skulking and slithering. Nevertheless, C now knows that D is slithering. But D doesn't know that C knows.

It doesn't make either good algebra or a good story. Oblivious to the needs of readers and writers, of course, participants Joe and Alice were excited. Joe said, "Following you? That makes it a four-car procession. Me, Sourpuss, you, and another car," Joe said. He was silent for awhile and becoming angry as he drove, before he said, "I'm on my street, now. I'm turning onto my driveway."

Alice: "I'm getting scared now. This is getting worse, no, crazier by the minute. We're still here on the highway. The car following us is light blue." It was another couple of minutes before she said, "We're moving again now. I can't see that blue car behind us any more. Oh, yes I can — he's tricky. I don't like this at all." And a bit later, "I can see your house up ahead — you just turned on a garage light. My god, Sourpuss is just sitting across the street from you in his car. He must be watching you. Is he waiting for the blue car? They're probably together."

Joe was in his driveway by the time he heard her say that. He got out of his car, stood in a shadow where Sourpuss couldn't see him, said into his cell phone, "This has gone on too long. I'm going over there. I want Sourpuss to tell me what he thinks he's doing."

"Joe! He might shoot you!"

"Naw, he won't. If he wanted to shoot me he coulda done it hours ago. These bums've got to tell us what they're up to."

"Then wait for me," she said. "I'll have the cab pull up and we'll confront him together."

"Yeah, but see what he does first. He might take off before I get to him. If he does you follow him and I'll follow you. Still see that blue car?"

"He's just hanging two blocks back. I don't think he knows I know about him. He might pull up and help his sourpuss friend. I can't take this. You've got to help me."

"Okay. If that blue car comes up any closer or he looks like he's gonna hassle you, forget about Sourpuss and just drive away fast as you can go. Then I'll get after the blue car myself. And we'll see if Sourpuss still follows me."

Joe didn't wait for her reply, he stomped straight to the street. There he started running toward the black van that was parked a short half block away. He was mad enough to punch Sourpuss. Before he got to the middle of the street Sourpuss's van was moving, accelerating toward him. Joe turned, ran back to his driveway. The black van shot past, accelerating.

As Joe was back in his car he was on the cell phone with Alice just as her cab was going past his house. He said, "You go ahead and follow him. I'm coming out again. I'm going to hang back and see what that blue car is doing. This whole thing is ridiculous."

Chapter 5

ARE YOU CONFUSED YET? Because this story just got even worse. Very quickly Joe was backing out and on the road and the reorganized chase resumed:

Sourpuss (now A) now was leading, followed by Alice in a taxi (B), skulking.

Alice (B) was followed by the blue car (C), slinking.

The blue car (C) was now followed by Joe (D), slithering.

Did Sourpuss (A) now know Alice (B) was skulking after him? Were Sourpuss (A) and the blue car (C) a team? Did A and C know that Joe (D) was slithering after C? Alice and Joe were still connected by cell phone. A few minutes later he told her, "I'm on the highway again, back of the blue car. I think it's a Chevy Camaro."

It was a procession that twisted and curved around Franklin's streets and wound up with Sourpuss's black van pulling into the parking lot of the Sheraton. "We're in the parking lot, too. He's going into the hotel," Alice said. "Good job, driver! He must think he's not being followed, because he's in no hurry. It looks like he's giving up. He's going home for the night. I don't know what to do next. Shall I wait for you here? Do you want to confront him here? Or do you think I'll be safe back at my own motel?"

Joe wanted to follow Sourpuss into the Sheraton, grill him, but it was too late now. Instead he said, "I'm too far behind, I can't catch up with him now. He could hide anywhere in that hotel. Go on to your place. I'll stay behind the blue car. If he tries to hassle you, I'll be right there to hassle him."

Her taxi pulled out of the lot. Ten seconds later the blue Chevy pulled out, following her. Four seconds after that, Joe drove out of the driveway where he'd been waiting and followed the blue car. "Just one guy in the blue car, that's all there is," he told Alice.

A three-car chase now, Alice leading. When the taxi took her to her motel, she said, "Joe, I'm so afraid. Now I need you here. We'll confront him together, I can't do it myself. You can back me up. Now I'm at the entrance, at the door. I'm going to stand here and wait for the two of you. Is he following me here? Hurry, Joe."

"He's not following you. He's driving away right now. I'm gonna see where he's going. I'm gonna hang up now."

"Wait, Joe! I want to go with you."

"Can't stop. He's stepping on the gas."

Alice, angrily: "Well, call me back and let me know what happens."

Over three quarters of an hour later Joe phoned her again, this time from his home. He said, "All I know is, I followed him to an office building. He parked in a private lot there and I saw him go in. The building was locked and all the lights were out except on the third floor."

"What's there? Do you know?"

"Naw. Gonna go back there tomorrow and find out, soon as it opens. Do you want to come, too?"

"I can't. I've got to be at the airport. You know, I'm so afraid. I told the desk clerk to not let anybody come to my room or call me. I've got my room door double-locked. I won't be able to sleep tonight. Oh, god. My plane leaves at eight. Will you know before then?"

"I don't know. Maybe. If the doors are open before eight."

"Call me on my cell phone when you know. I won't be able to answer on the plane, but you can leave a message."

After Joe hung up, he wrote on the menu card:

11 found bug on my car

12 sourpuss man tailed me

13 man in blue car tailed Alice

Back home, Joe was jumpy. Sourpuss, in his black van, must have been the one who planted the bug on his car, he guessed, since the blue car driver hadn't seemed to notice Joe's car at all. Joe paced his house, sat in a chair and looked out the window, paced some more, sat some more. Sometime after eleven o'clock he telephoned Herman, said, "It's real. I'm not crazy. You're not crazy." He told Herman about being chased by Sourpuss, who was chased by Alice, who was chased by a blue car.

Herman said, "Who's this Alice?" Joe told him. Herman said, "I know who Alice Kim is. I've met her." Joe remembered that both she and Herman were at Nora's memorial service. "Did you tell her I want to hire her to make sundidos?"

"Naw. She's got a job."

"You should've told her. Tell her tomorrow. Tell her I'll pay her better than her current job pays her. If she breaks her contract there, I'll pay whatever it takes to bring her here." Joe was sorry he'd mentioned Alice. She seemed to have enough problems of her own without getting mixed up in Herman's.

Joe wasn't afraid. For one thing he had his shotgun, recently cleaned, and shells in a back room where he could get at them quickly. He didn't really expect to use it before the next duck-hunting season. A couple of hours later he turned out the lights and just sat in the dark, thinking: were Sourpuss and the guy in the blue car both in the same gang? If not, which ones were the bastards who killed Nora? Sometime after that he took the wand and scanned his house and garage. The only bug was the one on his car. He went to bed after that and couldn't sleep, even though it was the first night he'd gone to bed without dredging up memories of Nora.

He lay in bed and thought, I said yes too fast. Finding out who killed Nora is too much for me. That's what police are supposed to do. Herman's important, he's a genius and everything. He should get the police to find who killed her. They'd do it for him, he's famous in Franklin, he's got money, he must have a lot, to start mass-producing sundidos. Alice Kim should call the police, too, find out who was following her. She's a big scientist out there in Colorado, she's a genius like Nora. She's so important, I bet they'd protect her.

Except for that conspiracy — and Joe was now believing, like Herman believed, that it was probably a conspiracy. Kemtrola Oil, the dye plant, the battery casings plant, those senators, if they're really connected to Nora's murder. Or the chase tonight, too. They're bigger than Herman or Alice, they'll get the police to stop any investigations. Look at Dr. Dryden, how important he is, how long has he been missing? Did they kidnap him? Did they get the police to stop hunting for him? No, can't trust the police, I got to do all this hunting myself. Without any resources. The job is too big for me. But I got to do it. I owe it to Nora.

Thoughts like those kept him mostly awake. When he did get to sleep, he dreamed he saw the long-jawed, black-eyed woman and the tall, stupid man in Herman's office and tried to scream to warn Nora to stay away. But he couldn't raise his voice, all he managed to do was groan, and his own heaving groans woke him up. About dawn he got out of bed and scanned the house and garage for bugs again; same result.

Chapter 6

IF INDEED A HUMAN SOUL is comprised of that human's desires, then Joe Heatley's soul could be said to have now shrunk. For one thing, when he and Nora had moved to Franklin for her new job, he had intended to complete his own university education, get a degree in computer science. After her death he hadn't even thought about enrolling in the university. Now, encouraged by Herman, whom he hardly knew, his sole wants were now to (1) bring her murderers to justice and (2) see that her dream of changing the world through her solar-cell batteries, her sundidos, would come true.

The day after that ridiculous four-car chase Joe didn't wake up until nearly ten in the morning. Forty-five minutes later he was eating the last of a dry breakfast bagel while paying a Mrs. Backstrom three hundred dollars cash to rent half her two-car garage for the next three months. He lucked out with Mrs. Backstrom. She was a retired waitress, a widow who walked with a cane, smoked brown cigarettes, lived alone in a small cottage half a block from the river on the edge of Franklin, hated police, and asked no questions about why he was leaving Nora's car — no bugs on it, he'd made sure of that — with her. In fact, she was so grateful for the money he paid her that she drove him back to his house in her own car.

There, he figured. If I ever need an unbugged car, a car they don't know about — whoever they are — I'll have one at Mrs. Backstrom's garage.

With last night's GPS bug still on the rear bumper of his own car he drove it back across the city thinking, I'm in over my head. What am I gonna do when I see that guy who followed Alice? What can I do if he won't tell me anything? Beat him up? Inside that driver's office building, finally, Joe looked on the rack next to the elevator. A surge of alarm shot through his bloodstream when he spotted which office was the entire third floor. Just at that moment the building's young security man approached him: "Can I help you?"

Joe jerked his head around at the man. He was tongued-tied for a moment before he answered, "Don't think so. I'm looking for, ah, Clinton And Gore Company, their office."

The security man frowned. "They're not here. The name sounds kind of familiar. I've got a phone book. Here, I'll look it up for you."

"No, don't bother. I'm in a hurry." Joe walked out, leaving the man puzzled.

Back in his car he had to calm down for a minute before he called Herman on his cell phone. "Last night was worse'n I thought. Remember I snuck back and followed that car that chased my friend, followed that guy to the third floor of that west side building? Well, that third floor is the Franklin office of the FBI."

There was a pause before Herman said, "The FBI, huh? Did they tell you why they followed you?"

"I didn't ask them. I didn't go in there. I don't want to deal with them."

"They can't arrest you. Tell them you're working for me. If they actually try to hold you, you have a right to call a lawyer. Call me right away, then. I have a good one and he'll spring you fast. If they don't arrest you, call me as soon as you can."

Joe wanted to say no, he wasn't going to do it, but Herman hung up too fast. Joe wanted nothing to do with the legal system, never, not at any level. When he was growing up his father had owned a tavern. As a result his father had been friends with cops, higher-ups in the police department, city inspectors, and Joe's policemen uncles had been friends of judges, prosecutors, defense lawyers. So though Joe's father had habitually broken laws, serving minors and staying open after the legal closing time, and police had had to break up brawls in the tavern, his uncles had seen to it that no charges had ever made it to court and that complaints had never even gone on the record.

No wonder, then, that for most of his life Joe had no use for any sort of cops, judges, lawyers. Avoiding them was not hard to do, he was naturally law-abiding. But now he had to deal with a federal cop. He had no faith in that alleged right to call a lawyer because he knew what happened to U.S. prisoners at Guantanamo and the secret CIA prisons.

The FBI agent who talked to him was a babe: tall, thick black hair not quite down to her shoulders, crisp white shirt, black pants. She could have been a nurse or a minister, with that concerned look on her pentagonal face, head forward, no smile, brows up over big eyes and bigger cheekbones, the crisp way she said, "How can I help you, Mr. Heatley?" I only want to be helpful. I would surely never imprison you, deny you your rights, deport you to a Middle Eastern jail full of sadistic guards.

They were in the FBI office, her desk, with a computer, phone, and some papers on it, was in a cubicle amidst a row of other cubicles. Some cubicles had other people sitting at them, talking on telephones, typing into computers. Those others paid no attention to her and Joe. In contrast to the 90-something degrees outdoors, here an air conditioner kept the big room at 64 degrees. Joe sat, hands on knees, in a chair next to her desk and said, "Why was some FBI guy following me around yesterday?"

"What makes you think one of us was following you yesterday?" I, a highly professional agent, am also so very caring. A nice girl like me would surely never attach electric clamps from my battery to your testicles.

"Cause I followed him back here to this building last night," Joe said. She was watching him with a concerned expression that said, Don't make nice, helpful me belittle your paranoia, Mr. Crazy Man. So Joe added, "It was ten o'clock last night. I followed him right back here."

"How could you follow him if he was following you?" Agent Helpful said it in a way that seemed she was interested, not mocking. Instead of arresting you, torturing you, I'll merely stick you in an asylum for the criminally insane.

"All right, what happened, he wound up following a friend of mine, she'd been with me all evening. So I followed him and watched him spy on her."

The FBI agent said prettily, "Before this conversation gets any more complicated. Alice Kim, your friend. That's who our agent was following all the time. Not you."

That shook up Joe. He sat up straight, said, "So you admit it."

"Of course. We're not hiding it from you. We would have preferred that you hadn't told her that she was being followed, but you really did no harm." Agent Concerned looked so cool, crisp, and trim, something about her screamed great health: perfect levels of muscle, cholesterol, heart rate, fat, blood cells, zero to sixty in a second. Maybe it was her sweat, which Joe could smell — she must have been working out and came in from the gym without showering that morning.

"I didn't tell her. What makes you say I told her that?"

"Maybe she found out on her own then. We'll have to tell our agent to be more careful. Both of you were talking on your cell phones as you were moving, so he took for granted you were talking to each other." Now aren't you grateful I condescend to be so very informative, you mere citizen?

"Wait. You telling me your agent knew I was following him?"

"Yes. That's why we're glad you came here today. It shows you don't know why we were following Miss Kim. Now that she knows she was followed last night, we'll watch her closely. If it's any comfort to you, we may decide not to follow her much longer." After all, we're your friendly FBI, all we want is what's best for you and your pals, whether you know it or not.

Joe figured the FBI babe was giving him a runaround. "How come you're following her? What'd she do wrong?"

"She hasn't committed any crime. She's not even suspected of any crime. But I can't tell you any more than that." Did the agent almost smile, with pale-red lips, at Joe after she said that? Such a healthy-looking unblemished face, too.

Joe felt his temper boiling up. He didn't like that, tried to keep it down. He knew he'd curse, stammer, and get red in the face when he got mad. "Well, talk to me. Are you protecting her? What danger is she in? Who's threatening her? Why don't you tell her?"

"We know now she's probably in no danger at all, Mr. Heatley. Now, really, I can't tell you any more than that." That almost-smile again, a look of, of course I care about you and Alice Kim and by the way I'm safe and secure here with my gun, and you don't have one, ha ha.

"What about your other FBI guy, the one in the black van that was following me?"

"The one who went into the Sheraton? He wasn't one of ours. We don't know who that was. The van was a rental, we learned that from the license plate. But that's out of our jurisdiction." She was back to looking concerned again, caring but cool and professional.

"What do you mean? What I did was none of his business."

"He didn't commit any crime last night. It's true, his trailing you was suspicious. But there was no hint of a federal crime, so we're not involved. If you want to file a complaint about him with the Franklin police, go ahead. And by the way, between you and me, I'd rather you not tell Miss Kim that it's the FBI that's following her." The pretty agent watched Joe as she said that, now with her head tilted a little back.

Joe couldn't take any more. He pounded a fist on the agent's desk. "God damn it! Between you and me! My wife got murdered and she never once harmed a soul in her whole life, never once. Me and Alice Kim got followed around the city last night and you won't tell me why. What's going on here? Did the U.S. government kill my wife? Are you covering it up? Is that why you're following Alice Kim and me? Why do you feed me this bullshit?" He was leaning over her desk and sputtering.

Agent Florence Nightingale was standing now. She looked like she was concerned for his mental health, like she was sorry but she was now going to call the guys in the white coats. She said, "I'm sorry about your wife, Mr. Heatley. That was a terrible thing. I wish there was something we could do."

"Yeah, I bet you wish. Bullshit! You probably held their coats while they killed her. Is anything you said the truth? What'd Nora ever do to you? What'd she ever do to the government? What'd me and Alice Kim ever do to the government? Your lying mouth — 'oh, we can't tell you anything about that' — bullshit! 'That's out of our jurisdiction' — bullshit!"

The bright healthy young agent still had that superior caregiver look on her face, and she extended her arms from her sides as if she were sympathetic but had to obey her orders. The look just made Joe more enraged. "You're nothing but a waste of time," he said, and started to walk away. But when he got to the elevator he stopped and turned to her, yelled, "Look out you don't suffocate to death in your own bullshit."

A number of people in the FBI office were watching Joe yell at Agent Sunshine. She gave him that sorry-but posture again. She was thinking how easily she could disable him for life with one blow of her hand. Which a good public servant like herself would surely never do. A couple of minutes after he left, back at her computer she called up all of the top secret FBI files on Joe, Nora, Alice Kim, Herman, and their families too, and reread them, beginning with the most recent.

Nothing makes a man feel more helpless than anger does, was Joe's experience. He went to his car, sat in the driver's seat, trembled, muttered, pounded the steering wheel for a few minutes.

He wiped tears from his eyes before he telephoned Alice Kim. She didn't answer — she's still on the plane flying home, Joe figured — so he left a message for her: "The FBI was who was following you last night. They're still following you. They say they're not gonna do anything to you and you aren't in any danger. That's what they told me. They're a bunch of liars."

He got out of the car and pulled the bug off his back bumper. He stomped on it with his heels a few times without damaging it at all. He saw a trash bin at the exit to the parking lot. He walked across the lot and started to toss the bug into the bin. Then he had a better thought, went back to his car, reattached the bug to his rear bumper. He pounded the steering wheel again a few times as he drove to Herman's shop.

Herman was at his desk reading internet movie reviews on his computer monitor. He sighed when he saw Joe: "That's a relief they didn't throw you in jail."

Joe told him all about the visit to the FBI office. He started to get angry all over again, too, and finished with, "That lousy liar didn't tell me a thing, not a thing."

Herman was feeling bitter about his fate that day anyway. Now the strength of Joe's insistence kicked him into his contradiction mode, or maybe it was his wise guru mode, the mode that used to get younger, impressionable girls hooked on him. "Sure she did," he said slowly. Now he was looking at the wall, the ceiling, but not at Joe or his computer. "Think about it. That bootylicious Jane Edgar Hooters told you a lot. She just didn't realize how much she was telling you."

Joe was sitting at Nora's desk. Was Herman's contrariness going to be as annoying as the FBI babe's dishonesty? "Yeah, well, now we know it was the FBI following us. Anything else?"

Herman stood up. "Not us. The FBI was following your friend Alice Kim. The guy who was following you wasn't FBI, she said."

"Sure, and the man in the moon is God. You can't believe her."

"The best way to tell a lie is to surround it with the truth," Herman said, in a tone like he was instructing an admiring college girl. "That's how good liars get away with it. So think about this. She admitted the FBI was trailing Alice Kim. That was a big admission. So after she admitted that much, why not admit the FBI was trailing you, too, if they were? If it wasn't the FBI following you, that at least verifies there's a third gang involved here — us, the government, and the third gang."

Joe groaned. "The guy in the black van, the sourpuss who wound up at the Sheraton, he's from the other bunch, the third bunch? Like that FBI girl said?"

Herman was now looking down, very slowly pacing the floor behind his desk — a small step, pause, a small step, pause — as he talked, his arms crossed in front, stroking his chin. "Yeah. So now we have a better idea of what we're up against. Another thing, she didn't say anything to you about Dr. Dryden. So they're not hunting for him. It means either they don't know he's missing or else they know where he is."

He stopped stepping because he was facing the wall. He turned around and began pacing very slowly in the other direction. He said, "The rest of it is about this Alice Kim. That means I'll have the FBI hanging around protecting us if I hire her to take Nora's place here. That's another good reason to hire her. Who else is there? "

Working for Herman, Joe realized, taking Nora's place, probably using Nora's desk right here. Herman went on: "She didn't commit any crime, right?, and they're still following her. She's not in danger — "

Joe: "They said she's not in danger. They were gonna say Santa Claus was after her to give her a bag of gifts, but I left before they had the chance."

Herman was feeling more and more like Sherlock Holmes, making deductions as he talked, and like Joe was dumb old Watson. He slowly paced, now in little circles, hands behind his back, looking at his feet: "Let's say they really believe she's in no danger and she didn't commit a crime. Then why else are they following her? How about this: Maybe they think she might know something and they can't ask her about it. Why? This is the tricky part: Because it's something she's not supposed to know. And in case she doesn't know she's not supposed to know it, they don't want to reveal anything by asking her about it."

Joe: "This gets worse and worse. What's the government's business in this? Who are the other bunch and why are they after us?"

Herman stopped circling, looked at Joe: "Yes, what? Who? Why? Right now, though, the main questions still are, who killed Nora and why is the sundido getting sabotaged? Once we find those out, the other ones ought to be easy to answer. I hope. Where's Alice Kim staying? I'll give her a call right now. I want to offer her a job before she leaves Franklin."

"She went back home early this morning."

"You should have told her I want to hire her. Who else knows as much as Nora about making sundidos? I'll hire them too."

Joe: "Alice is the only one outside of Dr. Dryden. Maybe she knows if there's anyone else who knows as much as she does."

"What's Alice Kim's e-mail address? And telephone number?"

"I don't have that stuff here," Joe said. He had that information at home, but he felt an urge to alert her, warn her, about Herman before the two of them talked. Just to end that line of discussion he told Herman he'd try to find out that information tomorrow.

"Well, find out. Don't put it off." Herman was annoyed with himself that he hadn't thought of trying to hire her when he'd seen her at the memorial for Nora. That made him all the more annoyed with Joe.

Chapter 7

JOE SAT AT NORA'S DESK. It still was her desk, the row of sundidos was still on top, some of her stuff was still in there: an address
book, two dictionaries; two paper copies and a flash-drive copy of
the unpublished paper by herself and Alice Kim and Dryden titled
"The Construction and Uses of a New Generation of Solar-Cell Batteries"; some reprints about photovoltaics from academic journals;
a Sue Grafton novel; three CDs, music by Mozart, Bach, and, yes,
an old one that Sicinski had given her of Charlie Parker and Dizzy
Gillespie playing, among other songs, "Bloomdido," the title that
had inspired the name "sundido." Nora had listened to it just once.
Joe copied the list of thirteen questions from his carry-out menu
to the computer, her computer. These thirteen are connected, he
figured, and whatever connected them must explain who the con-
spirators were, what was behind the conspiracy.

Ten minutes of searching Pennsylvania newspapers over the internet got Joe the names of the president of the company contract-
ed to make Herman's battery casings and the leader of the striking
union local. He added those names to number five on his list. In another ten minutes the internet yielded the names of the executives
at the dye plant that broke down. Those names went after number
four on the list. A phone call to the Franklin zoning board led Joe to
the alderman who had made the complaints about Herman's shop
breaking the law. The alderman wheezed over the telephone like he
was a fat man with asthma: "I just told the board what one of my
constituents told me. Doctor Darryl Newton is his name."

Darryl Newton proved to be not merely a professor of economics at the university, but a highly distinguished professor who was
famous among economics scholars. He sounded smug, snotty as he
told Joe over the phone, "Your business is on a lot that used to be
commercial. Now it's rezoned residential. So now there's no excuse
for you to be there. If you want to run a business in Franklin, it's
your duty to run it in a commercial location." Joe hung up, cussed
the self-righteous jerk Newton and the alderman, and added their
names to number six on his list.

A lot of Joe's search continued to be easy. He thought back to
his and Nora's university in Ohio and tried to remember the names

of the physics department chairman, the dean of physical sciences, the university president, and some of Dr. Dryden's fellow physics profs. He added these names to number eight on his list. While Herman happened to be out of the office, at a garage getting the air conditioner on his car fixed, Alice Kim called Joe's cell phone from Colorado. He managed to tell her about his experience with the FBI that morning without getting mad all over again. He also told her Herman's theories and asked bluntly, directly, "What do you know that the U.S. government doesn't want you to know?"

Alice hesitated before she said, "I can't imagine what. My god, how would I know that?"

Joe realized right away that he'd just said the wrong thing. "Yeah, I'm sorry I asked. I didn't mean to hurt your feelings. I mean, if you know something, you can't tell me, and if you don't know, how do you know it? I mean, you don't know me well enough to know if you can trust me. No, I mean — ah." He gave up.

"Joe, I'm not trying to keep any secrets from you. Really, I'm not. All I know is what you just told me, you know, that the FBI doesn't want me to know that they're sniffing after my butt. I can't do anything about that. Maybe it's even good for me that they're keeping an eye on me. You know, if there's really something weird going on. I mean, if that guy who went into the Sheraton, the guy in the van who was following you, you know, if he really is one of a dangerous group of people."

"Now you've come to think it's a conspiracy too?"

Alice: "I certainly don't believe that. But there sure is something weird going on with you."

Joe: "Something else. Herman needs somebody to work with him here. Somebody to take Nora's place. He's gonna call you and offer you the job."

"Just step in and take Nora's place? No way, I couldn't possibly. You know, I've got so much work to do here, this company has so many problems."

"Well, is there anyone else who could do it? If you can remember who, call me, will you?"

"Oh, Joe, now you're starting to get me frightened. The FBI! This is too much. I'm going to talk to them myself, see what on earth is going on."

After she hung up, after Joe thought awhile, he realized he should have asked her more questions. He thought, maybe I should have asked her about the place where she's working. What does Sonnes-trahl Systems do? What does Alice Kim do there? It's probably pretty important, seeing how important Nora was here. What're those problems she was talking about? Do Sonnestrahl Systems have government contracts? Is that why the FBI follows her? Since energy is apparently her company'sbusiness, they must have a connection with the government — what is it?

I should ask her all these questions, cross-examine her. Would she tell me anything? No, more likely it would make her mad or hurt her feelings and she'd swear at me and refuse to ever speak to me again. Nevertheless he dialed her number. She didn't answer and he didn't leave a message. He went on thinking: At least I could ask her who are names of those Kemtrola Oil people in that lawsuit against Sonnestrahl Systems. But maybe I can find those out myself.

Herman came back while Joe was searching the web for information about Sonnestrahl Systems. After about an hour Joe came up with next to nothing. The company's web site just said, "Sonnestrahl Systems, Finding Revolutionary Green Energy Solutions" and had generalizations about solar energy, wind power, fusion, a Boulder, Colorado address, a notice: "Watch this space for a major announcement soon to come" — all vague stuff. At least they had a web site, unlike Herman. But Joe did find, after more searching, the names of the Kemtrola Oil CEO and some other executives, including the people who were their main lawyers. He added those names to number nine on his list.

It was almost sunset when Joe left the office. Herman was still there and so was the black-bearded newspaper reporter Ted Sicinski. He had published articles about sundidos, he had met Nora, he was one of the reporters who had interviewed Joe briefly after her murder. Even at that late hour Sicinski and Herman were eating pizza and talking. "That was Nora's husband, you know. He's working for me now," Herman said.

"Poor guy. Captain Dahlman thinks he murdered his own wife," Sicinski said through a mouthful of baked cheese, spinach, crust, green peppers, onion, mushrooms, garlic, parmesan cheese, basil, bacon, and chili pepper.

Herman sat up, said, "Is Dahlmann going to bust him?"

Sicinski swallowed, said, "Not without evidence. Does Joe build sundidos too?" He swallowed some more.

"No, but he knows who does. I'm picking his brains," Herman

said, while picking bits of ham and sausage one by one out of his pizza slice. "He told me about this Alice Kim, who owns the other half of the sundido patent. I'm going to hire her. Don't publish that yet."

"Wasn't planning to," Sicinski said through a mouthful similar to the previous mouthful, minus bacon and green peppers but plus pepperoni and anchovies. He swallowed and said, "Have you met this new sundido woman you think you're going to hire?" He said that because he was familiar with Herman's grand schemes. They'd known each other a long time, he and his girlfriend used to live in a nearby small town, in a commune that was largely run by Herman and Herman's wife Ruth. Actually, she wasn't legally Herman's wife. They had been married without a license by another commune member, a minister who'd bought his theology degree and minister's certificate for $20 over the internet and who'd read texts by Madonna, Carlos Castenada, and Ayn Rand at the wedding ceremony.

The commune had rules. The members had to have jobs, all except Herman, who had kept the commune's books and conducted the commune's business. They had shared chores, the veggies they grew in their garden, some tools and appliances that they bought together. The goal was to live organically. Originally they'd hoped to buy a farm, but they couldn't afford one. So they'd bought a house in a small town near Franklin and rented another house a block away. The garden in back of the house they'd owned was so large that each commune member had a few personal rows to maintain.

Eleven people had started the commune. Three of them had moved out in the first six weeks. The month after that Sicinski had noticed that some personal items somehow had disappeared. For example, sometimes when he'd counted the money in his desk, a few dollars were missing. Other members had started missing items too, not just money. And then Val, Sicinski's girlfriend, had caught a member named Ed in their room stealing their marijuana. The next day when he had been out she and Sicinski had looked in Ed's room. They had found he had ripped off romance novels, panties, a brassiere — the underwear, they had figured, didn't even fit him. The commune members then voted Ed out; later they had found he hadn't had a job, either. After that the commune had given up the rental house and all the remaining members had settled into the house they owned. Cramped living, among other things, led others, one by one, to move out. Eventually the commune had consisted only of Herman, Ruth, Sicinski, and Val.

Herman ignored Sicinski's question about Alice Kim, picked a ring of onion out of his pizza, stuck it onto the pizza carton, and said, "You need to write another article about sundidos. You can make this one about how my company is rising from the ashes — "

"Your company still doesn't have a name," Sicinski pointed out, drank a long sip of pop to help him swallow better, licked the cheese on his moustache.

" — rising from the ashes, recovering from the loss of Nora, forging ahead despite all obstacles, to give hope to mankind smothering under the tyranny of the internal combustion engine." Herman pulled some anchovies out of his pizza, stuck them onto the pizza carton. "You need to show the greedheads who are trying to stop sundidos that they can't."

"Did I tell you what my editor said after the last sundido article I wrote?" said Sicinski, and bit into a triangle of pizza.

"Because they really are afraid of sundidos. They've got a vested interest in the suffering of the people. Their profits depend on destroying the air, the seas, the land. That's why they banded together to stop me." Herman said this while picking two mushrooms and some onion rings out of his pizza, sticking them onto the carton with his fingers.

"He said," said Sicinski through a mouthful similar to the previous mouthful but with Italian sausage and green peppers and without pepperoni and anchovies and mushrooms. He swallowed, said, "That I was," swallowed again. "Getting obsessed with sundidos and I should write about something else and he wasn't going to print anything more about you or sundidos." He licked tomato sauce off his lips and moustache.

"It's a conspiracy, you know," Herman said, picking green pepper out of his pizza.

"You told me that already. A number of times," said Sicinski and bit into his pizza again, attaining a mouthful similar to his previous mouthful but this time including chicken and hamburger and an anchovy and lacking Italian sausage and green pepper and onion.

He wasn't inclined to believe in Herman's conspiracy theories. When they'd lived in the commune they'd brought a cow to provide organic milk, kept the creature in the two-story garage. Their neighbors had protested its grazing on the lawns in front of their houses, wandering onto the street, dropping cowpies inside the town limits. The town cop had threatened to have the sheriff arrest everyone in the commune unless they got rid of the cow. Herman had called a meeting of the commune members, declared the townspeople were conspiring against the commune but that they would keep the cow and fight back and not bow to ignorance and provincial oppression. Later that night the only member who knew how to milk cows had moved out and taken the commune's only TV set with her. Herman had sold the cow the very next day.

"I'm going to prove it, now," Herman, picking bits of bacon out of his pizza, told Sicinski. "I've got Joe Heatley gathering evidence." He bit a bite of the pizza, chewed, complained, "This stuff doesn't have any flavor."

"Joe Heatley — poor guy," Sicinski said, thinking about how devastated Joe was over Nora's death, how Captain Dahlmann suspected Joe of her murder, and now how Joe had probably gotten suckered into working for Herman.

It was about that time when Joe phoned Herman. "I'm calling from my cell phone," he said. "Somebody's in my house. I'm a block away. There's a light on in my living room and I can see my garage door isn't quite shut. That's not the way it was when I left."

"Call the police," Herman said. "I'll come right over." He stood up.

"No, don't do that. I got a better idea. Is your friend Sicinski still there? Let me talk to him."

Herman told Sicinski to pick up the other phone, the one on Nora's desk. Joe said to Sicinski, "Call my home. Nobody's gonna answer, so leave a message on the machine. Say you're the Franklin police and you know I'm there and you have to talk to me. Insist on it — say even if I don't answer the phone, you're gonna send a squad car over there right away." He gave the number of his landline home phone.

Sicinski said, "If you tell me why, I might do it."

"There's somebody in my house. Maybe more than one. I want to scare him. Or her," Joe added, remembering the woman on Herman's videotape. "My answering machine is turned on so loud that whoever's there is gonna hear it. Herman's voice is already on the machine and they might know his, they mighta played the other messages already. But they don't know your voice. They hear you, they'll run out and I'll follow them wherever they go. And then I'll get the cops to bust the whole gang of them."

"That's nuts. You're completely out of your mind. So am I," Sicinski said, and twisted his mouth and looked at Herman. He dialed Joe's number on his own cell phone, waited through the recorded message, said, "Joe Heatley, this is Officer Thing of the Franklin Police Department. I know you're there, don't try to bullshit me. It's eight thirty-two p.m. and you're supposed to be at headquarters right now. We're not waiting any longer, I'm in the squad car, we're coming to get you right now. Wait there for me, don't go anyplace. Is that clear?"

Joe heard it all. Before he hung up his cell phone he heard Herman say, "Let's get over there now." Joe was in his car down the block from his house, within sight of it. He quickly went to his trunk, got out the tire iron, went back to his driver's seat, and waited. And waited. Whoever was in the house should come tearing out by now. But nobody came. Ten minutes. He finished his supper, his fast-food salami sandwich and lemonade. Fifteen. Just a minute or two later Herman's car zipped onto the street, parked in front of Joe's house. So Joe drove around and joined Herman and Sicinski. The light was still on inside. "Did you see them?" Herman said.

"Nobody came out," Joe said, getting out his key.

"Careful, they may still be there," Sicinski said and Joe unlocked the door.

The house was a catastrophe. Books thrown around, files tossed from the filing cabinet, contents of desk drawers dumped on the floor. In the dining room, cups, drinking glasses — only one broken — dishes on the floor. As the three of them looked over the scene, Joe's land-line phone rang.

It really was the Franklin police — no impersonation this time. In a voice much less imperious than Sicinski's phone call an officer said, "I'm calling from the Pacific Motel. We need your help right now."

The Pacific Motel was a grubby-looking place next to the Circle Highway that semi-circled the city. There in a dusty room, musty with nasty odors like urine and emptied bowels, a man sat in a wooden chair hunched forward, arms hanging loosely down, thin salt-and-pepper hair on his head that was lying forehead down on a white wooden table, blood seeping through a hole in the back of his shirt. A police officer pulled the man backward so Joe could look into his gray-bearded face. "Aw, no," Joe said, "God damn it!"

"Who is it? Do you know him?" Herman said. The cop let the man fall face forward on the table again.

"It's Professor Bert Dryden," Joe told the officer and Herman. "He's from Ohio and he's been missing for two weeks. He used to work with my wife. Oh, no, not him too."

"He's been dead for about eight hours," another cop said. "That means he got shot around one o'clock. That was shortly after he checked in here."

"He must've let whoever killed him into the room," the first officer said. That one had also investigated Nora's murder. "Did he know who they were? Did he know they were coming after him?"

"He had your telephone number. Did he call you today?" number two said to Joe.

"I don't know, I wasn't home to answer him. Maybe he left a message on my machine." When Herman heard that, he moved his lips incomprehensibly and glared at Joe.

The same police captain as before, Dahlmann, showed up at the motel and grilled Joe about his movements that day. He seemed to suspect Joe of this murder too, until Sicinski pointed out that Joe had been at FBI headquarters at the time Dryden had apparently been murdered. Dahlmann followed Joe as he drove home. Herman, Joe's passenger, said, "That cop thinks you killed your wife. You shouldn't have told him your answering machine was on. He's going to listen to your messages. And Sicinski's on there, impersonating an officer."

Joe didn't care. At home, he played his messages for Captain Dahlmann. The first was from Dr. Dryden at 12:42 p.m. "Nora, this is Bert. I need to see you right away. I'm in Franklin right now. Call me at the Pacific Motel so we can arrange to meet," and he left the motel phone number. The second call was from Dr. Dryden at 12:44. "Nora, this's Bert again. I have to talk to you about the batteries — I mean, the sundidos. It's extremely urgent. Call me from someplace where nobody can hear you, so we can figure out how to get together. I'm at the Pacific Motel," and he gave the motel number again. There was a third call at 1:07, again it was Dr. Dryden's voice: "Nora...?," and silence.

The only other call was the one from Sicinski at 8:32. "What was that about?" Captain Dahlmann said. When Joe explained the mess in his home and how he had discovered the break-in, instead of criticizing Joe, the captain surprised him by saying, "Good, you were using your head."

The tough cop was silent for a moment, looked away, thought: I know Sicinski, he's okay, so his friend Heatley must be innocent. If he is, do these phone calls mean he's in some more danger? Dahlmann finally said, "I think you have a serious problem on your hands." He had a buzzer to summon police with. It was smaller and thinner than the smallest mobile phone Joe had seen. He gave it to Joe, said, "I almost never hand out one of these. It's for emergencies only. It's quicker than phoning 911 — we can get to you in a couple of minutes." As he was leaving he suggested that to be safe Joe should stay at the Sheraton or the Holiday Inn, rather than at home, that night.

Dahlmann, after he left, realized that since he now didn't suspect Joe of killing Dr. Dryden, he also no longer should suspect him of killing Nora any more either. Not a good idea to take sides this early, he corrected himself, I should think of Joe as guilty until proven innocent.

After the policeman was gone Joe said to Herman, "What good would it do if I stayed in a motel? Dr. Dryden got killed in a motel. I'm staying right here tonight."

Herman didn't hang around long. Before he left, though, he told Joe, "You should get yourself a pistol. Whoever killed Dryden and tore up your home might come back. I've got one."

"I got a gun here," Joe said.

Chapter 8

CLEANING UP THE MESS IN HIS HOME didn't take Joe long. Before he was quite done, though, he sat in a chair and thought. His uncles were cops, he had grown up with his father's handguns in the house. He had a horror of them. Ever since one of those uncles and then one of his father's friends had committed suicides, years ago, Joe had never wanted to even be near a handgun again. He was aware of his own impulsiveness — who knew what he might shoot at if he had the convenience of a handgun? His feelings were hair-trigger these days, were especially in flux tonight, fear, rage, loneliness, pain that was actually physical, that shuddered through him whenever he thought of how Nora had died. And now Dr. Dryden too. But he only feared handguns. The idea of getting reckless with his shotgun, the gun he used for duck and pheasant hunting, had never occurred to him at all.

As exhausting as the day had been, he was not sleepy. Wound up as he was, he could not read or watch TV. He thought of that list he'd been compiling, of questions and of people who needed to be questioned. I need to know more about them, he thought. His first impulse was to call Herman's office to see if he had gone back there. So he called — only the answering machine answered. His second impulse was to call Herman's personal phone, and he almost did, but by that time it was after midnight. Instead, he picked up the key to Herman's office, Nora's key it had been.

He drove to Herman's office, went in, turned on all the lights, went to Nora's computer, really it was his computer now. He pictured Nora as she had looked sitting there, shook off the thought, opened his list of 13 questions and the names he'd added. He began looking up the names on the web, checking out information about each of them, copying it onto the file with his list.

He looked on encyclopedia web sites and who's-who web sites. He followed search-engine links to newspaper and magazine articles, to discussion groups, to blogs, to personal and corporate and university web sites. When Nora's face came into his mind again he stopped looking, thought about how much they'd loved and needed each other, started to cry a couple of dry, body-shaking sobs. On the verge of tears he microwaved water to make tea, took the tea to his desk, Nora's desk, and then searched some more as he drank the tea.

He checked out dozens of names, then checked out Nora's, Herman's, Alice Kim's, Dr. Bert Dryden, and his own names too. There would be more names to check out, but now he simply began reading. It was certainly dreary reading, too, and the various who's-whos were the worst:

Newton, Darryl Madison, b. Sidney, Arkansas, May 16, 1951; s. Curtis T. and Paula J. (Thornton) M.; m. Joan Bobak Sept. 2, 1975; children — Edward Wilson, Ivy Kennedy. B.A., S.U.N.Y 1972; M.A. Yale 1974; Ph.D. Columbia, 1979. Au.: A Modern Guide to Macroeconomics (with Mary Kaiser), 1974; The Volatility of Expocordal Models, 1989; Magnitudes of Logorithmic Fluctuations (with Gordon Barrie), 1993; Logocordal Instability, 1999; The Tyranny of Keynes, 2010. Instructor, Columbia, 1975-79; asst. prof., Northern U.-Franklin, 1979-83, prof., 83-. Awards: N E H fellowships 1977, 1987, 1995; National Inst. Economists Distinguished Contributor 1997, 2004, 2012; All-Freedoms Fdn. merit 2000. Member Schonberg Lutheran Ch., Phi Beta Kappa, Franklin Library, Cato Institute, Procida Society, Heritage Foundation.

Whitlock, Martin Jacob, b. Rochester, N.Y., Dec. 13, 1947; s. Jacob M. and Thelma D. (Luntzford); m. Helen Holiday June 20, 1970; children — Judi Ann (Fingers), Anita Dee (Herbert). B.A. Penn. State 1968; M.A. Penn State 1973. U.S. Army 1969-70. Penn. state sen. 1977-81. U.S. rep. Penn. 3rd dist., 1981-95. U.S. sen. Penn., 1995-. Committees: appropriations, commerce, military affairs. Awards: Best F.N.I, 1988, 2008; Outstanding W.G., 1992; F.O.L., 1994, 2011; Lions Gr. Na., 1998; Pittsburgh Arts H.F., 2002; Boy Scouts H.F.F., 2003; Ch. Bl. P. and T, 2006; Honorary Ph.D. Penn State 1994, Penn 1995, Haverford 2000, Beaver 2001, Sonoma State 2002, Shippensburg 2003, Pitt 2010, Reading 2013. Member St. Paul's Epis. Ch. of Pittsburgh, Intl. Lions Club, Intl. Kiwanis Club, Pittsburgh Sym., Pittsburgh Mus. of Nat. Hist., Pittsburgh Art Inst., Pittsburgh Hist. Soc., Phila. Inst. of Art, University Club, Procida Society, Sierra Club, USW, NRA, YMCA, ACLU, blah, blah, on and on, more and more tiresome the more Joe read.

Eventually, as pre-dawn was beginning to lighten the sky, Joe finally grew tired. He e-mailed a copy of his list and search results to his own e-mail address, closed down Herman's office, and drove home.

Late the next afternoon Herman was at his desk in blue jeans and a yellow WFSU t-shirt, thinking about the Nobel Prize that may be slipping out of his grasp after all. Would it be the Nobel Science Prize? No, more likely his would be the Nobel Peace Prize for the way sundidos end wars and bring about longer lives in the world. But he would only get the prize if he manufactured sundidos. Oh, how he needed some sundido expert to take Nora's place — and these thought brought him back to reality. Joe was also at the office, at Nora's desk, red-eyed and unshaven. He said, "I think I got something here." Herman did not like his reverie interrupted. He said nothing, did not even turn around to look at Joe, who said, "Google Procida Society."

"No, I won't. Tell me what you found out," Herman said. It was a cloudy day outside, off-and-on rain had come a little earlier. Reality was making him gloomy again. Some days you eat shit, he had come to believe, and the other days shit eats you. Seeing his employee looking so beat at the next desk only darkened Herman's mood.

"I want you to see for yourself what I found."

"Come on, I'm not playing some game here. Did you find out who murdered your wife and who's trying to destroy sundidos?"

"I got what looks like it might be our first lead. Our only lead up to now. Google Procida Society."

"Your one and only lead. All right," Herman sighed. "This better be good. Spell Procida Society." Joe did. A few seconds later Herman said, "Okay, this says 'A literary society devoted to the advancement of human progress and nurturing of,' and it stops there. Doesn't say what they nurture. Now I'm clicking on their web site. It says '404 Error.'" A few moments later Herman said, "The only other hits are some articles by someone named Richard Hoover. Titles are 'Regulating Conservation: A Survey,' 'Liberty in Crisis,' 'The Necessity of Moderation' — looks like deep stuff, we have to pay the web sites to read the articles. There's three, no, four of them..."

"See what it says about what this Dick Hoover has to do with the Procida Society."

"Only that under his byline it says 'Secretary of Procida Society.' Nothing here about him and solar energy. This is your clue? What makes it a clue?"

"Right," Joe said."Those're all I got on the Procida Society, too, from all the search engines I used. It's like they almost don't exist, from all the web doesn't say. But now get this. Out of these 74 people I got on my list, I found 61 of them belong to the Procida Society. That's what they got in common the most. Some of them come from the same places, got the same religions, went to the same schools, joined the same web forums, some of them belong to the same professional groups or fraternities or whatever. Mostly, they got nothing to do with each other and they got different political attitudes. But what 61 of them have in common is this society, whatever it is."

Herman said nothing, just looked at his monitor. Joe went on, "And those 61 are seven of the senators on the energy committee, and big officials of these car and truck companies and oil companies I looked up, and people like that. This Professor Newton, too, the one who wants the city to close down your shop, he belongs too. So, see, some of the most relevant people, relevant to your problems, they're members. I don't know, there's maybe more than 61, cause there's no way to tell about a lot of these people. Not enough information. Now google Procida, just that one word."

Herman did. "Okay, I see it. Here's a map. It's in the Bay Of Naples, Italy."

"And Naples is a corrupt Mafia city. That's famous."

"That makes your society a Mafia thing? You don't know that. If you don't have enough information about your Procidas," Herman said, "there's probably some other connections you don't know about. Maybe more than 61. Maybe more relevant than the Procida Society."

"Yeah, but all we can go with is what we know," Joe said. "I'm gonna hunt some more."

"Did you call Alice Kim?"

Joe was surprised: "No. I've been working on this."

"Ahh," Herman said. It was a sound of disgust. "Well, what is Alice Kim's e-mail address? And her phone number? So I can hire her."

Joe was preoccupied with the Procida Society and he would have preferred to evade the subject of Alice Kim. Instead he told the truth: "I'm not gonna drag somebody new into this mess before you know more about it yourself."

"Hey, hold on here. I hired you to help get this business going again." But Herman didn't pursue the Alice Kim subject for the time being. Joe was getting him, too, interested in this Procida Society.

Herman soon left for the evening. Joe did not want to go home, did not like to be there this evening when he was afraid he'd think about Nora even more. He stayed at Nora's desk and hunted some more on the web, checking out lists of clubs, city directories, phone directories, country directories. He got a cell-phone call from Alice: "There's an FBI office in Boulder so I went there today and confronted them. I'm afraid I lost my temper. They wouldn't tell me anything. They wouldn't even admit they were following me."

By then Joe wasn't thinking about the Sonnestrahl questions he'd meant to ask her yesterday. He told her about discovering Dr. Dryden's body last night and about the break-in at his own house, told her Herman was insistent about wanting to hire her. Joe was relieved, for Alice's sake, that she refused to let him tell Herman how to contact her. She concluded the conversation by saying, "You've made me so frightened about this conspiracy or whatever it is."

Joe kept working at Nora's desk till hunger became too much, then e-mailed his results to his own computer. He stopped at a restaurant on the way home, ate a hamburger, drank a chocolate milk shake. At home he went back to work on his own computer, a computer he had built himself when they'd lived in Ohio.

One thing wrong with making sundidos to save mankind was the the business occupied so much of Herman's time. He liked to live in university cities or towns. In places like that he'd go to the student unions or to coffee shops, bars, places where students and other smart young people went. He'd strike up conversations, gain the attention, then the admiration of young women for his explanations of the balance of nature, the ecology of mankind and nature, and by contrast how perversions like racism and sexism were as contrary to the ecology as air and water pollution.

He'd done some of that since he'd moved back to Franklin, but it seemed there were fewer exceptional babes these days, appetizing ladies aware enough to appreciate his vision. And especially lately he'd been so busy working with Nora and now with Joe that he had no social life any more. Now he realized he was missing the attention of admiring ladies. He was turning into a hermit monk. All that was now making him unhappy.

Herman spent the evening at home. He telephoned his parents

to give a progress report. His mother answered. She had trouble hearing and understanding Herman's problems, so the phone call was a struggle. Mom Sorg was Herman's original backer, the wife of a lawyer for a major developer. Herman had sold his parents on his plan to start a revolutionary photovoltaic corporation one day when they'd dropped acid together. It was Mom who had written the check that had set Herman up in business. Mom and Dad Sorg had in their youths been free spirits who had met long ago at an early Grateful Dead concert in California. They still had their collections of old *Mr. Natural* and *Fabulous Furry Freak Brothers* comics and they still grooved to Gregorian chants CDs on weekends.

Herman thought about trying again to hire Alice Kim, was bugged that Joe didn't come up with a way to contact her. He liked the fact that now the only person who could make sundidos was another woman. He had good luck working with women. He tried to remember if he'd thought Alice was one he'd wanted to sleep with.

He thought about what it would be like once she got his business running. Before long a Hollywood director would surely want to film a biography of his life. The love interest in the movie, Sandra Bullock or Nicole Kidman or someone like that, would surely have to move in with him, get next to him, in order to learn how to act her role right. As a result the papparazzi would flock around him and he would be interviewed on celebrity TV shows. Come to think, he would have the right to choose which actor and actress would portray him and his love interest. Which meant he'd have to select who she'd be by sleeping with the actresses who wanted the job. It's tough changing the destiny of mankind, he thought, but somebody's got to do it.

He was back to brooding about how events were turning against him when, sometime after 10 p.m., Joe phoned him. Joe said, "I found a private club register that repeats that bull about how the Procida Society is a literary club — "

"How do you know it's bull?" It was a sign of how pitiful Herman's life had become that poor Joe was the only person who seemed to be doing anything for him these days. On top of Herman's unhappiness about the sundido business, the phone call was interrupting his journey to the refrigerator for a bottle of beer. He was bugged. He said, "Do you read books? Maybe we should join this literary club."

"We can't join it. Membership is invitation only." Herman's laconic attitude bugged Joe, so he needled Herman: "Maybe you can get your Professor Newton to invite you."

By then Herman was at the refrigerator. He opened a bottle of Franklin Pride Beer before he said, "Maybe I can. Trying it can't fail any worse than anything else we've done lately. He and I could go to Procida Society meetings together. At least I could meet the enemy that way, see what he looks like." Herman got the beer out, closed the refrigerator door.

"You'd have to go to New York City for those meetings. That's the only Procida Society location in America. None in Canada, but there's one in Mexico City, or you could go to Paris or London or Zurich. Or Capetown, Cairo, Tel Aviv, Mumbai, Beijing, on and on like that. Far as I've found out so far, there's a Procida Society in about 50 countries in the world. Mostly bigger countries, I mean more population. Mostly in the capitals."

Herman took a drink from the bottle before he said, "That makes it a secret international literary society. Maybe they're a dirty book club, that's why they're so secret."

Was Herman trying to be funny? Joe didn't want that. He said, "Well, I'm gonna find out what they're up to, whether you like it or not."

"So do it. It's the nearest thing you've got to a lead yet. What do you mean like it or not?"

Joe said, "I mean I got their New York address. I'm going there. Meet them face to face"

"Sure. You've got nothing to lose. First, though, tell me how to reach Alice Kim."

"I told you already. She knows you want someone to replace Nora. She said she can't quit her job."

"Damn it, she hasn't heard my offer yet. Just tell me her e-mail and phone number."

"I'm not gonna do it. She said she doesn't want to talk to you."

What made Joe think he had the right to talk to him like that? "God damn it. I've got a sundido business to run. Give me her phone number and e-mail address or I'll fire you."

Joe's reply was immediate: "Okay, I'm fired. Good-bye. But I'm still gonna go to New York City and look over the Procida Society."

"God damn it," Herman said again, and then quickly, before Joe could hang up: "Okay, you're not fired. Go to New York tomorrow. I'll reserve a plane and a hotel room in Manhattan for you. But you'd better get the Procida Society or whoever it is off my ass." He stopped an instant before he said, "I'll contact Alice Kim without your help."

A little later Herman, after making plane and hotel reservations for Joe, thought, yeah, you go away to New York. Damn, the whole sundido revolution might depend on something you do or you find out tomorrow. It might be the turning point in freeing mankind from pollution, war, economic disaster. While you're doing that I'll just waste time here in Franklin. I can't get Sicinski to write about me, the other reporters are even worse. I'll call Alice Kim, she'll say she won't work for me. Nora, Dryden dead and the rest of the bastards have me stymied. Well, suffering is what makes a person soulful. And I sure have been suffering all my life.

He realized that, in contrast to his own gloomy situation in Franklin, tomorrow Joe might solve this whole conspiracy mystery. He was half tempted to call Joe and say he would join him in New York. Instead he just had another beer. More realistically, he also realized how much he wanted Joe to succeed and he hoped Joe was right about the Procida Society. The realizations made him more depressed. What obstacles did his peers, Galileo, Darwin, Freud, Hugh Hefner, have to overcome before they improved mankind?

The next day Joe didn't check out the Procida Society. That was only because his plane didn't land at JFK airport until late afternoon and it took two hours to get to where he was staying in Manhattan. Joe was unused to luxury when he traveled. Staying at a YMCA would have been his natural choice, but instead he checked into an expensive midtown hotel where Herman had booked him.

As the sun was setting beyond the ferociously hot city he took a bus to Fifth Avenue and got out at the Procida Society address. The society's building faced Central Park, which looked green and cheerful, with plenty of adults and kids about even that late. But the building itself was forbidding: A ten-story building, set back from the sidewalk, that looked like a fortress in the twilight shadows, with thick granite walls, in a comparatively dark place surrounded on three sides by much taller buildings. The long windows on the ground floor were so skinny, with various shades of dark-colored glass, that Joe couldn't tell if anything was going on inside.

Certainly he saw nobody go up the three wide marble steps to the arched doorway. Just inside, Joe could see there was a doorman in a uniform, with braids and epaulets, that an actor portraying an old European general might have worn in an old movie comedy. In fact, his fat face had such a stern, haughty look that for a moment Joe wished he had a custard pie handy. It was almost the first time Joe had smiled that day. That evening he walked over to Broadway, killed time in a bookstore, thought about Nora and became sad, and went back to his big hotel room.

The next day was just as hot. Joe woke up late and after a pastrami sandwich and egg cream breakfast he took a bus back to the Procida Society. In the midday light it was still in shadows, still forbidding. The doorman this time had a face that wasn't so fat, but as he looked down at Joe, who was actually the same height, this one too had a stern, snotty look and he too was wearing a uniform that looked like it belonged to a musical comedy general. The uniform must have made the doorman hot, the day was humid, sweaty. When Joe went up the three steps, the general made no move to open the door for him. But when Joe crossed the threshold, the general stepped forward, raised an arm in front of him, said, "I beg your pardon, sir."

Joe was taken aback. He said, "You don't have to beg. Drop your arm and I'll pardon you," and he pushed at the arm.

The arm didn't yield. The general said, "Only members are allowed to enter, sir."

"Yeah, well, I came here to sign up for a membership."

"Membership is by recommendation only. I'm sorry, sir."

"Yeah, sure. That's why I'm going in here now. I'm gonna get some of my friends to recommend me. You want me to tell my buddies Senator Glenwright and Senator Whitlock about how you won't let me in?"

The general hesitated slightly, for an instant. It was just enough that Joe was able to push his arm aside and walk into the Procida Society. He was in a dark lobby with a few dim lightbulbs on the wall, thick-carpeted floor, a few small chairs and two long chairs that looked like very old backbreakers — did anyone ever actually sit in them? At the front desk a fat, grey-haired clerk glanced at Joe, waved an arm toward the hall on the left and said, "That way, sir," and went back to whatever he was doing.

A little weird that the clerk seemed to recognize someone he'd never seen before. Joe looked back at the front door — the general hadn't followed him inside, but was standing at his post looking out at Central Park. So apparently he, like the clerk, had decided Joe was no threat to the club. That way, huh? Turning left, he tromped down a new-looking Persian carpet with an intricate design, to a door, opened it, entered. The door closed behind him, clicked shut.

The only person in this room was a slender black woman with hoop earrings and shining scarlet lips and fingernails who sat at her desk and looked up at Joe without the least curiosity. "Mr. Heatley, have a seat," she said and waved a bright red-lacquered fingernail toward a chair. "I'll tell Mr. Patrick you're here."

What? Joe took at least fifteen thoroughly surprised seconds before he said, "How'd you know who I am?" The chairs here looked less uncomfortable than those in the lobby. Joe sat in one, quite dazed and weirded out at what the woman had just said.

"He's here now, Mr. Patrick," she was saying into a telephone. When she hung up she said to Joe, "We knew you were coming. We've been looking forward to meeting you." Those were just words, she said it with something that might have been a smile on her face and a professionally warm voice, and went back to doing whatever she'd been doing at her desk.

What's going on? Is my phone tapped, is Sourpuss still dragging around after me, who, what? Joe watched her fuss with her computer and wondered what made them expect him. There were two doors to this room where he was waiting. It suddenly occurred to Joe to get up, go back to the door where he came in, try to open it — No. He said, "Hey, this is locked."

The woman, with a smile-like look on her face, glanced at him, said, "It'll be all right. Mr. Patrick's on his way," and returned to her computer.

Joe went back to his chair, sat. He felt a sudden rush of the familiar helpless feeling. His voice was almost steady, though, when he said, "How about Herman Sorg? Are you looking forward to meeting him, too?"

The woman looked up from the computer screen with another empty smile, or something like a smile. "Sorg — oh, yes. We want to see him too. Here's Mr. Patrick."

The other door, which was next to her desk, opened and Mr. Patrick entered. Or rather, he strode in, tall, thick, solid, in a gray suit, a smile on his face. Joe stood up and said to him, "How'd you know who I am? What made you think I was coming here?"

"Hello, Joe. I'm Maxwell Patrick. We know a great deal about you — we have very good, trustworthy sources." And Patrick chuckled. It wasn't a sinister chuckle, but Joe didn't like it, didn't like Patrick's smile, didn't see anything to smile about. At least Patrick didn't offer to shake hands. Instead he said "Come with me," and led Joe to the second door, past the woman at the desk, who was now typing something into her computer. "I know you're probably expecting something threatening or ominous about us — unfortunately, some people who come to look in on us feel that way. But that's not really what we're about at all. Basically, you'll find we're a humanitarian organization, which is why I hope you'll choose to join" — Patrick was opening the door for Joe as he said that.

As Joe walked in, three men in the room came toward him. They were in suits, too, and they looked as strong as Patrick, but they didn't smile like he did. One of them was Sourpuss. Patrick, who now had his big paws on Joe's back, said, "Now, Joe, everything's going to be all right."

"Hey, what's — what're you doing?" Joe yelped. He began a string of curses as Sourpuss and one of the other men gripped his arms. They managed to sidestep his attempts to kick them. The third rolled up Joe's right sleeve, rubbed some alcohol on Joe's arm.

Patrick now was holding Joe in a bear hug and repeating, "Now, Joe, it's okay, take it easy, don't make us use the taser now, Joe."

Joe continued struggling as the third big goon injected him with a hypodermic needle. "You bastard," he said as a back-kick finally landed on Patrick's shin.

"Ooh, no, Joe, don't," Patrick shot out as he lost his grip on Joe. "We just want to help you." Those were the last words Joe heard as he turned partly backward. He tried to yank his arms away from the two goons. Instead, his legs gave out under him. Patrick grabbed him again just in time to keep him from falling to the floor. By then Joe was no longer conscious.

Chapter 9

THE ROOM WAS SURELY COMFORTABLE: thick gray carpet, two plush chairs, a desk with a chair, computer terminal, printer, and keyboard. One wall was all dark-brown oak bookshelves full of books. There was a sink in one corner and a small refrigerator next to it, then a counter with a coffeemaker and a microwave. It was almost a pleasant room, almost inviting. Except it had no windows and one side had bars instead of a wall. The bars made it a cell, not a room. Joe came to consciousness there, lying atop a day-bed.

He lay there for a long time, still groggy from the drug, trying to will himself to get up and occasionally dozing off for brief spells. Eventually he managed to get to his feet and walked to the sink. He drank four glasses of water and splashed cold water on his face

He walked slowly around his cell. He went on walking. What he noticed first about the bookshelves was plenty of reference, poetry, philosophy, psychology books, plus religious works — Christian, Islam, Hindu, Buddhist, Taoist, Confucianist, plus studies of Native American, African, and other religions. He walked to the side with bars. Across the hall was a blank wall, painted yellow.

He noticed he was hungry. Nothing in the refrigerator. But on the counter he saw a package of ten oatmeal-raisin cookies and he began eating them. After awhile he sat at the desk. The computer showed that the time was 4:38 AM. There was an e-mail message on the screen with a subject line reading Attn. Mr. Heatley:

> Intranet mail
> Mr. Heatley:
> You have been checked out of your hotel and your bill has been paid for you. Your suitcase is next to your bed and your wallet is inside your suitcase.

Joe looked — sure enough, the suitcase was upright on the floor by the head of the bed. He opened it. Nothing seemed to be missing and nothing was missing from his wallet, either, not his money or credit cards or drivers license or other I.D.

Joe went back to the computer, deleted the message. Immediately a new message appeared on the screen. This one had the subject line FW: The Procida Society. Originally it had been sent to Herman. It read

Herman,
The Procida Society is not our problem. Just the opposite, they're great guys on our side. I'm going to stay here in New York a few more days, talk with them, and do research in the public library. I'll tell you all about it when I get back. Joe

Joe saw that the message had been sent from his own e-mail address on the day he had come to the Procida Society — was it yesterday? He deleted that message too and then typed a fresh e-mail as quickly as he could. His subject line was HELP and his message was

HELP I AM BEING HELD PRISONER AT THE PROCIDA SOCIETY, 1123 FIFTH AVENUE, NEW YORK CITY. PLEASE CONTACT FBI AND NY CITY AND STATE POLICE. JOE HEATLEY

He tried to remember as many e-mail addresses as he could. After racking his brain for fifteen minutes he came up with just a few — Herman, his sister, Alice Kim, info at his home-town library, a store that had once sold him size 10 shoes. Those would do for starters while he racked his memory for more. He clicked on Send. A window popped up: "Access denied for sending and receiving e-mails." At least the computer was connected to the web. He opened the Facebook site, tried to start typing his message. Again, "Access denied." The Twitter site, too. He experimented with some familiar web sites, beginning with the *New York Times.* The date on that day's Times was the day after he'd entered the Procida Society. He was skimming the index of articles when he had an idea.

He called up one of the *Times* blogs. The top entry was something about a coal-mine disaster in West Virginia and federal mine-safety regulations, something that Joe didn't bother to read. Instead he typed a reply that was a cry, the same cry as his e-mail for help. But when he clicked on "Submit" his message was not submitted. He clicked several times, waited. Nothing happened.

He tried to send the same cry for help to a solar energy discussion group he and Nora belonged to. A tiny window popped up:

"Access is not permitted from this location." He spent at least 40 minutes trying to send his message to various blogs, forums, and other web sites without any success. By then he had eaten half the cookies in the package and he wasn't so hungry.

He sat slumped in front of the computer and hardly noticed that he emitted a long groan: "Noooooooo..." A minute later he shot upright and onto his feet when he heard a voice say, "Hey! You awake?"

He looked around, walked to his cell bars, looked at the yellow wall. "Who's there?"

"That's a relief." It was a woman's voice. "I was afraid you were dead. I saw them carry you in yesterday. I must've yelled for you fifty times."

"Who said that? Where are you?"

"I'm in the next cell." Not a girl, not an old woman, just a woman, a soprano by her voice. "It took me two days to get totally conscious. That's a powerful drug, whatever it is, they gave us. Are you still fuzzy?"

"Getting better," Joe said. "Where are we? What is this?"

He heard her sigh. "I was hoping you knew. We might be in New York City. But I doubt it."

"Well, what're we doing here? Why're they holding us? How can we get out?"

"I've got a worse question. More important. What is sanity?"

"Huh? What? What's happening here is plumb crazy, I know that. Why'd you ask me that?"

She said, "It's the most important question for me right now. It's life or death. I've got to answer it. If I don't get it right, I don't know what's going to happen to me, if they're going to impair me somehow and then let me loose, or torture me first before they kill me, or how they're going to kill me, or what. So what is sanity?"

"Who wants to know? Why? Hey, is this some weird kind of job application, like for the CIA?"

"I just wish it was. But I don't want a CIA job. I don't think this is how they handle job applications anyway. I've been here three days. They snatched me right out of my office in Los Angeles in the middle of the day. I'm a lawyer, my name is Diana Watkins. I left my office to go to the ladies room and that's where they nabbed me. They tasered me and knocked me out. So I don't know much of anything about this place, whatever or wherever it is. Except that the Procida Society runs it. Anyway, what is sanity?"

Joe said, "I don't know and I don't care. I just want out of here."

"You'd better care. They're going to make you answer a question, too. If we don't get our answers right, the same thing'll happen to us that happened to the last guy who was in your cell. You should have heard him scream."

"What happened to him?"

"God only knows. All he said to me was 'Tell me, how do I know I'm real? I've got to tell them or they'll kill me.' That was the question they gave him. I heard him talk to himself a lot that day. He was there when they put me in here. The guards came after him twice. The first time, they took him away someplace and he was bawling when they brought him back. The second time, he never came back. Speaking of God, I've been praying a whole lot these last three days. We're going to need all the help we can get."

Killing, torturing, that question about sanity — "Hey, are we in some kinda nut house?" Joe said. "Psychiatrists don't say people're insane any more, do they? So there's no such thing as sanity either. Maybe it's just a legal word that doesn't mean anything." He had an aunt whom his grandparents had put into a booby hatch. She lived there a number of years and died there. He had met her just once, and as far as he could tell she was a lot more sane than her brother, who was Joe's father. She wanted out of there but she was forced to stay. Were Joe's parents the ones who made her stay there? Or was it because some psychiatrist or some administrator didn't want to free her? After all, their jobs depended on having inmates in the asylum, whether they were really insane or not. Joe knew that once you got put into a mental institution it was almost impossible to get out.

Is this a high-class kind of madhouse, with the nuts behind bars, in cells like this one, with books and a computer and comforts? Is putting people who ask questions about the Procida Society into madhouses the society's way of seeing they don't make trouble? It would be less trouble for them to simply kill him the way they killed Nora and Dr. Dryden.

Joe hardly noticed when he finished off the package of cookies. He was preoccupied with wondering what this place was, what he was doing there, why he and a lawyer were being imprisoned like this. For Diana Watkins's sake he also wondered what sanity was. All Joe's life he had managed to cope with every situation he was in

— wasn't that sanity? Except there in his cell he was helpless. Did not coping now mean he was temporarily insane? And he did stupid things sometimes, too, and regretted them later, and then he thought his whole life was stupid and he regretted that. Insane? No, it's not the same as stupidity.

But people with Alzheimer's think they're sane. The more confused they get, the more they think everybody else was crazy. Well, everybody is crazy. Everybody wants, wants, wants. Everybody thinks when you get lots of stuff you'll get happy. But when you get everything, you still want more. Poor addled meth fiends and crackheads and wineheads on the streets, those on the one hand, and the bankers and Wall Street greedheads that collect their billions of dollars for destroying people's jobs and lives on the other hand — and everybody else in between, too, they never can get enough, there's always something more they want. That's a delusion, that's crazy.

Look at all the people who despise anybody who're different from themselves, who look or talk different or who have different religions or different politics or who are richer or who are poorer. Crazy. Look how society everywhere in the world is based on lucky people exploiting other people who are less lucky. The whole world is crazy and the only sane people are the rare ones who go screaming mad in the streets.

"Hey, thanks."

Diana Watkins's interruption shook up Joe, who suddenly realized how upset and angry he was getting. He said, "For what?"

"For saving me. I just realized you answered my question."

"Huh?"

"I said, what is sanity? And you said that there's no such thing. Well, that's going to be my answer. They're probably going to kill me for it. But that's what I'm going to tell them."

Her words yanked the props from under his resentment, left a certain emptiness for a moment before his unhappiness at being imprisoned returned and filled that space again. Hungry, too, he laid on his bed again, looked up at the ceiling. Do these Procida Society people think they're sane? Something about that thought brought him off the subject of sanity and back to his own predicament. That was foremost in his mind awhile later when a guard showed up with a tray. He was a meaty guy with the muscles of a steroid freak under his uniform and he placed the tray through a slot in the bars. Joe took the tray, said, "What is this place, where are we?" The guard didn't answer, started to turn around. Joe said, "Why am I here?" The impassive guard walked away, back toward where he'd come from. "Hey," Joe yelled after him, "when am I gonna get to talk with somebody?" The guard didn't even turn around. Cold jerk.

But the food was delicious and plentiful. Eggs, ham, grapefruit, banana, pancakes with syrup and strawberries and sliced peaches — fresh and sweet, not canned — and whipped cream, a big glass of milk. Was this to fatten him up for the kill? The coffee was good, too. As he was drinking it a muscular-looking guard came again — the same guard? Joe put the tray, now with empty, dirty dishes, through the slot and said, "When're you gonna let me out of here?" Instead of answering the guard picked up the tray. "Hey, can you talk? Are you deaf or stupid or just a jerk?" Joe yelled at the guard's back. No response, not even to insults.

He was back at the computer and, for lack of any ideas about how to get out of that loony bin, playing and losing over $200,000 in an on-line poker game when he heard guards come in the hall. There were two this time, both tough, musclebound, and brutal-looking. "Hey, you two," he yelled at them as they pushed a wheelchair past his cell. "Can you talk? Can you think? Are you zombies, that why you act like that?" There was some relief in insulting them, so Joe went on: "You're a pair of sissies. You're gutless and stupid. You keep me in here cause you're such cowards you don't dare fight me."

Neither of them so much as looked at Joe or acted as if he had heard Joe's abuse. He stopped trying to get a rise out of them when they stopped at the next cell and let themselves in. A few minutes later Joe got to see what his neighbor looked like. Diana Watkins was a young black woman with curly black hair, thin and haggard-looking with a frightened, drooping expression on her face. She did not look at him as they pushed her, strapped onto the wheelchair, past his cell. He yelled, "What's the matter, you chickens? Got to pick on a woman cause you're afraid of a man, yeah?" They paid no attention to him.

He was losing over a million dollars at the on-line poker game by the time a guard returned. The guard pushed an envelope onto the tray in the cell's bars. "Hey, Gabby, can you understand English?" Joe yelled at the impassive brute. "Look out you don't frig yourself to death on that cob up your ass." He would have said more, but the guard was out of sight.

Joe opened the envelope, read the message that was inside:

Dear Joseph Heatley:

Your destiny will be determined by the way you answer a simple question. Of course you will want to give this issue your most thoughtful attention. A computer with internet connection and a library of books has been provided to aid you in your study.

The question is: What is your responsibility?

We will expect your answer tomorrow morning. Our decision will depend on how you reply — thus, your future is in your own hands. Choose your answer wisely, then.

And no signature at the end. Of all the freedom-of-choice garbage. "Your future is in your own hands" was as phony as lines like "don't make us use the taser" or "your money or your life," but more scary because no answer was implied. No, the note didn't threaten Joe. It didn't need to — being helpless in that pleasantly furnished cell might have been an improvement on torture or death, but it was still captivity. "What is your responsibility?" What a dumb question, and on top of a lie like "your future is in your own hands."

The more Joe thought, the more he became aware of what a desperate situation he was in. These people, his captors, were crazy as jaybirds on crack. Nobody at his hotel would be interested in him any more now that his captors had checked him out. What would Herman do? Would he try to e-mail Joe and would he get alarmed when Joe did not reply? But Joe's abductors were now using Joe's e-mail address and they'd come up with answers to anything Herman might try to e-mail to him. What about Alice Kim? Same thing, they'd reply to her e-mails in his name. In time they would dump his body someplace, maybe in the middle of the Atlantic Ocean where nobody would find him. Effectively, right now, Joe figured, he was as good as wiped off the face of the earth.

Could his captors get away with his murder? Sure they could. For all Joe knew the Procida Society might even be as powerful as the Mafia or a Latin American drug cartel or even a government, maybe even the U.S. government. There sure was no doubt any more that the society were the ones who were preventing the production of any kind of solar-cell battery that could be mass produced. They were the ones who had harassed Herman and everyone he dealt with, they were the ones who had murdered Nora. Heaven only knows what else they were up to.

What is your responsibility? Responsibility for what? I choose things all the time. So sure I'm responsible. For what? That's easy to answer if I'm helping someone who's sick or crippled or something like that. What about people like my old man and my old lady, mean buggers like them, relentless, was I supposed to somehow be responsible to them like they weren't responsible to their families?

Joe was thinking about responsibility when a stiff, silent guard brought him dinner. Since insults and nastiness had gotten Joe nowhere, this time Joe said, "Thank you very much." No reply to this one either, nothing even on the man's face to show he'd heard what Joe said. The dinner was very good, too, fried oysters, of all things, with red beans and rice and cole slaw. He was still thinking about responsibility much later when a guard brought him supper. "You got a tongue? Can you talk?" Joe said, and when the guard didn't reply Joe said, "Thanks for the delicious food. Do they punish you for talking with the prisoners?" to his departing back. The supper was great, too: steak, onions, mushrooms, salad, bread, and blueberry cobbler with ice cream for dessert. The condemned man ate a hearty meal, Joe thought.

What is your responsibility? Is that another way of asking, am I to blame for the human race? Despite all the books around, Joe was not in much of a mood to read. He pulled a Bible from the bookcase and started reading anyway: "In the beginning God created the heaven and the earth." Maybe it was God's fault. Or Allah's. Or, who were some of the other gods, Thor, Jupiter, Krishna, Buddha, Confucius? No, Buddha and Confucius weren't gods, were they? But maybe this Procida Society lot aren't religious.

What am I responsible for? Look at all the nuclear bombs around the world, the radioactive waste, the polluted water, the poisoned air, the fields and orchards in the country poisoned with chemicals, the cities poisoned with smoke, the lying, power-mad bastards who like everything just fine this way — am I responsible for any of that? Look at how the population explosion is destroying the world's resources, look at how the world's economy depends on the population continually increasing — am I responsible for that?

Yeah, maybe in a sense I kind of am, Joe figured. If I wasn't here I'd be driving my old car cause I can't afford a hybrid yet. My car that burns petroleum, a limited resource, and blows carbon monoxide out of the tailpipe. Before Nora invented sundidos I used to live in a house with natural gas heat, another limited resource. Electricity there, it comes from a coal-fired power plant that pollutes the air. Or maybe a nuclear power plant that makes radioactive waste. At least in the new house in Franklin I connected the electric and heating to sundidos. Okay, the metal in my car and house and my appliances and so on was mined by some poor devil in the third world, risking his life underground. And the clothes I wear were sewn by a little kid sold to a sweatshop factory in the third world, and the cotton in those clothes was grown by a starving peasant somewhere. So, yeah, in my own way I'm responsible for exploiting these people and these resources.

But absolutely not, no, I wasn't the one who exploited them, Joe thought. He remembered when he was a 15-year-old high school boy, rooming in an elderly woman's apartment and cutting his last class every day to take a bus across town to his job as a janitor in a hardware-supply warehouse. It was a social studies class in American history. He still got good grades on every test, which bugged his old, dreary teacher no end. "Suppose all the other students were as casual about class as you?" the guy had said. Joe hadn't answered that, but he'd known very well that he had no responsibility for what the other students chose to do. And now, he figured, I'm not the one who's sucking all the oil and gas out of the ground or forcing all the people who aren't as lucky as me to sweat and die so I can make a profit. If I was a billionaire I'd get everybody in the world a good education and a good job. I'm not greedy, I just use what's available to me. What's the alternative to living in a house and having to ride or drive to work? Should I live naked in the woods and eat berries instead?

"Your future is in your hands." The dishonesty of that grated on Joe again. It is why he decided that tomorrow any answer he might give would be as good as any other for these Procida Society bastards. He went back to the computer and googled for Diana Watkins. The computer came up with another ACCESS DENIED. He lost another $3,000,000 playing internet poker before the overhead light and the hall lights went out at midnight. He went to bed.

The next morning a guard brought Joe another big breakfast.

"Why don't you say something? What's the matter with you anyway?" Joe said before he ate the eggs and baked trout and the rest. Again he deliberately did not think any more about responsibility. Instead he tried to think how to deal with his imprisonment. Since those guards were the only people I ever see, I'm making a mistake insulting them. I got to get on their good side, start talking to them like I don't know they're evil bastards. That note yesterday says I'm going to talk to somebody else today, too. Whoever it is, I'd better agree with them, whatever they say. I got to change my attitude, be polite to these murderers, say yes to whatever they say.

By the time guards came for him again he had read newspapers on the web and lost a total of $13,000,000 of somebody's money, the Procida Society's, he hoped, playing internet poker. The guards were three more steroid-muscle brutes, maybe the same guards he had seen take away Diana Watkins yesterday. They did not grab him and shoot some kind of knockout medicine into him. They did not taser him. But one of them finally did speak — he said, "Come."

"Congratulations. That sounds like human speech. You must be the one that's evolving." Joe regretted it as soon as he said it because he had resolved to try to be cool. They didn't say any more as they surrounded him, and neither did Joe. They led him down the hall and through a door. They took an elevator to the fourth floor of the building, to an office where a smiling man waited in a large room. He was tall, his balloon-belly extended into a ledge over his pants, and several long strands of his brown hair were combed over his bald head. He stood in a gray suit, white shirt, and red-and-silver striped tie behind a mahogany table and said, "Have a seat, Joe. I'm Senator Martin Whitlock."

Chapter 10

JOE SUPPRESSED THE URGE TO SAY, Why am I here and why did you murder my wife? Instead he said the edited version: "What'm I doing here?"

Whitlock smiled. "Have a seat," he said again. "We need to talk."

"We sure do," Joe said and sat down in a chair that one of the muscle-men held for him. "You didn't have to kidnap me just to talk to me."

The smile on Senator Whitlock's face now turned into a look of concern, eyebrows tilted up, peaking above his nose. He said, "I'm so sorry for your loss. The death of your wife was a tragic, tragic event — "

"Her murder. She was killed. Assassinated. In cold blood." The hammy look on Whitlock's fat face only bugged Joe.

Whitlock said, "Her — her murder, yes. It never should have happened. If it's any consolation to you, we in the Procida Society know who killed her — "

"Who did it?"

"Two rogues hired by a competitor of Herman Sorg. As you probably know, there are others besides Herman Sorg who are attempting to build solar-cell batteries to power automobiles and for other uses. If it's any consolation, I can tell you in strictest confidence that both of the — the killers have been apprehended and dealt with already. Permanently and as severely as humanly possible. Nobody will ever be bothered by those two men again."

"It was a man and a woman who killed Nora — "

"I mean, that man and that woman. That pair."

"You mean you killed the ones that killed Nora?"

"The Procida Society doesn't kill people. But I know that your wife's killers have been executed. That's right, executed. By whom, I can't tell you, I'm sorry. The Franklin police haven't even been informed. But that case is closed."

Joe didn't say anything for awhile, for as long as it took this new information to sink in. He didn't know Herman had a competitor. Just the opposite, Nora had told him that she and Herman had been cooperating, sharing information with other solar-battery researchers and technicians in American and other countries. What competitor hired murderers? How did Whitlock know that the murderers had themselves been executed? Who, what was the executioner? A government agency, the Mafia, a gang? Had the Procida Society hired someone to execute for them?

It was the fat senator who broke the silence. The smile was now back on his face. "As for the present, please remember that we didn't harm you. And we need to learn a number of things about you in depth and urgently. Believe me, I'm sorry if we inconvenienced you."

That nothing smile of Whitlock's bugged Joe. It was a fixed smile, the smile of a politician shaking voters' hands or lying on television. It was settled on Whitlock's face so it looked smug, like nothing could harm him. He was one guy who would never get kidnapped, drugged, and held in a cell somewhere, God knew where. Sure, I'll forgive you. The day after I do the same things to you that you did to me. Inconvenienced! Sorry! All Joe said was, "Then how come I'm here?"

Across the table from him, Senator Whitlock still smiling but now with eyebrows upraised again in that look of concern, said, "We need to know if you qualify for membership in the Procida Society. We had hoped to enroll Nora as a member, too, but now, obviously, it's too late."

"You mean you were gonna grab her like you grabbed me and put her in a cell?"

"We had expected to approach her openly and invite her. Perhaps in her home or her office. As I say, I'm sorry we had to apprehend you as we did."

Had to! Sorry! How many times had Whitlock said he was sorry? The senator was one sorry bastard, but Joe had to remind himself that he had intended to try to act cool today. "I"m real careful about what I join," came out of Joe's mouth spontaneously. But he thought an instant before he said, "Membership? What do I have to do to become a member? First, what's the Procida Society?"

"Vision, responsibility, and intelligence are the sole qualifications. Race, religion, sex, wealth, status, educational achievement, things that may concern other organizations do not concern us. For instance, we have many members of all beliefs and races in the Procida Society, here in America and in other countries. Which brings me back to your first question — the reason you're here. Yesterday we asked you a question — what are you responsible for? Do you want to answer now or do you want to think it over some more?"

Joe had his answer ready: "I'm responsible for what I say. Or do. That's all. Just my choices."

Whitlock looked concernedly at Joe for a few moments before he said, "That's all? That's your entire answer?"

"Yeah. I got nothing to add."

"Mm," Whitlock said and then was silent. The nothing smile and the concerned upraised eyebrows were gone now. Instead he was frowning, his head was tilted a little back, and he was looking up as if Joe was not there. Now he looked scary. Joe watched, thinking, okay, okay, don't put me in your stinking club, kill me now. The silence in the room lasted so long that Joe finally said, "Is that all? Are you gonna let me out now?"

Whitlock finally spoke: "Joe, the Procida Society is not just a club in the ordinary sense of the word. It's a benevolent society, but even that description doesn't encompass enough of our mission. We're an elite group — so elite that many presidents and prime ministers and other government leaders, and all dictators and many Nobel Prize winners haven't been invited to join. The reason we're so elite is because our mission, our purpose is so important. Ours is a lonely responsibility. And it's a responsibility to the entire human race."

The responsibility of benevolent murderers, Joe thought. The senator went on: "We are the ones who have to guide the world through all the chaos and insanity that surrounds us every day. The great mass of people need guidance. It's easy to see that most of them don't have the necessary intelligence or understanding to choose their destinies. A greater problem is the genuinely understanding, intelligent people. The vast majority of them lack the vision to guide humanity."

"This how you do it? By kidnapping people?"

Whitlock ignored that and went on: "Even among those with vision, too often their vision is fatally flawed by points of dogma or perhaps a point of intellectual misunderstanding, a misinterpretation, or simply character flaws or poor health. Against all this is the Procida Society. It's very important that we have no ideology, no dogma, no governing theories. We are totally pragmatic."

Nazis, Khmer Rouge, Revolutionary Guards, Joe thought. A society of Fascists. Bloodthirsty ones. "We can't become an institution like the ACLU or the NRA or the Heritage Foundation or the American Enterprise Institute for the same reason we can't begin a political party," Whitlock went on, "simply because no majority of people in any democratic country in the world would have the superior understanding and vision to accept and support our guidance. It's important that we serve in, well, not wholly in secret, but in the background, purposely. We don't even have publications or a web site, so that we won't attract attention to ourselves."

He looked so sincere and concerned that Joe, for an instant, considered spitting into his face. He continued: "It's true that many Procida Society members are leading politicians like me who get elected specifically to further objectives or to eliminate potential threats. For example, for my first term I faced a threat to the nation. I had to run in order to negate a very unstable man back in my state. His exceptional charisma was likely to have gotten him elected U.S. president in a few years. Even with a large campaign fund that the society secretly raised for me, and even though my campaign claimed that he was a pederast, an atheist, a drug addict, and unpatriotic, I only defeated him by less than one percent of the total vote. Nevertheless by being elected I saved the United States from unimaginable crises."

"How come you guys want me for a member?" Joe asked.

"We have three reasons. The first is very simply that you had the ingenuity to see the influence and importance of the Procida Society. Of course, that led to your coming here, which is especially high in your favor. The second reason is your wife's working with Herman Sorg on the sundidos. Third, now you're working with Herman Sorg. All of these factors demonstrate your crucial vision and intelligence. The only real question remaining is your responsibility."

"That why that quiz about responsibility?"

"It was a consensus of us, not just me personally, who chose to ask you about your responsibility."

"So was my answer good enough?"

Whitlock said, "The membership committee will decide that. I'm on that committee. I'll tell you frankly that I found your answer somewhat unsatisfying, but your answer is not the sole indicator of your responsibility. I have to say that while your crude and insulting behavior toward your guards is understandable, it still suggests instability that tells against you, too. Again, the full committee will weight these factors and decide whether or not to accept you. And now I have to leave you for today. But you'll be in the capable hands of our Mr. Hoover."

It occurred to Joe that if he ever got out of this place, he would try to find Senator Whitlock and get revenge. He got up as if to follow Whitlock out the door. But two of the guards came in the room when Whitlock opened the door. As he left they stood between Joe and the door. Joe sat down again.

So my answer was unacceptable. So my behavior toward these sewer rats is crude and insulting. So I'm unstable. So these scum really are watching me in my cell. For the first time in his life Joe, since he now figured he was doomed to die there anyway, wished he could become a suicide bomber, to blow up the Procida Society along with himself. As he sat the strong feelings of anger and fear gradually subsided enough that he was back to thinking he should not insult any of these Procida Society people, whoever they were, but agree with them in hopes of getting sprung.

As he was thinking these thoughts a bearded man in a grey suit and white shirt and blue-and-green tie came in. The salt-and-pepper beard was razor-trimmed, the kind of beard an executive wears to show he is a very important nonconformist. "Hi, Joe, I'm Dick Hoover," the man said and held out his right hand. As Joe shook hands Hoover said, "Have you eaten lunch yet this noon?"

"No," Joe said. He suddenly realized he was hungry.

"Okay, I'm going to have them send you a meal. You and I can have our talk after that."

A guard was left with Joe as he ate alone at the big table. They brought him a big hamburger with swiss cheese melted on it, onion rings, potato salad, a big milk shake. Like the other meals the Procida Society had served him, this one was delicious. Joe ate and drank it all. The guard took away the empty dishes and glass and Joe thanked him. Joe was feeling a bit drowsy and reminding himself to act cool toward the next people he saw when Dick Hoover came back in the room.

Hoover sat down at the table across from Joe in the same chair Whitlock had sat in. Hoover did not lay a Whitlock-like smile or concerned expression on Joe — none of those Whitlock looks that had virtually screamed "I am a fraud." Instead his expression was noncommittal and his attitude was businesslike as he held a recorder in one hand and extended the other, holding a microphone, toward Joe. He said, "What is your opinion of me, Joe?"

"I hate your stinking guts already and I want to kick your ass from here to the North Pole, you son of a bitch." Joe said it rather quietly. He didn't raise his voice or look angry as he spoke. In fact, he was surprised at what he was saying even as he said it.

Hoover stayed expressionless as he asked, "What do you think of Senator Whitlock?"

"He's a lying suppository. I want to rip that fake smile off his face and stuff it down his throat." Joe spoke calmly and thought, why am I saying this? I should be trying to act cool.

Hoover smiled momentarily before asking, "What do you think of the Procida Society?"

"A bunch of fascists and paranoids and other arrogant jerks. Your bullshit about secretly running the world is nothing but superiority complex. You're liars and murderers and kidnappers and thieves and every other kind of self-important goons." Joe was answering in a normal tone of voice and trying to remember what he'd just said. He was telling Hoover exactly what he thought, yet he felt somehow detached from his rage.

"Senator Whitlock said he hoped you'd join the Procida Society. Will you?"

"If that's what I got to do to get out of here. I'll do anything if it gets me out of this sewer. If I got to act like I don't know you and Whitlock and all those others are filthy ruthless liars, then I'll act that way." Truth serum. They put some kind of truth drug in my food. "You stinking weasel, you doped my food with some drug."

"A temporary stimulant that removes your inhibitions. It has some similarities to alcohol, except without any of the intoxicating effect. Effectively it leaves you powerless to resist the impulse to answer my questions with the first thing that comes into your mind. Naturally, the first thing that comes into your mind is your true knowledge, your true feelings — the truth, in other words. So you can't help telling me the truth." Hoover calmly said all that, without any expression on his face.

Joe started to stand up. Suddenly he felt so dizzy that he couldn't see straight and the delicious meal he had just eaten rose up in him in a gorge. He gagged on the acids and the undigested bits of food in his mouth as he stumbled forward at the table.

He did not quite actually vomit. The guard grabbed him before he fell on the table. The guard gently lowered him back into his chair while he called the guard a musclehead and a steroid freak. Once Joe was seated again his nausea gradually subsided and the room stopped spinning around. He tried to remember what he had just said and done. All he could recall for sure was that he had been fed some kind of drug that made him say what he really felt and thought instead of what he wanted these bastards to believe of him, and that the pig across the table from him was named Dick Hoover. "You pig, you killed my memory."

"The drug only cancels your short-term memory for a brief time. You'll have temporary amnesia, but only about our time together this afternoon. Outside of that you'll be back to normal by evening."

That was the beginning of what seemed to Joe like a very long afternoon. He felt almost delirious, as bad as being drunk. Even so he spoke clearly and answered Hoover's questions calmly, truthfully, and insultingly. Some of them were kid questions: What movies do you like? What are your favorite songs? Favorite books? Favorite subjects in school? Some of Hoover's questions were pseudo-intimate, about his attitudes toward religion, do you believe in God?, sex, women, girlfriends, potency, masturbation, do you lust in your heart for women you're not married to? Some questions were too intimate, about Joe's childhood, his family, his marriages. Joe told Hoover things that he'd only discussed with Nora and Liz and, years ago, an army psychiatrist. He talked about these at length and every sentence was full of curses and filthy insults, all directed at Hoover and the Procida Society.

After awhile a thin woman, blond, short hair, square face, long jaw, and deep-set black eyes, came into the room and joined Joe's guards while Hoover stepped out. When Hoover returned she talked with him so quietly that Joe couldn't hear them. She was the woman who'd killed Nora, she'd looked evil on Herman's video, now she looked just as sinister up close, and she was not there very long. She only glanced at Joe, she didn't notice the shock of recognition on his face. The questions kept coming, then, from Hoover. How do you feel about this, about that, what are your politics, ideology, your attitudes toward conservation, energy, ecology. He told them how he worked to get Nora through graduate school, about

Nora's work in solar energy research, about Doctor Dryden and his colleagues in the university laboratory, about how Nora got the job with Herman, about Herman and his laboratory, about his search for revenge for Nora's murder.

He couldn't help himself. Every question Hoover asked him aroused an impulse to answer, and to tell the truth, too, an impulse so strong that Joe couldn't resist, no matter how much he wished he could resist. All afternoon he sounded cool, serene as he told how about how his parents had brutalized him and his sister, his wife had been murdered, all his pains and shame and guilt, too. He was also placid as he called Hoover, the Procida Society, and everyone connected with it all kinds of vilenesses and obscenities.

Three different times as Joe answered questions, a guard brought him a glass of water. Joe didn't want to drink the stuff, he knew very well the water was drugged, but his mouth and throat were so dry that he drank it anyway. Eventually his answers grew shorter, with fewer descriptions of Hoover's sexual and excrementory perversions. When Hoover asked him where Herman had acquired the money to run his business, Joe finally was too exhausted and too dry to answer that he didn't know or to curse the questioner.

"There's a depressive side effect to the drug you've taken," Hoover said. "We're giving you a mild anti-depressant to counteract it." A guard brought him a glass of water. Joe was too thirsty to not drink it, with whatever was dissolved in it. Within a few minutes he was asleep in the chair.

He woke up back in his cell, on the day bed. He tried to remember what Hoover had said to him that afternoon and what he had told Hoover. Couldn't remember anything he'd said, not one thing. There were a few things he recalled very faintly — that the guards had been there awhile, that he'd been fed drugs, that he had been terribly dizzy, nauseous, that he was sorry he'd talked so much even though he had no idea what he'd talked about.

He got up and was surprised to find he felt steady, clear-headed, no nausea. He went to the computer screen, saw that the time was 8:37 p.m. How long had he been there? He hated that computer. He was hungry. Looking around, he saw a package of oatmeal-raisin cookies, like the cookies he'd eaten yesterday? Two days ago? Three? More? He ate the cookies and even though his alimentary canal did not protest this time, he still hated every bite. He went back to the computer, called up the headlines on a newspaper web site, tried to read articles about the heat waves across North America, Europe, Asia, protests against the new wind turbines in Minnesota, and the prime minister of Norway threatening to sue Great Britain over its oil spills into the North Sea, and the ruination of the Atlantic Ocean by the oil spills, and a ruptured natural gas pipeline in Venezuela. It was hard to concentrate because he hated heat, protests, Minnesota, wind, turbines, the coast, the Atlantic Ocean, oil, and the spills, with such a terrible fury, and he hated Norway, its prime minister, Great Britain, the North Sea, Venezuela, pipelines, and natural gas every bit as furiously. He rammed his fist onto the computer screen, tried to destroy it. He only hurt his fist. He wished there was something in his cell heavy enough to pound on the computer, to smash it.

A guard brought him food. "You filthy garbage, you've been spying on me," he screamed, and screamed curses well after the guard was out of earshot. The meal was barbecued ribs, one of his favorites. The choice of food enraged him and so did the guard for serving it. Joe gobbled it down and viciously hurled the bones out of the cell, into the hallway. He lay on the day bed, hated the lights because he could not turn them out, tried to sleep anyway. After the lights went out he was furious at the darkness. He could not sleep for rage at everyone he could think of, even at the memory of Nora.

As he lay there he realized: This isn't natural, all this anger. This must be the result of that awful truth serum and that stinking antidote drug. This is no way to have to live. Are they going to keep drugging me? Am I going to be helplessly angry like this for the rest of my life? Hour after hour he lay shaking with anger until he finally drifted off to sleep, complete with nightmares that his parents and the Procida Society were attacking him and Nora again now that he was helpless.

When he woke up he tried to will himself into not thinking about subjects that made him angry. Before long there were periods when he wasn't enraged and as the day went on those periods grew longer. When breakfast came he threw a grapefruit and a banana at the guard who brought it and screamed, "Eat me, you pig pervert." But later when another guard brought him a sandwich and salad he surprised himself by quietly saying "Thanks" for the first time since he'd been back in that cell. He saw then that he was recovering, even though he was still shaking.

Chapter 11

FINALLY, THE NEXT DAY when Joe no longer shook at all he was taken to the conference room where Hoover had already grilled him. Hoover was there again, along with a tall, barrel-chested man with a stupid, vertical face, long, thick nose, and dark hair in a widow's peak. It was Joe's first direct look at the man who'd killed Nora. It reminded Joe of the one thing he remembered from yesterday's interrogation — that he'd seen the woman who'd killed Nora there. So he knew the senator had lied to him: the Procida Society hadn't killed Nora's assassins. "How do you feel?" was the first thing Hoover asked.

"Like a prisoner, of course. What you expect?"

"Veli, I need to talk privately with Joe now," Hoover said to Tall and Stupid. T. & S. took a last look at Joe as he left. Hoover continued, "The drugs you were given, the one to make you talk and then the mild anti-depressant to counteract it, should be worn off by now. You should be clear-headed and steady."

"Mild, huh?" Joe said, remembering the extent of his helpless anger. "I'm not clear-headed. I don't remember anything you asked me yesterday. Or what I said."

"That's to be expected," Hoover said. "Don't worry. Your amnesia is only about that one afternoon. You won't be afflicted with any more memory lapses. You've been through a lot and now it's time for your reward. You have been accepted into the Procida Society."

"Big deal. I never wanted that. I wouldn't treat a rabid animal like you guys treat me."

Hoover looked away and seemed thoughtful. Then he turned to Joe and said, "You have every right to be angry with us. You would be unnatural if you weren't. But right now we have some final matters to settle. Can you put your anger aside just long enough to hear me out? You may even find yourself in sympathy with us."

Final matters? Are they finally going to release me? Or kill me? Joe exhaled. He said, "Go on, talk. Procida's an island off Italy. You some Italian bunch?"

Hoover said, "A few of us are Italian, yes. But nationalities are misleading. Are you familiar with the Byzantine empire in the 13th century?"

"Yeah, I took World History. The Crusaders about ruined the empire. It wasn't so rich any more."

Hoover: "Even so, in its decline, surrounded by enemies, the Byzantine wealth was the envy of its neighbors, especially of Europe. But it was far, far more than wealthy. It was the most civilized empire in the western world at the time, the highest developed culture. Do you remember the emperor Michael? Or Charles of Anjou?"

Joe: "No. They're something about the Byzantines?"

"Michael was the Byzantine emperor who recaptured Constantinople from the Crusaders. Charles was his enemy. He led the French and conquered Italy. He intended to destroy the Byzantine empire once and for all. He was stopped by a rebellion in Sicily and a Spanish navy. Do you realize how important it was to prevent him? To preserve Byzantine civilization? Europe was still barbaric. After 12 centuries of Christianity most Europeans were scarcely more than savages. If the French had won, there would have been no Renaissance and Western civilization might have disappeared."

It sounded like nonsense to Joe, who said, "What's this got to do with Procida?"

"In 1282 Charles's French navy was set to sail from Italy two days after Easter, to attack Constantinople. He would have destroyed Michael's empire, no question about it. On Easter Monday near Palermo, Sicily, there was a riot when local people killed some French soldiers who occupied their village. The rebellion spread fast to the cities and around the country. The rebels sank the French ships off Messina. Charles had to postpone his invasion of Constantinople in order to try to restore his rule in Sicily. And then the Catalan fleet attacked the French. It was the beginning of the end of Charles's rule of Europe."

At first Joe was resigned to listening to a long, boring story. But he was becoming interested as Hoover talked on: "It was a revolution. Michael's secret agents had been all over Sicily before that, spreading discontent with the French occupation. Michael had to wipe out the Byzantine treasury to bribe King Peter of Aragon to sent his Catalan navy to attack Charles's. It was worth it, too — the rescue of Byzantine civilization was the major event of the 13th century.

"But here is the most important part — saving the empire wasn't Michael's idea. Michael was desperate. The only faint glimmer of hope came from an exile from Procida. A doctor named John was the one who had the depth of insight to realize how important it was to preserve Byzantine culture. John of Procida came from a noble family and he was also a gifted diplomat. He was the one who traveled in disguise from country to country. He formed a hidden network of agents, he bribed local officials, he negotiated with the kings and the rulers of his time. He was the one who actually planned the revolution — not Michael. He talked Michael into recruiting those secret agents, paying bribes, spending whatever was necessary. He was the one who talked Peter into taking Michael's money and fighting Charles.

"And after his triumph with the Sicilian rebellion, he and a few fellow intellectuals founded our society. At first we were Christians and Muslims and Jews from Europe, Africa, Asia. We were a small group because there were so few responsible intellectuals in that benighted age. We've stayed small by choice ever since."

Hoover was silent for some moments after telling that long story, he looked down, seemed almost reverent. It fascinated and disgusted Joe, but he didn't say anything, just watched. Then Hoover looked up and said, "I know Senator Whitlock has mentioned to you the Procida Society's mission to mankind — our responsibility. Christopher Columbus was a member, even if Ferdinand and Isabella weren't. Our Procida Society predecessors were powerless to prevent African-American slavery or direct the French revolution. But we were able to foment the Industrial Revolution and spread the use of the steam engine. We inspired the American revolution, too. And we guided George Washington in his victories and later as he formed the first U.S. government. It was the Procida Society that guided Abraham Lincoln during the Civil War. Eight U.S. presidents were members. We brought about the American interventions that ended the First World War and eventually ended the Second World War as well.

"More recently we set in motion the forces that ended racial segregation in America and broke up the Soviet Union. Right now the Middle East, Iran, Afghanistan, Pakistan all seem to be in a chaotic condition. It's our members in those countries who are seeing to it that no single ruler or party or religious sect is able to dominate the region. Are you getting an idea of how necessary the Procida Society is?"

Joe remembered that he had heard something like this once before. A politically minded friend of Nora's had once dragged her and Joe to a Communist Party gathering over in Cleveland, Ohio.

That night he'd heard some gray-haired old guys congratulate themselves about how they'd been the ones who'd ended racial segregation and various wars in America. But the Procida Society had no ideology and otherwise didn't sound like Communists, either. Joe said, "I get it. Talk some more. Why couldn't your society stop this global depression that's going on?"

"We don't want to. It's necessary."

"Huh? Necessary? To put all these millions of people out of work? Make them homeless?"

Hoover said, "If we don't have our depression now, to clear out economic dead wood around the world, something far, far worse would follow very soon. Something like that is why we've been interested in your wife Nora and Herman Sorg. Why we hoped she would join us and why we still want Sorg to join us. And you too, of course."

"How come your society didn't stop those mile-deep oil wells in the oceans? When everybody knew how sloppy those oil companies are?"

Hoover shook his head, said, "Sometimes we have to accept that accidents happen. These oil spills seem like a terrible price to pay, but sometimes we have to accept crises like those in order to keep civilization running. Of course, if we let the U.S. government regulate industry any more than it does, the cost to freedom of enterprise would lead to a different kind of crises, far worse crises."

It was an answer that sickened Joe. Instead of disputing Hoover, though, he asked a question that was more important to him: "Senator Whitlock said the society knows who murdered Nora. Who did it?"

"A man and a woman who worked for a solar energy company in Texas. It holds a patent for a process of building batteries similar to Nora's patent."

Joe said, "Whitlock talked like the society had them killed. That true?"

"No. We're not murderers. But Nora Heatley herself would have been valuable to us. So we saw to it that the pair who killed her were executed themselves."

"You hired killers. Hit men."

"Yes," Hoover finally said. "Nora Heatley was too important to lose. We had to make an example of her murderers."

Joe felt the anger rise in him, opened his mouth to curse Hoover, to make him admit that Nora's killers were alive right then, there. Instead he forced himself to swallow, to try to keep from showing his disgust on his face. He managed to speak as if he didn't know Hoover had just told a terrible lie: "What made Nora so important? Her patent?"

"More than that, her work with Sorg. This is why your sense of responsibility is so crucial. The problem we face, we, the human race, is that progress toward renewable energy is proceeding far too fast. We need Sorg to redirect his efforts from his large-scale plans, his grand designs, I call them, to replace the internal combustion engine. If he redirects his energies onto a smaller scale he can do far more good and make a profit, even in the present economy."

Joe felt himself beginning to sweat with the effort of keeping down his anger. He said, "What you mean, solar energy's coming too fast?"

Hoover said, "Do you know how many people are out of work now? Do you know how many more will be out of work if everything is powered by renewable energy? Ten million Americans work for the oil industry alone, and the livelihoods of another sixty million directly depend on them. Do you know how many governments will collapse, how many people will starve to death, how many wars will result if mankind doesn't need fuel for internal combustion engines? The human race can't handle universal, inexpensive solar power yet.

"Now that we're in a global depression the prospect of cheap cars that don't run on gas would be irresistible to millions of people, immediately. More likely billions. Add on cheap fuel to heat homes, run businesses, factories, to light cities — do you see what I mean? But for instance Saudi Arabia, Iran, Iraq, Russia, Nigeria, Venezuela, other countries that depend on selling energy will be plunged back into poverty and the Dark Ages. The catastrophes will follow each other like falling dominoes. In the current global economy they'll happen fast enough to begin regional wars. Some Asian countries have nuclear weapons, which means World War III would be inevitable. The result could mean the end of the human race. It definitely would mean the end of civilization."

Joe was concentrating on Hoover's words, forcing down his own feelings. "It's not gonna be the end," he said. "Lookit what laptop computers and the Internet and cell phones started. That was a revolution and it was all peaceful."

"And components of laptops and cell phones depend directly and indirectly on extracting oil. Fuel is the basis of civilization, especially fuel for internal combustion engines," Hoover said. "Without fuel, mankind dies. Look at it another way. Did you know an oil company bought the original nickel metal-hydride battery patent from an auto manufacturer?"

"Yeah, I know. To keep them from making electric cars that use those batteries."

"No. The oil company executives are not fools. They know that the widespread use of electric cars is likely. They'll no doubt eventually get out of the oil business and manufacture those car batteries or even solar-cell batteries themselves. But they don't want to do it suddenly, faster than the human race can absorb this economic and cultural revolution."

Joe said, "Does the Procida Society back them?"

"We have no financial interest in any oil company or any other energy producer. What we want is to prevent World War III and the end of civilization. But if Herman Sorg continues on his project, it probably would be the beginning of that end — a small beginning, you may think, but all beginnings are small. Now do you see why we wanted Nora Heatley with us and why your answer about responsbility was so inadequate?"

"Not good enough for you?"

"Your answer was disappointingly narrow. Your responsibility is to the whole human race, not just to yourself."

Any minute now Joe was about to blow up at Hoover, but he managed to say, "Yeah, Herman's responsibility too?"

"We want him to redirect his energies. Just like you," said Hoover. "Surely you understand the importance of what we're doing. That's why we're offering you the opportunity to join the Procida Society."

Joe sputtered, "You still want me to join? After you said I wasn't good enough?"

"Your answer about responsibility was unsatisfactory. But you obviously have the intelligence to contribute to our group. You don't have to make a decision right now. Think it over. I know you can't help thinking about what you've been through here. But also think about what I've just said and about your responsibility to humanity. Whether you want it or not, you have it. Right now, though, you're free to leave."

Joe was startled: "Free to go? Just like that, huh?'

"Your suitcase has been packed and a private jet has been reserved to fly you directly back to Franklin. Here's my card. Call me at any time, day or night. I certainly hope to hear you say you want to join the Procida Society."

A guard led him out of the room and to the front door. As relieved as Joe was, he wasn't about to relax until he was safely out of the Procida Society's clutches. He wasn't surprised to see that the door didn't open onto Central Park or a New York City street. He was surprised at the hellish summer heat, from the sun almost directly overhead, as soon as he stepped outdoors. The countryside was wooded, rocky hills in all directions and with no buildings in sight except for the three-story grey brick building he'd just stepped out of.

The windows of the air-conditioned limousine that took him to the airport were blacked, he could not see out. It was a silent, fifty-eight-minute ride with a lot of curves and turns. Joe quickly gave up trying to note the car's turns or when the car slowed and speeded, and there was no way to guess where the driver was taking him. When the limo finally stopped the driver blindfolded Joe and walked him to the plane, helped him up the steps. It was only after he was in a seat that a guard took off the blindfold. The plane's windows were blacked out. The Procida Society did not want its passengers to know where they were.

Chapter 12

IT WAS A STRUGGLE FOR JOE to keep his mind on other subjects but he managed to not let himself think about his anger until he was back home in Franklin. The first thing he did there was yank the GPS bug off his rear bumper, toss it in his garbage can. He did not know how long he shook with rage, he screamed inside his house until his ears hurt and then felt silly for screaming, he cursed but did not cry. He also pounded walls with his fists or shook, screaming, cursing, or silently, standing with his back to the front window, sitting in the wooden rocking chair that used to be Nora's favorite chair.

When his shaking subsided the first person he tried to phone was Herman Sorg. Herman did not answer at his home or office. Joe left messages, drove to the shop. It was locked. Joe let himself in. It was late in the hot, hot afternoon, the office smelled old, looked dusty. Herman's computer was turned off.

Joe turned on the lights, tried to call Alice Kim from the office. No answer there either. He was relieved at that, he didn't want to talk to her but realized he had to. He telephoned his sister Liz. She said, "I've got a date tonight. He's the nicest guy. It's the second time he's taken me out. He took me to the city, bought me dinner in Greektown last week. He's a salesman, he works for the cable — "

"Liz, I just got home. I was kidnapped."

It took awhile to tell her what the Procida Society had done to him. He kept getting mad at her, too, because she kept interrupting with cracks like, "Why'd you go to work for that jerk?" and "How do you keep getting yourself in these crazy situations?" and "That's crazy, no U.S. senator would do that." When he was done she said, "That's the craziest story I've ever heard. What makes it worse is, you're my own brother. Anybody else but me would lock you up in the nut house."

"Lookit, I'm just telling you what happened. It's the truth. I'm not asking you for anything."

Liz said, "You think you're so smart just cause you married a genius woman. Well, look at you now. Beaten and kidnapped and nobody can help you. It's what you get for not minding your own business."

"What you mean mind my own business? Don't you know I got to bust up this gang who killed Nora?"

Liz: "Oh! You great big hero, you. You're crazy. You claim they're senators and scientists and everything and you're just one guy who thinks he's smart. Joe Blow from Ohio. You don't even know anything about solar-cell batteries. That was your wife's business. Except, now you know the trouble they make you."

Joe: "So just forget it. Forget I ever said anything. I'll never talk to you again."

Liz: "That's a relief. I can't afford your hospital bills and funeral expenses and I won't bail you out of jail."

"So good-bye." But then he relented: "Good luck with that date tonight. "

Liz refused to be pacified: "Just stop acting crazy. You're driving me crazy."

No comfort or sympathy or whatever from Liz, then. Joe drove to a restaurant, ate a bowlful of noodles alone while large families at two other tables chattered and laughed, worked up his nerve to phone Alice Kim again. He did when he got home — again no answer. He left a message on her machine and went to bed exhausted. He dreamed he was watching Nora walk toward Herman's office and tried to scream a warning at her. He couldn't get the scream out and as she reached the door he woke up groaning, "No! No! Don't..." Later when he fell asleep again he dreamed Nora was a prisoner in the Procida Society, watching the long-jawed, black-eyed woman come toward her with a gun. Again he woke up. He was starting to cry gently as he fell asleep yet again, and this time he did not dream.

When he awoke he still felt tired, groggy. He was about to go out to buy something for breakfast when his cell phone rang. "This is Alice," she said. "Oh, my god, I'm so glad to hear you. I've been so afraid this week that I haven't been able to work or go to sleep. Are you all right?"

Now she's going to bring me some bad news, he thought to himself. What he told her was, "I just had an awful ordeal. I got kidnapped and attacked and put in a jail and they gave me the third degree. They fed me a truth serum sort of drug."

Alice all but cried into the phone: "Oh, Joe, I'm so sorry. That's what I was afraid of. I know now, you know, you were right, there really is a conspiracy against sundidos. That drug, did it make you say the first thing that came into your mind? Almost like you were drunk and couldn't help yourself?"

He was still far from fully awake, he had to think about what she'd said before he answered, "Yeah. Except it didn't make me drunk."

"Oh, Joe." She was silent for a moment, he thought he heard her sob, before she said, "I know all about that drug. It's called nyalhis. It's supposed to work on the inhibitions like alcohol but without the intoxication. I was afraid of something like that. Ever since I learned that the Procida Society wanted you and Herman Sorg. I'm so sorry. I wish you'd told me what you were doing."

This call was already too much for the part-foggy Joe. "What's this about Herman? Are you a member of the Procida Society? How'd you know they wanted me?"

"Joe, we have got to have a serious talk because I'm terribly afraid and there's too many important things to talk about over the phone right now. I'm going to fly to Franklin today. I should get to your place by late afternoon."

What on earth was she yakking about? Joe didn't like what he was hearing at all. He didn't like that she even knew the Procida Society existed, let alone that she knew the society had held him or that they wanted Herman. She was probably one of those people on the other side. Even before Alice telephoned he'd decided he didn't trust her any more. He didn't expect to trust what she was going to say to him when she arrived at his home. In fact, Joe began to think that now the only person he could trust was Herman Sorg. Who was now missing.

Late that hot afternoon Alice Kim thought, Oh, god, this is going to hurt Joe. It's going to kill him, he's going to hate me, he won't ever speak to me again. But I have to tell him, for all I know I might save his life. What she said, and she sobbed as she stumbled on the words, was, "I'm a, I mean, I'm a member of the Procida Society."

They were facing a residential street, sitting in the shade on a bench on the otherwise sunlit bright green lawn near an entrance to the Arboretum. Joe had chosen that location because the street had little traffic, they could easily see from there if anyone was following them. Across the street a fast-striding woman was pushing a baby stroller, half a block away a boy and a brown spaniel were dawdling. Even though Joe hadn't said so, Alice knew he didn't want to talk to her in his home or at Herman's office because he didn't trust her, didn't want her around, wanted to send her back to Colorado that same day. "I'm not involved with society activities, but I know a few of the other members. Oh, my god, Joe, I'm so sorry."

"Sorry about what?"

"Sorry I didn't warn you. Sorry I, you know, didn't pay attention to what's going in the society. I didn't find out what it was going to do to you and Herman Sorg until too late. You know, too late to try to do something to stop it. I found out you fell into their lap there in New York and I know they took Herman three days later. They picked him up here at his office."

"You mean the Procida Society's got Herman now?"

Alice was sitting half-turned, facing Joe. She was thinking, once again, the same question she'd been asking herself for several days: How can I be so unaware, how can I be a member of something but not know what that something is, does? Joe was looking at the street and thinking that Alice looked serious and she seemed to be sincere. Not like the blatant fraud of a senator or the snotty businesslike Hoover he'd met at the Procida Society prison. That must mean, he figured, she's a better actor than they were. She said, "Yes, right now. He's in the Daryl Newjoy Memorial Institute for Psychiatry and Psychoanalysis. The same building where they held you. It's in northern Connecticut."

Joe didn't look at her as he said, "Do you know who it was killed Nora?"

"Yes. I know now. I know their names. It was a woman and a man. Velma Snell is the woman's name and Veli Kokola is the man. They live at that psychiatric building in Connecticut." Alice's eyes were wet, looking at him. She took a handkerchief out of a pocket, blew her nose, wiped her eyes.

Joe thought, Velma Snell — she would be the short, skinny, blond woman with the long jaw, and Veli Kokola would be the big, stupid bruiser with the big nose. He asked a crucial question: "Are they still alive?"

"Yes!" Just then a girl and a boy on bicycles, absorbed in their own conversation, came riding out of the woods, rode past Joe and Alice. When the pair were past, Alice said, "Did you see them there? Do you want to have them arrested?"

Alice now realized how tense Joe had been because his whole body seemed to unwind after she said that. He sat back, his legs stretched out, he looked at her, heaved a sigh. "I'm glad you said that. Cause that blackout drug they gave me, that truth drug — "

"Nyalhis," she said.

Joe must have realized his eyes were wet because he wiped them with his thumbs and forefingers. Alice wiped her own eyes with the ball of her hands while he said, "I found out yesterday and this morning that the amnesia from that nyalhis wears off. So now I remember what that Dick Hoover and me said. And I remembered something weird — he never asked me about you, nothing. So that means you're in cahoots with them."

"I'm a member, yes, I'm, you know, sorry. But oh, god, I don't sympathize with the rest of them at all."

"I know you're telling the truth about that woman and that man. I know cause I saw Herman's videotape of them when they killed Nora. I sure know what they look like. They were both there at that Procida Society place."

"It's worse than you think," Alice said. "Worse than I thought. I found out they killed Nora on purpose. They didn't just, you know, kill her because she happened to come there during a break-in. But if you and Herman have a videotape, that should be evidence enough to get them arrested. You know, the Procida Society has important lawyers but you have proof on your side."

Instead of replying to that, Joe changed the subject: "The FBI, they still on your trail?"

"They sniffed around my butt back home in Boulder for a day or two after that night I dragged them around Franklin. I haven't seen them since. Maybe they've gotten better at hiding themselves. I'm more worried about myself and you and the Procida Society right now."

"Yeah. Did your friends in that society — "

He didn't finish the sentence because a girl in blue running shorts was approaching. The girl ran past them on the path into the woods. Alice thought irrelevantly that the grass on the lawn was so green it was almost dazzling in the burning sunlight. She was the one who spoke, then: "They're not my friends. I know some of them. I have to act friendly to them. But you know, my god, don't think they're my friends."

Her words didn't seem to placate Joe at all. He said, "Not your friends? What do you get out of it? How come you joined?

"Well, at least it wasn't my idea. I never heard of the Procida Society till this spring. My employer, you know, signed me up. One day the president of Sonnestrahl simply told me that since I was vice-president, they were now making me a member. I thought it was some kind of professional sorority or fraternity or something. I didn't have to go through everything you did. I was only there a day, I mean, they didn't hold me against my will. But they did give me that same truth drug, nyalhis, and I think I've still blacked out some part of that afternoon. I'm still mad about what they did to me. You're probably lucky you recovered your memory. The drug must work differently on different people's metabolisms."

"If you don't like it, don't like them, why don't you get out?"

Alice: "Oh, for god's sake, Joe. Can't you see what a bind I'm in? I didn't want to be a member, but I couldn't tell Mr. Sonnestrahl that I didn't want to be a member because, Joe, I, you know, have to keep working there. We're not making sundidos yet but I can't make them anyplace else. The other reason I can't quit the society is because I've got to survive. I, you know, don't want to end up like Nora." Oh, god, I said that wrong, no wonder he's hurt and mad at me. She said, "And as long as I'm a member, I mean, I hope I can find out more about their dirty work. And put a stop to it."

"So you do know some Procida Society people. Do they talk to you? Did they tell you they were gonna follow me again?"

Alice: "Nobody said that to me. But you didn't join them, so they probably don't trust you, and especially after the way they treated you already, you know, I expect they really think you're important enough to follow. Did they give you their story about how sundidos would start the third world war?"

A panting girl in red track shorts came running out of the woods, almost stepped on a squirrel that suddenly came out of nowhere, darted across her path. When she was past them Joe said, "That's what that Dick Hoover told me, yeah. You know him?"

He's accusing me, Alice thought. How can I possibly show him I'm on his side? She said, "Yes, I know Dick Hoover. You know, don't act like it's my fault, I can't help the people I know sometimes. I know him well enough to know you can't believe anything he says. He's grandiose and he flatters people he thinks are important so he can think he's important too."

"Yeah, well, he drugged me and made me sick for I don't know how many days. He's important enough to cause misery."

The squirrel was now on its rear legs, looking at them, tail quickly wigwagging, belly palpitating. Roof rat, Alice thought, and said, "You know, it's like rats weren't important unless they were the rats that had the fleas that carried the bubonic plague." She could see her comparison didn't make any sense to Joe. She waited until a fat man on a bicycle rode out of the woods and past them, while the squirrel returned to four legs and crouched, before she went on: "Dick Hoover thinks he's important because the Procida Society has him do some of their dirty work. Most of the senators and congressmen and other politicians are power freaks like him. Power groupies, you know? The real powers are some people who make decisions at oil companies, utilities, weapons plants, car factories — not necessarily the CEOs, but the real deciders. Hoover believes everything the Procida Society says is, you know, pure gospel, as the saying goes."

"What you mean 'gospel'? Are they religious fanatics?"

"They're not that kind of fanatics. Just the opposite. They claim their members represent all kinds of religions." She saw the squirrel turn 180 degrees in an instant, run off to nowhere. "But I've seen enough to see the ones who run the society believe in, you know, some sort of archaic wild frontier morality. I don't know how to explain it, it's, you know, something like the morals of *The Sopranos* or the Godfather movies, you know? Do you know I know tae kwon do? That'd be too religious, exotic for the Procida Society, if they knew."

Joe said, "The stuff you're telling me doesn't make any sense." Now they were watching a girl and three boys, all Spandex-clad bicyclists, zooming down the street, bearing down toward them

"Damn it, Joe, now you're trying to mess with my mind. I'm telling you the truth. Of course it doesn't make sense. That's the way it is, there's no sense to it. Don't you understand that?"

Joe: "Lookit, they got senators and bosses and professors." He paused while the cycling quartet zipped in front of them, then said, "Why do they want a little guy like me? Or even Herman? He's helpless, now, without Nora."

Alice, wiping sweat off her face with a thumb: "For the same reason they wanted me, of course. They're afraid. They want us for members because that's how they think they can control us. They're scared of what photovoltaics will develop into. I think right now they're also scared of what you might uncover about Nora's murder and of what you might say to others."

"Do they control you?"

Alice was aghast. "Don't say that! Don't do that to me!" She yanked herself up, started to walk away across the lawn. He just watched. Fourteen paces later she turned back, and when she got to Joe she said, "All this entire afternoon I've been trying to tell you. I'm sorry I got put in the Procida Society. Once I got put in, I'm sorry I didn't pay any attention to what the society really does. I really am. I'm sorry I didn't find out about what the society planned to do to Nora or what it's doing to you and Herman. I thought it was some sort of honor society. I didn't know it was a matter of life and death. I'm sorry I have to stay in that society to protect my life. What do I have to do to make you believe me, Joe?" She was standing there, arms at her sides, looking down at Joe on the bench. He just looked at her. She added, "As long as I'm a member, I'm not only safe from them, you know, maybe I can throw a monkey wrench into their works some day."

Joe looked expectantly up at her — she thought, does he like my idea of sabotaging the Procida Society? He said, "So your society has all their power and they're these great big, important politicians and bosses and stuff. But they're nothing but scared little bullies."

"Yes!" Alice said, shaking her head. "You've got that right. That's what they are. I saw some of these people close up. Some of them are charming, they have charisma, some of them know a lot of facts. What blew my mind when I got to know them and got to hear them talk, was their, you know, mediocrity. The worst part of it all, they really really believe in their own brilliance and they want to completely stop progress toward depending on renewable energy. And they're getting away with it. Their senators and congressmen are selling the public on the idea that since we're in a deep economic recession, the government can't afford the money to support solar energy." She wiped sweat off her face with her thumb again.

Joe said, "That's why your club killed Nora."

"Damn it, don't keep saying it's my club." Alice heard a faint sound, looked down, saw that the squirrel was back, now on four legs, tail switching, looking at them. She looked back at Joe, thought before she said, "Of course they don't want my company to make photovoltaics either. I found out, you know, that's the real reason Kemtrola Oil is suing us — to push our stockholders into demanding we should stop, you know, work on photovoltaics. That's good enough for the Procida Society, and my boss and Kemtrola's officers are all members." Not good enough for the squirrel, apparently, since it again turned and ran off.

The truth was, this day's conversation with Alice was a big relief to Joe, now he was beginning to believe her again. He was glad that she seemed to be just as relieved that she was confiding in him. They had enchiladas at a restaurant and she stayed in the guest room at Joe's house that night. Joe couldn't sleep. He watched the news on television, all about the fierce heat wave in the west and south and east, even though it was only in the 90s in Franklin, and about the United Nations having a special session to decide what to do about an African country where the dictator, backed by his personal wealth in bribes from an oil company that exported oil from there, was slaughtering a pro-democracy rebellion.

He got out of bed at about one in the morning and went out the back door in his pajamas. Another clear night, the moon was nearly full, so he could only make out a few faint stars overhead. A warm, humid summer night, now and then a bit of a breeze from the west where city lights glowed above the horizon. He thought about the Procida Society and about Alice Kim. He was still having spells of mistrust about her, thoughts of, what was she keeping from him? ever since she had said she was a member. But her admission led him to mainly trust her in spite of those passing doubts.

He thought about Nora, how she used to enjoy summer nights like this, how when she and he were young they sometimes went swimming after work or rode down the river with friends in a motorboat, ate ice cream in the park in the dark, and how while they were married she almost never got to do those things because she was so busy with school, with inventing sundidos, and then with her new job here with Herman. He went back indoors, sat at the table by the window and looked out. Some time later Alice, in her pajamas, came out of her room and sat across from Joe at the table. He said, "Would you like some tea?"

"Yes I would." She said it softly, not looking at him.

He made two cups of mint tea. She thanked him. She was frowning, her face looked unhappy in the moonlight as she looked at him, looked out the window. He had no way of knowing she was thinking about herself and Nora and Dr Dryden and the sundidos and himself. She said, "Do you remember the car-battery sundido that Nora shipped to me?"

"Yes."

"I've got it working. I cut off the gas tank on my hybrid car. I bypassed it, you know, so now the car runs entirely on the sundido." Joe had nothing to say to that and that was the extent of her talk. She drank the tea slowly and then went back to her bed. Eventually Joe went back to his.

In the morning when Joe was driving Alice to the airport she said, "You really need to join the Procida Society, just to protect yourself. If you do, you'll be safe. Because then they'll think you're on their side."

Joe despised that idea. "They killed Nora" was his reply.

Joe went to Herman's office that day. Herman again did not. There was no sign of anyone else. He went out to Herman's home. Nobody there. So the Procida Society had abducted Herman. Was he still being held at the Procida Society's Daryl Newjoy Memorial Institute for Psychiatry and Psychoanalysis? Did he answer their silly question about responsibility or sanity or whatever? Was he even alive? Maybe they'd rejected his answer and, for all Joe knew, were torturing him to death.

No phone calls or e-mails from Herman. Several times that day Joe had a strong impulse to go downtown to the Franklin police or the FBI and tell them where to find Nora's and Dr. Dryden's killers and that the Procida Society was holding Herman against his will. Each time Joe had that idea he remembered what had happened when he was a boy — how his father, helped by his uncles, had been able to talk a little blarney here, give a few donations there, and jolly police and officials into ignoring his violations. And his father was just one man, not a whole club or society or gang of politicians and bosses. Besides, by now Herman may just be taking a vacation — he may need one after the Procida Society's assaults on his mind and body.

But damn it, there was that video of Nora's murder to show the police and the FBI. Surely they'd arrest the killers once they saw it and Joe told them where the killers were. What had Herman done with that video? Where was it? Without it Joe figured he had nothing. What would happen if he told that bootylicious FBI babe that his wife's killers are in that psycho place in the woods and hills of Connecticut? That he'd been kidnapped by the Procida Society, held in a dungeon, seen his wife's and Dr. Dryden's murderers hang around, had to listen to a U.S. senator tell lies. What, a U.S. senator? Yes, they've always had senators and presidents and kings and queens, too. Because the Procida Society has been around since before Christopher Columbus and it runs countries, fights wars, and kidnapped Herman and me, too. Why did they kill your wife and kidnap you two? Because our battery will change the world and make the internal combustion engine obsolete.

And the FBI babe would look at me like she pitied me and say sorry, nothing she could do, her hands were tied, and besides it's time for her to go to the gym and do her healthful exercises. Forget the police and the FBI, when did they ever do me any good?

Joe spent the afternoon mostly swimming in Franklin's lake. Each time he got out of the water and sat awhile on a park bench under a tree, he started thinking again about what to do next. If the Society killed Herman, what would happen to Herman's lab, the batteries, the deals to build cars to run on those batteries? Who were Herman's heirs? No, where did Herman get the money to operate? Would all his property go to some bank?

Back at Herman's office, where Herman was not, Joe could not get into Herman's computer to read the e-mails — he did not know Herman's password. Joe went through the piles of Herman's mail, did not even find a single letter that looked promising enough to open. It was hopeless, Joe knew he could not go on like that. He decided that if Herman wasn't back by tomorrow morning he would try to get the police and FBI to take action, despite his own better judgment.

He ate fried perch at a restaurant, drove home, thought about Nora, about times when they'd been enjoying sex and she'd teased him: "You're such an animal, I should have you arrested for bestiality." He was tired of thinking, weary of thinking about the Procida Society, wished he could never hear of it again. Nevertheless, while the evening twilight was still a bright glow he got three telephone calls. The first was while he was in the kitchen reading a newspaper article about a fight over Russia cutting off electricity to Lithuania and the radio was playing a Beyonce song. The caller, in a reedy contralto voice, said, "Mister Heatley? Joseph Heatley?" Yes. "Oh, I'm so glad you're there. This is Mildred Baugh. I'm so sorry about the death of your wife — "

Who was this woman? Joe had no patience with euphemisms on that evening. "She was murdered — "

Mildred Baugh interrupted him: "Exactly. She was murdered by ruthless lunatics. Mister Heatley, I was terribly worried about you ever since I learned that the Procida Society was holding you. Did they damage you?"

How did she know so much? The answer to this stranger's question was none of her business. Not only that, she had an imperious way of talking that made Joe dislike her immediately. He said, "Who are you?"

"I'm Mildred Baugh and I must talk with you. Please. It's tremendously important. Have you heard from Herman Sorg today?"

"No, I haven't. He — "

"You'll see him tomorrow. Let's you and I meet after that. Don't tell him you're coming to talk with me. I live at 2109 Maple Cliffs Drive. We can get together at eight o'clock tomorrow evening — "

"Hey, wait. I'm not making any appointments. What makes you think I'm going to see Herman Sorg tomorrow? Who are you? Why are you sticking your nose into my business? Don't tell me you're Mildred Baugh again."

"Of course you're entitled to answers. I'll explain it all when we meet tomorrow." She hung up.

Of course Joe wasn't going to meet her tomorrow. He was having enough trouble with Herman and Alice and the FBI and the Procida Society. He did not want to add the snotty-sounding Mildred Baugh to his complications and he hoped if he never talked with her she'd disappear. But he also hoped she was predicting accurately about Herman returning tomorrow. Then they could get their heads together and figure out some idea of what they would do next. Or more accurately, get done to them, since the Procida Society seemed to have the situation completely under their control.

The next call came less than a quarter-hour later, while he was in the front room watching a TV newscaster tell about the prosecution of energy-company bosses and how former U.S. government officials were now living in Dubai, becoming Dubai citizens to escape criminal prosecution over here for letting those energy-company criminals set American energy policy, and Joe was simultaneously trying to read an article about thousands of deaths from the current heat wave in the U.S. The guy on the other end was a baritone who sounded young and said, "Joe, you don't know me but I'm a friend of yours. I know what you went through when you were held at the Procida Society. It's not often we find someone who takes a principled stand as you did."

"Who're you?"

"Who I am isn't important. Let's just say I'm one of a number of concerned citizens who think the Procida Society wields far too much influence in America. And not only here — "

"Just tell me who you are, hell with your Procida Society talk — "

"Yes, exactly, the hell with them. As I was about to say, we believe the Procida Society wields far too much influence not just in American life but also in world affairs. It's a left-wing radical organization — "

"How come you're calling me? What do you want from me? Tell me or hang up."

"We want you on our side. We see you have the necessary courage to oppose the society and we want you to join us."

Joe was emotionally beat, he did not want to hear any more. He hung up. Within ten minutes, while he was reading about the rising price of gasoline and a TV reporter was describing a nuclear power-plant accident in France near Mediterranean seaside cities, there was another telephone call that began, "Hi, there! This is Betty Bluebird and I'm calling to ask if you and your loved ones are getting enough — " He hung up before the insanely happy woman could tell him enough what. A lousy end to a lousy day. Somewhere a loony bin, probably the Procida Society's own loony bin in Connecticut, must have fallen down and all the loonies escaped and somehow they got his telephone number and were calling him. That night he had the nightmare about Nora in the Procida Society again, only this time the skinny long-jawed woman looked even more vicious and dangerous.

"Yeah, they drugged me too and put me in their silly little jail and asked me their dumb little question. A lot of cheesy melodrama. I had to make up some answer to 'How can I know I exist?' At least the meals were good."

They were in Herman's office the next day and Herman was telling Joe about his experiences during the last four days. First, four men from the Procida Society had come calling at that office. They had drugged Herman and flown him to the Newjoy Memorial Clinic in Connecticut. There Herman had gone through pretty much what Joe had gone through. Herman looked tired. He drooped, he didn't move much, he jerked when he did move. He talked slowly, as if he was struggling to think and remember.

"You're lucky you're still alive. Now you're back," Joe said, "you can back up my story. See, the police and the FBI may not believe what happened if it's just one guy. But now the Procida Society kidnapped two of us, we can go to the cops this afternoon and tell them where to find those two who killed Nora."

Herman just stared incredulously at Joe before saying, "Where?"

"What do you mean 'where'? They were walking around that Procida Society psycho institute, bold as can be. Their names are Velma Snell and Veli Kokola. Didn't you see them?"

Herman thought before he said, "No. Are you sure those drugs didn't make you hallucinate?"

Joe said, "They musta affected your brain. The drugs, I mean. Those two were right there while Senator Whitlock and Dick Hoover were dumping their manure on me."

Herman looked at the ceiling, said slowly, "Hoover and Whitlock, yeah. Whitlock claimed the Procida Society began during the Middle Ages in order to start the Renaissance and it's been trying to protect the world from ignorance ever since. He claimed the society is just being pragmatic and has no ideology. Apparently he thinks cryptofascism isn't an ideology."

"Did they give you their truth drug, nyalhis?"

"You mean the drink that makes impulses irresistible. Yeah, Hoover put it in my coffee."

"Did you black out like I did?"

Herman yawned before he said, "Yeah, but eventually the amnesia wore off. Now I can remember just about everything they asked me. Let me see, was I phobic? Was I afraid of girls? Was I afraid to undress in front of others because my penis is too small? Did I have nightmares about being ignored? Questions about movies, art." Herman yawned then went on, "Books I read, what I thought of Plato's *Symposium*. My religion and politics, my childhood, adulthood. If Hoover's publishing my life story, I ought to get paid." He was looking at the floor, he seemed to be talking to himself.

Joe said, "They said they asked all those questions to see if we were good enough, or something, to join the Procida Society. The ones who aren't good enough, they just disappear."

"They don't really. They return to their normal lives, or as normal as possible." Herman yawned again before he said, "Hoover told me a few of them went home and tried to sue the Procida Society.

The three that actually got so far as a court trial all lost their suits. He implied the others dropped their suits after awhile or else made some out-of-court settlement with the Procida Society."

"Yeah, well, too bad Diane Watkins didn't know that. They had her in the cell next to mine. She was scared out of her mind they were going to kill her if she gave a wrong answer. I saw them drag her off."

Herman sighed as if educating Joe was a hard chore. "No. I heard about her. They didn't kill her and there was no reason to frighten her like that. If the Procida Society has been around for seven hundred years, they ought to find cheaper and less complicated ways to recruit members. Or not recruit them."

Joe said, "And there was no reason for them to kill Nora. You know, we can prove they're not — "

"No." Herman finally looked at Joe and said, "We can't prove anything. We can't prove the society murdered Nora. All you have is your word, and you were drugged when you think you saw those killers." He sounded more alert when he said that.

Joe was stunned at that. Even more stunning was what Herman said next: "And the Procida Society really are brilliant people. They do have a vision. They want the same things we want — a world without poverty or war or pollution. Of course it sounds like heaven on earth. And they'll have to work through a lot of problems to get there. But so would we." He shrugged at Joe, hands at his sides, palms up, as if to say, what can I do?

The astonished Joe managed to say, "But that's not true. You've got a solution right here. You're gonna mass-produce sundidos and they aren't."

"No, they aren't. But they won't oppose my doing it." Herman sat up as if he was pulling himself together. "There's a difference. A lot of what Hoover said is complete nonsense, but he's right about some of the most important things. We could mass-produce sundidos. Auto makers could produce millions of low-priced cars and trucks and S.U.V.s that use them, in every country, within eighteen months. A country like China could convert all its heat and light to our sundidos just about that fast. Other countries that depend on coal and oil will want to do the same."

"Yeah, yeah, I know. Nora and I always said that. Before they killed her."

Herman shook his head, said, "It'll destroy the world banking system if it's not a gradual transition. The key factor is in the timing, in not delivering sundidos until the world is ready for them. Introducing sundidos now will make the changes happen too fast. So fast that Hoover is right that it's even going to begin wars. They might claim to be righteous wars, like Bush claimed about his war in Iraq. Or Russia will try to revive the Soviet Union. Really, though, they're just going to be wars about energy again. Only this time instead of fighting over selling oil to America, they're going to fight over smaller and smaller markets. And as soon as one shoots off a nuclear bomb, the rest are going to follow. There's no way America can keep out of the next war, either. That'll be World War III."

"Aw, that's so, that's — how can you fall for Hoover's garbage? Even though they killed Nora, they can't stop progress."

Herman pounded his desk, snapped, "What do you mean they can't? What do you call this place? A hive of activity? The dye maker breaks down, the workers at the factory that makes my battery casings are on strike, I can't get supplies, the city of Franklin says I'm breaking their zoning laws. Most of all, Nora's been murdered and I can't go on without her. Progress here is at a total standstill."

For Joe this conversation was one amazement after another. He said, "Well, it sounds like you're giving up. Quitting." Herman just looked back at him, so he added, "After all the Procida Society did to you."

Now Herman looked tired again. "I'm not quitting. Kemtrola Oil is offering to buy me out." Now Joe was worse than astonished. He just gaped at Herman. "They have the money and the clout to do everything I can't do now. They've offered to keep me working on photovoltaics."

Joe had to absorb it all before he shook his head and said, "Kemtrola Oil tried to buy Nora's patent. She turned them down to work for you instead."

Herman just looked at Joe with sad eyes, finally said, "And your point is?"

"What's going on here? Are you gonna back me up when I get those two killers arrested? The ones who killed Nora?"

Herman just looked at him some more before saying, "What're you going to do? Call the police?" When Joe had no response to that. Herman said, "Go away. Leave me alone."

After Joe left, Herman thought, the Procida Society made a mistake when they tried to recruit him. He's simply not intellectually advanced, let alone emotionally advanced, to our level. Herman went on to imagine the interview he would be doing in a few days, after all the lawyers' work will be done and his contracts with Kemtrola Oil will be signed. While the TV cameras would record or, better yet, broadcast live, the chick with the big hair would reverently say, "I'm speaking with Herman Sorg, the sundido entrepeneur who today announced his partnership with Kemtrola Oil Corporation. Mr. Sorg, how did you acquire your profound genius and depth of vision, so that you're changing the course of human civilization?" And he would modestly reply, "I'm only one simple man doing what I can, for the benefit of us all." And she would be so overcome by his prophetic brilliance and humility that she would say, "Would you please have sex with me?" He thought of phoning Sicinski, letting him do the first in-depth interview, then instead decided to call his lawyer again and then Mildred Baugh and Barbara.

Chapter 13

JOE LEFT THE SHOP. He knew better than to go to the police and the FBI with his story. A half hour after he had left Herman's office he went back there to argue with Herman, harass him for being a quitter, maybe punch him. By then Herman's car was gone and nobody was there.

At a quarter of eight that evening Joe parked his car in the semicircle drive, under the portico in front of the mansion at 2109 Maple Cliffs Drive. The sun hadn't yet gone down but the place looked dirty and dark, in the shade of big, old maple trees and poplars with drooping, heavy leaves. It looked dark inside, too, he saw no lights through the oversized picture windows on the first and second floors. Nothing good is gonna come of this, so why did I come here? he asked himself. He was beginning to see how alone he was and that he had no more than a faint hope that this Mildred Baugh might shed some light on what he could do next, if anything. But in a mansion like this, something out of Edgar Allan Poe, withered and sere, whatever sere was, she was probably as crazy as she'd sounded on the telephone.

The woman who met him at the door was even like Poe's Ulalume, at least to the extent that she was slender, clad in black, and had a vaguely serious look on her face. But she was suntanned, brown-haired, short-haired, and wore big black-rimmed glasses above a long nose with a tip so pointed it could drill holes. The black clothes she wore this time were black jeans and black McDonald Observatory t-shirt, and she looked taller yet less willowy, more substantial than a Poe woman. Maybe the evening shadows were why he didn't recognize her immediately. What she said was not exactly inspiriting: "Come enter into the Dank Tarn of Darkness. Cool, you're early."

"I met you someplace," Joe said. "What's your name?"

Not-Ulalume, scratching the tip of her nose — sharpening it? — said, "Sure, you met us. Herman took us to the memorial for your wife Nora, remember? I'm Barbara Fleming."

Oh, yeah, she was one of the ones there, Joe thought. Barbara led him into the twilit house, into a large room. A too-large room, in fact, the scale was excessive — the ceiling was too high, the filigree carved into the beams was too elaborate, the glazed ceiling light fixtures looked like the wings of some huge extinct birds, the crummy painting on the wall, showing Indians shading their eyes and looking up to a mountain, was faded and oversized. Hard to tell, the room was so dark, but Joe could see a couple cobwebs in the gloom and there were surely more. The room looked dusty, dirty, old, and not just because of the evening darkness.

Joe couldn't see the painting very well anyway despite the picture window and the light in the room, in a corner, from a floor lamp next to where Mrs. Baugh, a bony old woman with thinning white hair, sat like a queen in a throne-like chair with a back that was a foot taller than herself. She was thin and had a vertical face, too, and she wore a too-big skirt with faded squares like a quilt, and a black long-sleeved blouse. The net effect was to make her perhaps seem taller than she actually was. She leaned forward on a cane, watching him eagerly. He looked up in the grayness over her head. Was a raven roosting somewhere up there, about to quoth "Nevermore"?

He recognized Mrs. Baugh, of course, she was the other woman Herman had brought to Nora's memorial. So these two were friends of Herman. Having met them already with Herman led Joe to feeling a certain provisional distrust. They didn't look alike, were they mother and daughter? "I'm so pleased that you came, Mr. Heatley," Mrs. Baugh said in an annoying reedy voice as he sat down on a similar chair facing her. "Especially since I have so few visitors. Now that I'm in my declining years most people find me depressing."

"Why'd you call me here?" From there he could see out the picture window. Past the maple trees and down the hill was the big lake, where at least a dozen boats were still on the water and with distant city homes in a half-ring around it.

"We have no need for electricity or gas here. Instead I'm grateful to your poor wife Nora, God rest her soul. She and my associate Barbara" — nodding at the younger woman, who was sitting down demurely in a smaller chair next to her — "installed sundidos to replace them."

Joe was not surprised: "She did that for Herman Sorg too."

The regal Mildred Baugh said, "We discovered something today to add to your woes. Barbara, would you please show Mr. Heatley what you printed?" The younger woman silently handed Joe a sheet of paper. Mrs. Baugh said, "That is from today's *San Francisco Chronicle* web site."

Drowning Victim Identified
The woman whose body was discovered in the Pacific Ocean
near San Luis Obispo yesterday has been identified. She is
Diane Watkins, a well-known Los Angeles civil liberties attorney and activist who had been missing for the last ten days.

The article went on about how Diane Watkins died was a mystery and that she had appeared worried and apprehensive in the
days before her disappearance, according to family and friends and
coworkers at the California Citizens Action Institute. Joe did not
read the entire article. When he looked up Mrs. Baugh said, "Barbara, would you please bring Mr. Heatley and me each a cup of
coffee?"

Without so much as a nod or a raised eyebrow Barbara left the
room Mrs. Baugh said to Joe, "I understand Dr. Watkins was a
prisoner of the Procida Society at the same time you were in their
clutches."

"Herman said the Procida Society didn't kill her. Who are you?"

"Nevertheless, they killed her. What do you think of Herman
Sorg now that he's back from his ordeal?"

Even though this woman was apparently Herman's friend Joe
did not spare whatever good feelings she had about him. "He was
brainwashed," Joe said. "He believes all the stuff they told him and
he's gonna sell out to Kemtrola Oil. Look, why am I here?"

"Oh, dear. I'm afraid it's far worse than that," Mrs. Baugh said in
that reedy voice that had irritating treble gravel in it. "Poor Herman
joined the Procida Society. What he said about what happened to
Dr. Watkins was the official society version. And his lawyer and the
oil company's lawyers are drawing up contracts this week."

Joe was not surprised. He said, "What do you care about all this?
How do you know all these things?"

"Mr. Heatley, this is how I know the sad story," she said, leaning toward him on her cane and frowning as if she were regally ad-
monishing him. "Three years ago Herman Sorg was unemployed
and living in his parents' home here in Franklin. He had failed in
his previous job, which was operating a macrobiotic restaurant in
Grand Haven, Michigan. Now, how could he afford to set up a
business as ambitious as his photovoltaics works without money?
His mother loaned him some to start. But it was my vulnerable husband who was so excited by Herman's plans to save the human race

from itself that he gave him the money he needed to proceed. My husband was the famous philanthropist and state senator Osbert Baugh, you may have heard of him." Joe hadn't.

Mrs. Baugh sighed, looked down. "In his way, my husband was tragic. It was the last investment of his life. After his death my Barbara learned about Dr. Dryden's sundido research and led Herman to recruit your wife Nora. So you can see we were the ones who were responsible for Herman. I gave him the money to operate, to hire Mrs. Heatley and set up his office and laboratory. And who fully expected to continue to finance all his future sundido adventures. Until now that he's sold out. That's why I care about him and why I despise and mourn all these shenanigans with the Procida Society. Does that satisfy you?" Now she even looked as if she might cry.

Joe was beginning to glimpse how seriously Herman had betrayed this woman. Maybe it had been almost as much as he had betrayed Nora's memory or Joe. He was even beginning to feel a very little sorry for this skinny woman with her annoying voice. Now she was not looking at him. After some silence he said, "Talk to me some more. How come you know so much about the Procida Society?"

"My husband was a member, God rest his soul. I'm afraid it didn't get much rest on this earth. Chasing after inventions and politicians and priests and gurus and prophets. Especially prophetesses and guruesses. To his masculine sorrow and I'm afraid to the prophetesses' profit, events proved he never had the opportunity to conclude his chases." Was that a momentary smile on the face of the unhappy woman?

Joe was certainly becoming interested in her. Now she leaned back and looked past him, both hands resting on her cane. Maybe because her face was so wrinkled, she looked very sad again. She was stuck in reminiscing mode: "Maybe poor Osbert's weaknesses weren't his fault. He was an idealist, he always sought truth and enlightenment. The problem was, he believed that he could achieve power to do good without becoming corrupted. And then he joined the Procida Society."

Barbara was back and setting cups of coffee on the end tables next to Joe and Mrs. Baugh. Barbara also set a spoon, sugar bowl, silver creamer, and a plate of what looked like small molasses cookies next to Joe, then sat down without taking a cup or a cookie for herself. Behind those incongruously black-rimmed, big eyeglasses she had alert eyes. Her nose was obviously red from, not gin blossoms, but the sun and she had the thin pale lips of what, a censor? She didn't seem to smile easily, unless that odd curve to her mouth was the hint of a secret amusement. "Thank you, dear," Mrs. Heatley said and smiled a quick smile of thanks at her, then resumed:

"Joining the Procida Society fortified Osbert's faith in his own integrity. So he became able to rationalize every compromise of his principles. He sincerely believed each compromise was a necessary, temporary sacrifice that would lead to a permanent higher good. As a result his compromises compounded until they became virtually his career as a senator. Some of the quacks he enriched were quite charming. But he achieved very little of the good that he originally set out to do. Of course, in his failure he unwillingly realized his likeness with the rest of humanity, since desire and failure are the destiny of human existence.

"Even so, he continued to try to transcend his fate. Hence his aiding Herman Sorg." She glanced at Barbara, who was looking at Joe's feet during this tale of woe. Then she said, "Mr. Heatley, what are you doing about your wife's murderers?"

It was none of their business, of course. But Mrs. Baugh did not seem to want to damage him and Barbara seemed to follow her lead. He was hardly aware that he was beginning to trust them when he answered, "I want to get them busted. Cause I saw them at that Daryl Newjoy Memorial Institute for Psychiatry — the Procida Society's jail. But — "

Barbara said, "Did Herman see them there too? Will he i.d. them too, along with you?"

"Naw, he's not gonna do a thing. He said so today. If anything gets done, I got to do it myself. See, the FBI and the police won't lift a finger. So it's nobody but me against the Procida Society."

Barbara said to Joe, "There's a good cop who might help you on the Franklin police force. Captain Dahlmann — Mrs. Baugh's known him a long time. Twice he arrested swindlers who tried to bilk Senator Baugh."

"Yes indeed. Captain Sven Dahlmann. Mr. Heatley, my husband could easily afford to be swindled. In fact he often was, by lawyers and corporations and other legal means," Mrs. Baugh explained. "It's only when he was cheated illegally that he could strike back. Of course, illegal thieves are those so poor in finances and friendless and otherwise poor in body and spirit that they can't pass laws legalizing their crimes. Their opposites are legislators and the rich people who buy them."

Barbara said to Joe, "Tell Captain Dahlmann that your wife's murderers are agents of the Procida Society's larger conspiracy. You may not have to take on the Procida Society all by yourself." She was looking intently at Joe, hunched forward, hands folded in front of her, tapping her feet.

"So true," Mrs. Baugh said. "Tell him I sent you. If necessary, I will be glad to verify what you tell him. If he thinks your story is ridiculous or he refuses to help you for some other reason, well, at least you can be more certain that your problem is unsolvable than you are now."

Joe didn't have any idea what to do. He said, "Oh, yeah? Thanks, Mrs. Baugh. But look, aren't you afraid of the Procida Society yourself?"

"My contacts in the Procida Society think I'm a sympathizer," said Mrs. Baugh, "as well as a harmless old schemer. A feeble old broad."

"Helpless," said Barbara.

"Foolish," said Mrs. Baugh. "Intellectually challenged."

"They think she's morally on their debased level," said Barbara.

"I purposely feed their vanity," said Mrs. Baugh. "I despise them for how they destroyed Osbert. Of course, if the Procida Society hadn't corrupted him, others would surely have done it. Dear Osbert was too eager to feel potent and important and to show he was more than merely a rich man's son. So he was easily corruptible. Nevertheless, I'm prepared to go to any length necessary to help you fight the Procida Society's conspiracies."

Joe was getting an idea of why she had instigated this conversation and he didn't like it: "Is that what you want? Me to get revenge for you?"

"Surely not revenge, Mr. Heatley. Justice, don't you think? Of course, revenge and justice are the same, aren't they? In practice, of course, if not by definition. But please believe me, I don't want to tell you what to do. I want to help, if possible. Only if you want help."

The young woman frowned, shook her head, murmured, "Mildred, the sundido patent."

"Yes indeed, most important," Mrs. Baugh said and turned back to Joe: "And now something else. Who holds the patent on the process of manufacturing sundidos?"

"Me and Alice Kim."

Mrs. Baugh said. "Are you going to continue to work for Herman Sorg?"

"Yeah. Since I own half the patent," Joe said, "Herman needs me to make sundidos. He hired Nora after she turned down an offer from Kemtrola Oil. She said they wanted to bury sundidos instead of build them."

Barbara squinted, shook her head yesyesyes, said, "She was right. See, even if they make him a partner in name, the ones really in charge will be pulling Herman's strings. So now he won't need the patent, unless he and Kemtrola're scheming to use you and it to bury sundidos, like she told you. What work are you doing for him?"

"All he actually asked me to do was to find out who killed Nora."

Mrs. Baugh said, "Dear, dear. And now that you've found out, he won't go to the police with you. Oh, my. As far as you know, then, does he want you for anything at all besides the sundido patent?"

Joe had to think a moment before he said, "Nothing. Today he didn't even say if he wants me to go on working for him."

"Then we have a proposal for you. But don't breathe the least word of this to Herman Sorg. You don't have to answer us right away. Although at my great advanced age my spirit may depart my body at any time. So I'd prefer an early answer. Is that clear?"

"Yeah. What's your proposal?"

"Now. Mr. Heatley, as you may know by now, I'm very wealthy. Poor Osbert had inherited an enormous fortune before he married me and after we were married I inherited another enormous fortune. Even after the stock market crashed in September, 2008, we were shamefully wealthy."

Barbara, looking down again: "Obscenely wealthy. Sinfully wealthy."

Mrs. Baugh: "Sickeningly wealthy. Repulsively wealthy."

Barbara: "Oh, criminally wealthy."

Mrs. Baugh: "Yes, criminally too, even though we broke no actual laws. No one, of course, acquires so much money without doing a great deal of damage to the planet and to her and his fellow beings. After my husband's death I continued to back Herman's mad, wild-eyed scheme to mass-produce sundidos. It's partly penance or reparations, or shame, for my and Osbert's families' damages. Also, after all, if I die rich it means I've squandered my life."

Barbara, still looking down: "Frittered it away."

Mrs. Baugh: "Farted it away."

Barbara: "Pissed it away."

Mrs. Baugh: "Yes, or otherwise wasted it. All rich people, after all, are wastrels, is my experience. Although to be honest, I surely would have wasted my life anyway even if I had been poor."

Even though Barbara had surely heard this story often enough before, she now looked intently, concernedly at Mrs. Baugh. Joe didn't care how rich or ashamed Mrs. Baugh was, so he took his first bite of cookie — it proved to be a ginger cookie — and swallowed his first swallow of coffee. Mrs. Baugh went on: "So if you're willing to help carry on the work that Mrs. Heatley started, we will hire you. I mean to transfer my support from Herman to Barbara here. What you'll have to do is see to it that inexpensive solar cell storage batteries — sundidos — are mass produced, just as Herman and Mrs. Heatley were originally going to do."

"You mean Barbara's gonna start a business and run it with me? Even though I don't know how to make a sundido?"

He looked at Barbara, who said, "See, you know your wife's fellow physicists, right? The ones who did sundido research with her. So you can find someone who does know to make them. Isn't this what Herman originally wanted you to do? Alice Kim understands the process. So you can pay her or another person who knows to work any way they want. Either permanently or just long enough to train others to make them."

Joe was startled, confused, by what the two of them were saying. He felt like they were assaulting him. He tried to sort out their offer, finally said, "What do you want? Me or the right to make sundidos?"

Barbara, hunched forward, foot tapping, looking intensely at Joe, said, "Even if you only want to be a figurehead, we mostly need you for the patent. How much you get involved in the business is up to you. But — "

Mrs. Baugh: "You seem smart and serious. I really do hope you choose to work with Barbara."

Barbara, not even noticing that she was tipping her chair forward: "Look, we're in a mess. We need you. You can see we need all the help we can get."

"Yeah, I see. Thank you..."

Barbara: "There's one big thing, though. Mrs. Baugh and I agree that it's important to start the sundido business, with her money, outside the United States. We think Canada would be best. Ontario's already the biggest photovoltaics market in the world."

Mrs. Baugh: "The Procida Society has no influence at all there. You can operate free of harassment." She looked at Joe as though she was trying to make herself smile, said, "And now, Mr. Heatley, I wish you the best possible success when you speak to Captain Dahlmann."

The conversation left Joe surprised, confused. Barbara saw that, was concerned as she walked him to the front door. Outside, she said, "Before you go. Look, don't be fooled by appearances. I know this place looks like it rose up out of the Dismal Bog of Desolation and Despair. But Mrs. Baugh isn't a silly old rich lady with too much imagination. Just the opposite. She's one of the sanest people I've met in this mad world. I've been her assistant for seven years."

"Oh, yeah, I figure she means it," was what Joe said. His feelings were agitated, he was still stunned at the enormity of the offer Mrs. Baugh and Barbara had just made to him.

"Well, she was willing to give Herman Sorg just millions of dollars if he needed it. He turned out to be a bad investment, so now she's chosen me and you. For her sake I hope you don't blow it like he's doing."

The force of Barbara's intensity, her seriousness unnerved Joe, made him feel, what?, afraid of saying something hurtful? He said, "I'm gonna think about it. You heard her say she doesn't expect my answer right away." He did intend to think about it, even though he expected to still think her offer was ridiculous when he woke up the next morning.

"I really want to know what you decide to do. Obviously. Since it'll make such a difference in what I do next. Another thing, are you going to the police tomorrow? About that man and woman who murdered your wife?"

"I got no idea what to do," Joe admitted, and as he said that he realized he was trusting this earnest young woman with an intimacy. "The FBI agent I saw tried to bullshit me. You can't trust cops. I've known them all my life."

"Captain Dahlman is probably different from the ones you remember." Behind those forbidding black-rimmed specs she had seemed thoughtful all evening, and now, again, she was looking eyebrows up at Joe with what he thought was real concern. She said, "He was fired from the St. Paul police for being too honest. Now he's so good at his job that they can't get rid of him here too. She says he's smarter than the senators and CEOs in the Procida Society. But she says that about a lot of people. She probably thinks the same thing about you." Did that odd curve of Barbara's lips now edge over into a faint, momentary smile?

After Joe was gone Barbara said to Mrs. Baugh, "I definitely want him. I can see that already. I can tell you want him. I think he'll come along with us after he gets justice for Nora Heatley's murder."

"Avenges. Gets vengeance."

"Retaliates. You've been through this already with him."

"Gets closure. An eye for an eye."

Barbara sighed, said, "A slip off a hip could sink a ship."

"Oh, dear," Mrs. Baugh said. "It's so hard to know the right thing. But I'm sure we're doing it."

"What else can we do?" Barbara said. "We've racked our brains over this. The only alternative is to do without sundidos."

"As the rest of the unhappy world beyond our decaying doors does right now. A world of sundidoless pain and sorrow." She would have continued but she saw that Barbara was now leaving the room.

After Joe left, he realized, they complimented me, offering me that job. But the big-brain egomaniacs in the Procida Society tell me I'm a big brain like them. Is that a compliment too or are they all trying to scam me? But what is these women's scam? That night Joe had a dream about Nora and himself together as teenagers in love. As dreams do, this one transformed into another nightmare about the Procida Society. This time he was prisoner again and the skinny long-jawed woman and the tall, stupid man were advancing on him.

Chapter 14

BABYLON THE GREAT IS FALLEN, is fallen, and is become the habitation of devils, and the hold of every foul spirit, and a cage of every unclean and hateful bird. And this is Babylon right here and now, this whole world has become one great big Babylon, everyone's in it together, connected by a pulsating hell of cell phones, the internet, TV, oil spills, greed, and lust.

Captain Sven Dahlmann of the Franklin police believed that. He was determined to be among the ones raptured up to heaven when the time comes, whenever that will be. Pretty soon, he figured, because the signs were proliferating in the 21st century. He couldn't keep count — who could? — of all the wars going on around the world, Asia, Africa, Europe, South, Central, North America, right now this very day. Or of all the earthquakes, plagues, oil spills, hurricanes, droughts, and famines going on. Or of the greed, lovelessness, lying, brutality, and all the other kinds of wickedness among mankind. Or of false prophets and their followers. On top of everything else now you could learn how to make nuclear weapons over the internet, and so many crazy people now had them that Revelation, the last book in the Bible, surely must be coming true

His job was to try, as much as one cop could, to keep a lid on the damage. He knew God said vengeance was His. When Captain Dahlmann first thought about that, he realized he had a moral conflict. Because in his daily work he had to use his judgment — did that mean he had to play God? His conscience eased when he concluded he was not punishing people, he was simply protecting them from each other. Far from judging and meting out punishment, which was God's job, he was just doing His preliminary dirty work.

Now that Captain Sven Dahlmann had become a born-again Christian, his new attitude proved to be good for him in his police work. His tough exterior was now tempered with a degree of tolerance, even as he remained as professional and honest and mistrustful as ever. Now he had some pity as often as anger for the hapless souls he dealt with, lawbreakers and victims both, even punks who cursed him the worst. Maybe most people do the best they can under the circumstances, he'd come to believe.

123

That did not mean he had become exactly forgiving. After all, God gave everyone the choice between right and wrong. So everyone had to accept the consequences of their choices. To whiny miscreants he liked to repeat an old, probably non-Christian saying: Don't commit the crime if you're not willing to do the time.

On the morning after Joe had met Mrs. Baugh, Captain Dahlmann said to him, "One more time. You're telling me that there's this secret society, this Procida Society, that murdered your wife and Dr. Dryden and kidnapped you and Herman Sorg. And they did it to prevent Sorg from building his sundidos. And that you know where to find the murderers. Quite a story. Is that all?" He was looking at Joe as he said it.

They were at Franklin police headquarters, at the captain's desk. Joe said, "There's a whole lot more I don't know about. But I know that much." He thought the story he'd just told the captain sounded crazy, the captain probably figured he was a loony.

What Dahlmann actually thought was, don't feel bad, Heatley, thy time is not yet to know what the great serpent doeth. That was another image the officer remembered from the Bible. What Joe was saying about the secret society, the Procida Society, actually fit suspicions the captain had been nourishing in recent years, made his vague imaginings about a demonic conspiracy take shape, seem real. He said, "Mildred Baugh phoned me before you came. She claims anything you say is gold and I can put it in the bank. Her bank, that is, one of the banks she owns. So you must be good. Most people would think your secret society story is too far out. I wouldn't be talking to you if she wasn't backing you up."

He had his eyes on Joe as he said, "But I talked with Herman Sorg, too. He said he went to the Procida Society headquarters in New York two days after you. Said it's a philanthropic society and he was so impressed by the work they do that he joined. He says you're probably confused about that club cause you've been so upset by your wife's murder."

Joe blew up at that. "Confused? What's he talking about? They did the same things to him they did to me. He told me so himself. Lookit, I can prove everything I told you. I can prove I flew to New York, I stayed at a hotel, I got receipts, I can show you the Procida Society building, the guys who cold-cocked me there. I can show you that lunatic asylum in Connecticut where they held me, where Velma Snell and Veli Kokola that killed Nora are, you saw them murdering Nora on Herman's video, I can show them all to you. In person." He was glaring at Dahlmann, mouth open, and his face felt like it was getting red.

Dahlmann liked to stir people up, liked to manipulate them using the "Let's you and him fight" method. So he liked the way he was handling Joe, was pleased to see Joe was mad. For one thing, it set Joe apart from Herman, who was probably going to go to hell for his pride. He said, "So you have a wild story. Mildred says she knows it sounds crazy but she backs you up. Sorg's known you longer than she's known you and he says the story's crazy because you're going crazy."

"Going crazy!" Joe said. "He said I'm going crazy?"

Dahlmann said, "Not quite. What he said was, you were so upset by your wife's death that you believed things that weren't true."

Joe stood up. "That's the same as saying I'm crazy. That's, that's, how could he? He knows it 's not true. I knew I shouldn't'a come here. I knew you wouldn't believe me. I knew you — " He was almost yelling, he was on the verge of cussing out Dahlmann. Instead he looked around for the exit.

"Sit down!" Dahlmann wasn't actually angry, but he said the words so sharply that Joe turned back to him. "Sit down, we're not done yet." Joe sat, but he was biting down his anger. "Okay, your story's crazy. But you have a few facts to back you up. Some of it Mildred Baugh verifies. Sorg disputes you and he's vague. For instance, where was he for the whole four days he was out of town, supposedly in New York?"

Joe: "He told me he was in the same place I was, that insane asylum in Connecticut. First he went to find me at the Procida Society building in New York and they took him to Connecticut like they did me. They did the same things to him they did to me. That's what he told me"

Dahlmann took no pleasure in trying to sort out the conflicting stories about the Procida Society. Right now Joe's story was the one he wanted to believe, but he had to stay impartial until he knew more. He said, "Herman told me he joined the Procida Society there in New York. He didn't say what he did the rest of those four days. Okay, I'll look into your story. God help you if you're lying to me. God help Herman Sorg if he's lying. The first thing I'm going to do is contact the police in that place in Connecticut. We'll find out about that Kokola and that Snell woman." And just to get back at Joe because this conspiracy yarn was going to make more work for himself, Dahlmann added, "Don't leave town. You started something and now you're going to have to help push it on."

After Joe left Dahlmann thought, no wonder he's mad. Too bad for him, he's been deceived. This case is getting too complicated. If he's telling the truth, the Procida Society're a secret society of infernal schemers, devils. So they say they secretly rule the world, do they? There's another angle I can't overlook — are they some kind of Murder Inc., is that what they do? Then who would hire them to kill Nora Heatley and Dr. Dryden? Dahlmann was glad he had the authority to investigate such problems. Liars and slanderers and blasphemers and unholy schemers, ha!, he thought,

"You went to the police today? After all you've been through with police? And you told them that story about the Procida Society?" Herman Sorg said.

"You knew I was gonna wind up there," Joe said. They were in Herman's office. Herman was seated at this desk and Joe was standing beside it. Herman looked so smug that he made Joe mad, with anger that showed in his frown and his voice: "You told that policeman, that Dahlmann, that I was crazy. Why'd you make up a lie like that?"

"Do you think cops are going to believe what you say about a secret society that hates sundidos and keeps their own private insane asylum? That sounds like some kind of fraud — the Turner Diaries mixed up with James Bond or The Body Snatchers. A conspiracy theory." Herman didn't sound tired this time. Just the opposite, he sounded feisty, eager to argue.

"You know what the Procida Society did to you. Same as they did to me. You can't deny that. You got to tell the truth."

Herman said, "Got to do what? What I'm going to do, what I'm committed to do, is manufacture solar-cell batteries. Before now I was going on alone, on my own resources — "

"Not your resources," Joe said. "You had — " Joe almost said "Mildred Baugh' s money," but remembered she didn't want Herman to know she and Joe were talking. Joe said instead, "You woulda been nothing without Nora."

"That's what I was gonna say before you interrupted. Without Nora I was going on alone and I was a joke. Even with her, the media, if they mentioned me at all, they made fun of the guy who was going to replace internal combustion engines. That's all different now. Now the Procida Society is the first important bunch of people who recognize how important my work is. Thanks to them, now I'm a vice-president of Kemtrola Oil and I've got more responsibilities and these solar cell batteries are going to expand. Everything's changed from what it was a week ago."

"Is that why you're not gonna tell the truth about the Procida Society?"

Herman aimed a smug smile at Joe and said, "What is truth?"

That smile raised the anger level in Joe. "Then I've had it with you," he spat out. "If you won't tell the truth, I won't let you use Nora's process and you can't call them sundidos. If you can't tell the truth, you can't have anything. So now you're alone and you've got less than nothing. Unless you tell the truth about the Procida Society."

Herman just looked calmly at Joe and said, "You want truth, huh? The truth is, getting rid of the internal combustion engine isn't the most important thing I can do for the world. It's not going to stop global warming anyway. The damage that's already been done to the environment is irreversible. The real problem is the population explosion."

Joe: "That's a whole other subject."

"No it's not. Fossil fuels aren't the only things the world's running out of. Don't forget metals, forests, fresh water, food — especially water. The deserts in Africa and Asia are getting bigger every day. Two hundred thousand babies are born every day on Earth. Only a hundred and fifty thousand people die every day. That's adding a million more people to the world in less than every three weeks. They'll consume more and more of less and less stuff. There's the byproducts, too — sewage, garbage, junk. There's disappearing species, too. Remember toads, frogs, bats, butterflies? All the human development upset their ecologies and drove them off the planet."

"What does that have to do with the Procida Society?"

Herman was thoroughly enjoying this conversation. "Crisis management, that's what it's all about. We can't hope for a natural disaster big enough to get rid of enough humans. So we'll have to create the disaster ourselves. Could be a world war or famine or a pandemic like the Black Death. Hundreds of millions of people'll die — "

"Good Lord."

"Some terrorist or some group nobody ever heard of will get blamed for starting the war or the epidemic. These are just some of the solutions the society's come up with so far. They're asked me to help develop some more ideas on how to handle overpopulation."

"You're crazy. The Procida Society's totally nuts."

Herman: "Don't call me crazy. Or us, don't call us crazy. What we are is super realistic. As for my shop here, I'm closing down and moving to Fort Worth, Texas. That's Kemtrola Oil's headquarters. They have their own patented process of making inexpensive solar cell storage batteries."

Joe said, "So you admit it. They bought you out."

"Admit, hell. I'm proud of it. They bought me out. I'm, I mean we're going to use their process, not Nora's, to make those batteries. And yeah, they won't be called sundidos, either. I don't need you any more. Give me your keys to this office and lab. And then go away. And stay away."

There was a message from newspaper reporter Ted Sicinski on Joe's cell phone. The message was, "SKREEK! call me. I want to ask you some questions about sundidos," and his phone number. Joe didn't call him.

That afternoon Joe saw photos of Velma Snell and Veli Kokola on Captain Sven Dahlmann's computer screen. "I got these from the police in Dunning, Connecticut," Dahlmann said. "They're the same two that're on Herman's video that shows them murdering Nora. So you were telling me the truth about that. The officer who e-mailed me back said that mental institution, that Daryl Newjoy Memorial Institute, is their address. They're employees and they apparently live there. He says the place is in the country five miles from the nearest town, in the middle of some woods. Says he's seen both of them but hasn't talked with them. Seems those people at that Memorial Institute keep to themselves and don't socialize with the local people."

"Are you gonna arrest them?"

"I'll have Dunning, Connecticut arrest them. And then have them extradited back here," said Dahlmann, who thought, he seems like a nice fellow. Too nice to hire that pair to murder his wife. That Memorial Institute has got to be more dangerous that those Connecticut police think. A place in the woods and they secretly rule the world from there? A lot of people seem to be possessed by devils these days — are this Procida Society possessed too? What about the antichrist, are these people ruling the world for him? Dahlmann knew about the antichrist, the imposter who would deceive people into sin and then hell. What form would he take, or what form was he taking? Was there more than one antichrist? The Bible wasn't clear about that. Maybe he was a she, maybe he or she had been around a long time. More likely, Dahlmann thought, a lot of antichrists were running loose these days.

It was the weirdest thing. Joe had just arrived home, was using the wand to sweep his car for GPS bugs — it had become a habit with him by now — was thinking, this is a waste of time, when he found another one. This second bug was on the under side of the rear bumper, almost where the previous bug had been. How long had it been there? Joe tried to remember the last time he had used the wand, decided it had been in the morning before he had left to see Dahlmann. The only places where he had parked since then had been at Herman's lab and at a grocery.

Did someone have the nerve to plant the bug on Joe while he was at the police headquarters? Or had someone planted the bug while he was with Herman? Surely Joe would have noticed any suspicious characters around that place. Had someone followed Joe from Herman's to the grocery, planted the bug there? Who? The Procida Society, the FBI, even the Franklin police? If the Procida Society knew Herman was making trouble for Joe, they didn't need to plant the bug. Maybe they didn't know about Herman and they planted it because they suspected, correctly, that Joe didn't intend to join. If the FBI planted it, maybe they wanted Joe to lead them to his accomplices before they busted him. Well, what did they learn about Joe? No secrets, not that day.

Joe figured it was the FBI's bug. Should he just leave it there on his bumper, like he'd left the previous bug? Suppose he wanted to pay a visit to Mrs. Baugh. It wouldn't hurt for the FBI or even the police to know that he had someone as important as her on his side. Who knows, maybe it wouldn't hurt his case for the Procida Society to know that too. Problem was, she'd told Joe she didn't want people to know she was talking with him.

Inside his house Joe found he had another answering-machine message from Sicinski: "Joe, call me, let me know when we can talk. I want to ask you some KAAUCK! I want to find RRAWW! sundidos," and again gave his phone number. Again Joe didn't call.

Barbara Fleming had good reasons to be loyal to her boss. Seven years earlier, when she'd applied for the job as Mrs. Baugh' s assistant, she was new to Franklin then, unemployed, almost completely broke, afraid, had just left her grimly jealous husband, and was living — hiding out, in fact — in a motel. It had been a devastating marriage, her self-confidence had been shredded by his insistence that she was a human wreck who couldn't get along without his magnanimous direction. He couldn't find her so he had harrassed her with phone calls, until she got a new cell phone. He had harrassed her with e-mails until she got a new e-mail address. Mrs. Baugh gave the inexperienced and by now frightened young woman not only employment but also a place to live, in a room in the mansion.

One day Barbara's husband learned where she was living and came to fetch her. His bravado leaked out when the senator answered the door and described the state's anti-stalking laws to him. A good lawyer might have told him that the senator was exaggerating those laws, their penalties, and the rigor of their enforcement. But the senator's words, as well as the fact that a state senator was Barbara's protector, had scared him, he had become too ashamed to tell a lawyer that his selfless attempts to save his wife from herself might be considered stalking. He didn't fight Barbara's divorce suit, either. Instead he moved west — to California, the last Barbara had heard.

Barbara was a fast learner. While she threw herself into her work for Mrs. Baugh for seven years, she both outgrew what was left of her innocence and gradually recaptured her premarital independence of spirit. Even as her self-confidence increased she continued to be naturally self-effacing, out of gratitude to Mrs. Baugh. After the senator's death mutual aloneness became a closer bond between the two women. Once she told Mrs. Baugh, "I never understood why you hired me in the first place."

Mrs. Baugh' s reply was, "It was four very true things that you said when I interviewed you. You mentioned that justice is unnatural, there's no justice in nature. So instead of praying for justice, you prayed for mercy. And then we were discussing philanthropy and you said, if you give a hungry man a fish, he'll eat today. If you teach a man to fish instead, he may starve to death before he catches anything. In my declining condition I forget what the other two were, but your proverbs were so very wise that I knew immediately I needed you."

Which one believed more strongly in sundidos, Barbara or Mrs. Baugh? If Herman was the one who had made them enthusiastic about photovoltaics, Mrs. Baugh was the one who had learned about Dr. Dryden's research at a university in Ohio. And Barbara was the one who had started the discussions and made the contacts that led to Herman hiring Nora.

Monday was the day after Joe had gone to Mrs. Baugh's mansion. It was also the day of a coal mine disaster that killed 34 miners in Kentucky, of more deaths in Houston from air polution, and anti-government protests, by protestors paid by oil billionaires, all around the country in favor of more ocean oil drilling and an end to regulation of oil companies. On that day Barbara rode a bicycle from Mrs. Baugh's mansion all the way across Franklin to Joe's house. He was at the dining table trying to decipher Nora's old notebooks when Barbara rang his doorbell. She propped the bike by his front door. She wasn't dressed in black this time, but in tan bermuda shorts, red and white shirt. He was glad to see her and being glad was rather a surprise to himself. "Isn't that dangerous? All the traffic in this city?" he said when he saw her vehicle.

"Not for me. I ride it all the time. There's bike paths and I know the side streets. It's better than a car because it gets me more time out of that gloomy old mansion. Look, here's a cell phone for you," she said. "It's got a new, unlisted number for you. It has Mrs. Baugh's private phone line and mine stored."

"What's all this for?" Joe said.

"Do you understand how someone can tap your telephone?"

"I already got a cell phone. They can't wiretap that."

"They wouldn't have to. Your cell phone broadcasts on radio waves — "

"Oh, yeah, that's right," Joe said. "All they got to do is park nearby and tune in to the frequency I'm on."

"Then frequently listen to your frequency wherever you frequent," the bespectacled bicyclist said, deadpan. "But see, the frequency this phone is on is outside the range of the Procida Society's receivers, or the police's or the FBI's or almost anyone else's, for that matter. It blocks outgoing caller IDs, too. It has a new unlisted number for you, but it's in Mrs. Baugh's name and she's paying for it. You can call us and make other calls that you wouldn't want the Procida Society to know about."

"Okay, thank you. Maybe I'll use it," Joe said. It felt like Mrs. Baugh and Barbara were making decisions for him, and he didn't like that.

Barbara sensed he didn't like that, said, "Do what you want, of course. What're these notebooks?"

"They're Nora's. They're her notes on the sundido process," he said, and immediately thought he was talking too much. So he added, "It's none of your business."

Was Barbara maybe just a little startled by that? Because back of her big glasses was a rise of eyebrows, curiosity. "You're correct to object. Abject apologies," she said, deadpan again. "I'm being intrusive. I used to be cool. But I've worked for Mrs. Baugh so long that she gave me some of her uncoolness."

"Talk about intrusive, I found another GPS bug planted on my car this afternoon."

As Joe was about to tell Barbara about the bug his old telephone rang. "You didn't finish your conversation with me last evening," the young-sounding baritone voice at the other end said. "As you know, we've been admiring your stand on the Procida Society." Joe turned the phone speaker on and the volume up, beckoned Barbara with a finger. She came over to him, they looked at the speaker and listened. "We're like you," the guy said. "We know what you went through at the Procida Society because we were imprisoned and tortured like you were. Some of us tried to sue the society and we lost because of crooked judges."

"Talk to me," Joe said. "Who are you? What you want from me?"

"Like I tried to tell you, we're patriots and we're concerned at some of the left-wing policies of the Procida Society and the way they have been carried out. It's obvious from your experience that you have rare vision, responsibility, and intelligence. What's that sound?"

That sound was a choked, bitter laugh by Joe. He said, "How do you know about me? Say, are you calling from Connecticut? Are you one of those guards from the Procida Society?"

"Certainly not. I just told you that we're opposed to the Procida Society."

"Yeah, well, I heard that same junk about vision and responsibility and other stuff when I was a prisoner there. Stop beating around the bush. What do you want from me?"

"We want you to join us in fighting the Procida Society — "

"You mean I should join you in a lawsuit against them?"

"No lawsuit. It should be obvious that legal attacks on them don't work."

Joe said, "Come on, say what you mean. I should fight them with fists? Guns? Bombs?"

"To put it simply, yes. We need to talk this over. What was that sound?" Barbara, who had been listening in bemused silence, had just chuckled softly, without smiling. "Is someone else there? Is someone listening to us?"

"So let's talk it over right now."

There was a momentary silence at the other end before the guy hung up. Barbara now looked at Joe, and once again he thought, was that crooked turn of her lips a smile trying to break onto her face? She said, "Who was that character? By the way, you invited me to listen to his call, so this time I'm not being intrusive."

"Yeah," Joe admitted. "He called two nights ago just after Mrs. Baugh called. I thought he was crazy."

She looked intense again: "He sounds crazy and dangerous. Did you tell Captain Dahlmann about him?"

"Dahlmann already says he doesn't know whether to believe me. If I told him about this, he'd think it would just be more madness from me."

"Mad, huh? And that caller wants you to join him? I can't imagine you as a mad bomber. Or even a sane bomber." She said it while looking worried.

"Not me. I'd rather do face-to-face hand-to-hand combat."

"I kind of thought that would be more like you. Let me know if that guy calls you again. And if you join his gang." The intensity of Barbara's look actually disconcerted Joe. Then she looked at Joe's feet then, and he felt an even more awkward silence before she said, "I hope you stay in close touch on your new phone. Mrs. Baugh can be a lot of help if you let her. She likes you already. I mean, we like you."

He said, "You mean you like what she likes?"

"Or do you mean you'd like me to repeat my compliment?" was her quick comeback.

Being in Barbara's proximity this evening must have been what made Joe talk like her. Because what he said, with exasperation that was half unreal, was, "I don't know what to think about you. You got a stone-face look and a stone-face way of talking. You're inscrutable. Why can't you be scrutable?"

Now suddenly, surprisingly, she really did smile for a moment. But then she said, "Seriously, I mean, I don't mean — look, just because I work so close to her all the time doesn't mean I share her opinions. But this time it's true, I agree with her. I've decided I want to begin the sundido business in Canada. I want you, I really hope you'll come up there and work with me."

Not long after Barbara left Joe began thinking. Something about her got to him. She dressed plainly, had what seemed like shy ways of speaking, of looking at him, of looking down, but he had already seen enough of her to know what she had wasn't really shyness. Instead, what she was was very serious, in spite of her whimsical sense of humor. Most of all she seemed intense: She seemed to feel strongly, she was passionate, or maybe she was obsessive.

Could this intense, worried person run a big business like the sundido operation she and Mrs. Baugh conceived, or like Herman and Nora had begun? She wasn't a bossy type like them, not edgy and nervous like Nora or a glib salesman like Herman. Still, from what Mrs. Baugh had said, Barbara had been the brains behind most of Herman's moves. Another thing, he thought: When was the last time someone said they liked me? It would have been Nora who said that. But when? Joe tried to remember when was the last time he heard Nora say she loved him, or even liked him.

As Barbara bicycled back home to Mrs. Baugh's fusty, musty, dusty, rusty mansion she realized that she didn't feel so sorry for Joe and his loss, not as much as she'd felt before her visit. For the first time she saw that he had some inkling of a sense of humor. He was a bright guy, she'd told the truth when she'd said she liked him. She had no idea if she and he were the right people to operate a big corporation like the one their sundido factory was likely to grow into eventually. But that was no problem, she could hire the right people, hadn't she discovered Nora for Herman Sorg? Joe seemed to be changeable, like herself — why had Herman underestimated him? Joe probably believed she was a nerd or a geek — she thought that because she sometimes considered herself a nerd or a geek.

The first call Joe made on his new cell phone was to Alice Kim. He told her about Mrs. Baugh's and Barbara's offer to him, about Herman's joining the Procida Society and selling out to Kemtrola Oil, about the impending bust of Nora's killers in Connecticut. "Does Kemtrola Oil really have their own solar-cell storage battery?"

Alice said, "They have one. It's a lot more expensive to make and sell than sundidos and it doesn't store as much energy. It's going to fail as a consumer product. That's, you know, what they want, to ruin the market when someone introduces a better product. Are you going, you know, going to take this Mrs. Baugh's offer? Will you help start a company to build sundidos?"

"I won't. I don't know anything about that. You should take her offer. You must be the only one who knows how to put them together."

"I know that. I won't have a job here much longer, too, and making sundidos is what I want to do most of all. But I don't know your Mrs. Baugh or your Barbara Fleming, so I wouldn't work there without you. Because I know at least you're honest. But remember, you can't trust me, you know, I'm a member of the Procida Society. And I've probably got the FBI on my trail, sniffing my scat. You've got to be sure you really, you know, want to work with me."

"The only way I'll go to work for her is if you do too. I'm gonna tell Mrs. Baugh that and tell her you're gonna be available."

"Joe, try to understand what a fix I'm in. I don't know who I can trust any more, except you and just a few others."

"Well, I'm in the same fix. These two women are the only other ones I trust." And I still have doubts about you, he didn't say.

Alice: "I dearly want to help you start a sundido company. But you've got to understand, I might just end up bringing your new venture more grief. And if you tell your Barbara Fleming and Mrs. Baugh about our conversation, you know, please don't tell them how to reach me, all right?"

He told her about the phone call he'd gotten from the patriot who wanted Joe to join his anti-Procida Society group. She said, "That sounds like something called the John Wilkes Booth Brotherhood. I know all about them. They're just as crazy and dangerous as the Procida Society. But at least they don't have any power. Not yet, anyway."

Sicinski left yet another message: "I need your help. Please call me back and let's make an appointment to KAWWWK!" Again Joe did not call him. Instead Joe went out for supper at an Italian restaurant alone. Within five minutes after he got home Sicinski was at the door. Joe took him into the kitchen. "I've been waiting for you," the reporter asked. "What is going on with you and Herman? You disappear and then he does, and you're both gone for a week. And now you've turned 180 degrees backwards and you're working for Kemtrola Oil."

"Not me. Herman is."

"Don't you work for Herman?"

"Not any more. So I got nothing to do with Kemtrola Oil either."

"Damn," Sicinski said and frowned in puzzlement. "Well, was he brainwashed? I mean, from the first he's been telling me energy companies were the enemy. Now you both've come back from your mystery hiatuses, he's in bed with an oil company. And you say you're not. What's going on?"

Joe did not answer because the teakettle was whistling. While Joe poured tea into two cups instead of answering, Sicinski said, "I put out for Herman. For you too. I had to talk my editor into letting me write the first story about the end of the internal-combustion engine and the revolution it'll cause. He thought I was nuts. Then I pestered the police for the stories about your wife's murder and Dr. Dryden's. I thought you guys were real." Joe said nothing. "Herman won't talk to me. Now I'm going to write about how sundidos are a scam."

Joe: "Not a scam. Who got scammed? Sundidos are real." Sicinski cursed. Joe said, "Yeah, Herman got brainwashed. They tried to do it to me too." He gave Sicinski a cup of tea and sipped from his own cup.

So what if it all sounds crazy? It's time to tell the world about those pigs, Joe figured. So he told Sicinski about the Procida Society, how he discovered its existence, how he went to New York, was drugged, kidnapped, imprisoned, and wound up in Connecticut. He told how Herman had gone through the same thing and chose to join the society. It took a long time and Joe made them each another cup of tea. He didn't mention Mrs. Baugh. He did say he had found Nora's murderers and he expected they were going to be arrested imminently.

Sicinski did not take notes, did not turn on a recorder. He said, "Oh, yeah? You've been holding out on me, then."

"You didn't ask," Joe said. "You only know cause I volunteered to tell you right now. Anyway, that's now police business."

"That jerk Herman. He's stabbing us in the back. How could he sell out like this?" Sicinski shook his head. "It's not the worst stunt he's pulled. I've known him since I was at the university, so I've seen some of his tricks."

"You mean he's done worse?"

"Lots. He and I used to live in a commune. Bought a house in Mount Ives, you know it?" Joe didn't. "Little town west of Franklin. I was new at the newspaper then, the *Daily Tribune*, R.I.P. We were close enough to Franklin that I commuted every day, no hassle. We had this big garden and we were supposed to live on organic food. No pesticides, no chemicals. So rabbits and bugs and mice and God knows what else ate the hell out of the vegetables. So he hung a bright light up over the garden. Turned out that wasn't enough. So he used to stay up all night out there shooing the critters away. He wound up sleeping during the day, and that's when the birds and squirrels and rabbits and mice really ate up the food."

Joe: "Why are you telling me this? What makes it Herman's worst stunt?"

Sicinski: "A year later Herman and his wife and my lady Val and I were the only ones left in the commune. Then he decided he wanted to marry Val. He didn't want to take out papers on her — he said marriage was a holy sacrament between two people and God, and making it legal was sacreligious. He wasn't going to leave his wife Ruth for Val, either. See, it was only society and the law that said it was wrong to have more than one wife.

"I got pissed off. I said, then I should have rights to Ruth's sexual services. He agreed, said I was right. He knew Ruth didn't like me and I wouldn't take her with a million-dollar dowry and covered with chocolate syrup and whipped cream. Val didn't want him, either. She got so pissed at both of us that she moved out. I don't know if that was Herman's worst stunt, but losing Val sure tore me up. So I left too."

Joe: "Was that the end of the commune?"

"Yeah. After that he and Ruth went to Florida, started another farm. They just had five acres, but it was more than he could handle. Especially after she left him. It still might've worked out for him, but a hurricane came along and wiped out his goat, his chickens, everything he planted. That was the end of Farmer Herman."

Joe: "Did he start the sundido business after that?"

"Yeah, a few years later. In between he got a few jobs. The job that lasted longest was running a vegetarian restaurant with one of his girlfriends. It was in one of the resort towns on Lake Michigan. It got popular, too, even after the county board of health closed it down the first time. They closed it down three times. After the third time, he and she broke up and he closed it down for good. By that time there weren't enough customers left anyway."

"Well, what were you doing while Herman was failing in his different businesses?"

Sicinski: "I worked for the *Daily Tribune* till it went out of business five years ago. I've been on my own, writing for other papers and magazines ever since."

Joe: "After all he put you through you still stayed friends with him anyway."

"'Friends' might not be the right word for it. I was still pissed at him when he moved back here three years ago. He called me because he wanted publicity for sundidos and he wanted me to do an article. I thought manufacturing and selling sundidos all over the world was a great idea — still do." Joe thought, so he doesn't really believe sundidos are a scam. Sicinski continued, "So now you know everything worth knowing about Herman Sorg. Back to the present — can you prove all the things you just told me about the Procida Society?"

"Sure. I'll take you to their headquarters in New York, they can brainwash you too."

"That's one hell of a story. Something like that's exactly what I've always thought was going on. You say they invited you to join. Are you going to?"

Joe said, "Course not. They murdered Nora."

Chapter 15

ANOTHER NIGHTMARE ABOUT NORA and the Procida Society
that night. The next morning's newspaper included news about the
current heat waves in America, Europe, Asia; a photo of the evacuation of Miami, to prepare for a forthcoming hurricane; news that
the U.S. Supreme Court ruled that preventing the death of the Gulf
of Mexico from oil spills was not a valid reason to stop drilling for
oil there; and an article about illnesses and deaths from oil spill-dis-
persant chemicals. Late that morning as he was opening his garage
door two cars suddenly swerved onto his street with vicious squeals
of brakes and shuddered to sudden stops in front of his drive with
screeches so loud they set dogs barking for two blocks in all directions. Seven men and a woman, all in black jackets despite the hot,
humid morning, leaped out of their cars and ran to Joe. The first
four to reach him had guns drawn and the other four were quick
to join them in surrounding him. "Drop it. Hands up. Come here,"
one of them said.

Joe opened his hands, raised them, palms toward his captors.
Nothing fell out because he had been holding nothing. "Smart-aleck. Thinks he's smart," another said. He was a stern thin guy with
close-cut hair who looked like a male model in a TV ad for a criminal justice college course. That one must be the bad cop.

A third one held a handgun with two shaky hands, pointed it at
Joe's chest, said, "All right, put your hands on the garage door and
spread your legs."

Joe said nothing. He was glad he didn't happen to have the spare
cell phone on him, the one Barbara had brought him yesterday.
They probably would have taken it from him. He saw that FBI was
printed in white on the back of the jackets. He was a little surprised
that he wasn't surprised at being rousted at his own home — surprised at his own fatalism. He did what he was told. As two of the
FBI agents patted him down and went through his pockets the fe-

male agent said, "Aren't you going to read him his rights?" She must be the good cop, Joe guessed.

Yet another agent said to Joe, "We're not charging you with anything. We're just going to question you about the murders of Nora Heatley and Dr. Bert Dryden. You have the right to remain silent. You have the right to an attorney. Anything you say may be held against you in a court of law."

"Her," Joe said as they surrounded him.

"What was that? Who?"

"I said her," Joe said, pointing a finger at the female agent. She was the bootylicious Jane Edgar Hooters who had humbugged Joe up in the FBI office a few days before. Even now she had that concerned, eyebrows-up, superior caregiver look on her face. "Hold her against me." He was angry and he hoped it would bug these FBI creeps.

The male model said, "Fucking smart-aleck. Put him in my car. Let me take him back myself." He was a walking cliche machine. The others didn't respond to his words. He and the tootsie made quite a team.

Nobody assaulted or spoke to Joe on the ride across town, in a car with four agents, and he kept silent the whole way. At the FBI office the earnest babe was the one who questioned him while two others looked on. "So you finally realized Nora's murder is in your jurisdiction after all," he said coolly.

In spite of her caring look, she wasn't acting like Agent Florence Nightingale today. She said, "It always was. We actually tried to be protective of her, just because of the work she did." Joe snorted at that, almost said something obscene. "I couldn't tell you about our keeping an eye her until now."

"You incompetent fools," Joe snapped. "Some job of watching you dummies did. Blind and deaf people coulda done better. Do you blundering idiots have any idea what you're doing?"

The FBI babe said, "Mr. Heatley, do you understand how serious this situation you're in is? You've been identified as the person responsible for those two murders."

Mister, yet. Joe blurted, "You know I couldn't have killed them."

"We know you didn't do it with your own hands. How did you have them murdered?"

It was hopeless, Joe figured, but he decided to tell her about the Procida Society anyway. It was the same story he'd told Sicinski the night before. Sure enough, one of the agents interrupted him: "Are you saying a U.S. senator was holding you prisoner?" So Joe had to explain the Procida Society has always had senators and presidents, kings, queens, dictators, too. That's because the Procida Society has been around since before Christopher Columbus, running countries, starting wars, fomenting revolts. One more time, to one more bunch of people, Joe said that the reason those people killed Nora and Dr. Dryden and kidnapped Joe and Herman was because the sundido will change the world and make the internal combustion engine obsolete.

"That's enough bullshit. You make all this up yourself or did you read it in a comic book? You fucking smart-aleck, you think we're just ignorant cops. Let's put him away till he gets some sense," the male model said.

"We already know about the sundido and about your wife's work on it," the babe said to Joe. "We also know that she and her employer Herman Sorg were having an affair and that you were jealous — "

"Slander!" Joe shouted, pounded her desk, started to stand. An FBI agent pushed him back down in his chair while he said, "You slander Nora cause she isn't here to tell the truth. To talk that way about a woman you never met. You've got a filthy mind and a toilet mouth — "

" — and she'd had an affair with Dr. Dryden, too. You were jealous and you have a hot temper. So you hired two people, a man and a woman, to murder her and then you murdered Dryden yourself. Where did you find the hit man and woman?" Her telephone rang. "Just a minute."

Joe sizzled while the FBI babe talked on the phone: "Yes, he's right here, right now in fact. Who did you say you are? Franklin?" She looked at Joe as she listened and he figured she must be talking about him. Talking to who? Guessing at that began to distract Joe from his anger. "But — "she said, and a few moments later she said "But — " again. Then, "Yes, I know. Your jurisdiction. Who was with him?" and "Sorg? But he's the one who — he contacted you too?" After listening some more she said, "All right. We'll bring him to you."

When she hung up she looked at two of her fellow agents, not at Joe. She said, "That was Captain Dahlmann of the Franklin police. He's taking over the Joe Heatley case."

"Shit!" barked the male model agent as he leaped up. "Fucking ignorant local cops. You watch, this smart-aleck is going to slip through their fingers."

To Joe, Agent Caring said, "We've got our eyes on you. We're very interested in what the Franklin police are going to do with you. Whatever you do, don't try to leave town." She believed that busting Joe was the key to breaking up the sundido conspiracy. She had never once lost that concerned, superior, caregiver look.

Franklin police captain Sven Dahlmann had started as a cop up north in St. Paul, Minnesota, an old-fashioned, hard, unforgiving cop who was also smart, hard-working, and thoroughly honest. After fourteen years there he'd been fired soon after arresting a state senator's daughter for drug possession. Mrs. Baugh knew about that.

What she didn't know was how Dahlmann worked. Some miscreants liked to think they were too smart to fall for the old "your buddy is ratting you out" line until they were actually in custody, desperate, and Dahlmann in his subtle way convinced them they really couldn't trust each other. One night in a basement two drug dealers had shot each other to death because Dahlmann had told each that the other was moving in on his territory. That worked so well, in Dahlmann's opinion, that he pulled it another time on two rival gang members. But thugs have notoriously lousy aim and this time when they fired at each other it was at a business intersection in broad daylight and they badly wounded some innocent people. Dahlmann's role in this incident was the one that had actually gotten him fired.

At first he'd just been shocked at getting fired. After all, he'd worked on some difficult cases, had arrested some vicious characters. Dahlmann had even had moved his family to a new suburban home because of death threats from some gang members. He'd been shot at himself — one night a stoned meth freak had fired at Dahlmann just before leaping off a three-story-high roof and crashing to his own death on concrete. Obsessing over his own courage and achievements soon made Dahlmann bitter at the ingratitude of the department that had fired him.

His wife, who worked as a beautician, had been a religious woman all her life. She and his daughters had become his refuge from the madness he dealt with each day, the only people whose sanity and intelligence he trusted. Everyone else, even his fellow officers whom he had to depend on, was more or less unreliable until proven otherwise. Now their girls were grown and living in Texas and Oregon and Captain and Mrs. Dahlmann were living in Franklin. There she'd joined an evangelical Christian church and she'd drawn him into joining it too. He'd become born again and baptized again.

The rapture was Captain Sven Dahlmann's current obsession. He'd pored over his favorite book in the Bible, Revelation, was in awe of the grandeur of the horrors it described. He'd also read a fair amount of the conflicting interpretations of Christ's second coming. Revelation was confusing enough and the interpretations disagreed with each other. He couldn't make out exactly when the rapture was going to come. All he knew was, it was surely going to happen soon, the present era are the end times. So he and the rest of the Dahlmann family would zoom up into heaven at the moment of rapture.

He knew he'd be chosen to go to heaven because he was so honest and conscientious and so were the rest of his family. And when the Dahlmanns get raptured he would not feel sorry for the non-raptured, all the commandment breakers who would have to suffer the Apocalypse.

He was now preoccupied with the Nora Heatley-Dr. Bert Dryden case. He had never heard of the Procida Society before yesterday. As it happened, just last night at the church service Dahlmann and his wife had attended, the minister preached about the sufferings of the early Christians. For a moment it made Dahlmann think of Joe's captivity in the Procida Society, except of course he didn't know if Joe was born again or a heathen, or just one of those wavery Christians who would not go to heaven in the rapture. Dahlmann by now had seen and heard enough of Joe to provisionally believe him. But Dahlmann couldn't dismiss the FBI's story. Maybe the feds knew something he didn't and weren't telling him.

So who was the Procida Society? A conspiracy, a mystery, is it some kind of fancy street gang or organized crime outfit, ha, could they be devils or are they mere humans? Do these people secretly run the world, like Heatley says they claim they do? If they do, is the Procida Society the invention of the antichrist and are the members his deceivers? Or his dupes? To Joe he said, "The accusation against you is that you murdered your wife and Dr. Dryden. The same as your federal case, or almost-case. Herman was the one who

143

gave you up to us and the FBI both. He called me yesterday and then came up here. What the FBI thinks is, you hired those two people, that man and that woman, to kill her and then did Dryden yourself. Herman didn't disagree."

Joe: "You think I killed them too? That why you took me from the FBI? You want to be first to arrest me for murder?"

"Not yet. I'm just telling you what Herman claimed. I told that FBI agent you couldn't have killed Dryden by yourself because he was getting killed at exactly the same time the same day you were at her joint bringing joy into her life. A little friendly service from me, your friendly public servant. Before long you can be sure they'll think you hired this mysterious Procida Society to kill your wife and Doctor Dryden — "

Joe: "Oh, no."

"And maybe they kidnapped you in New York because you hadn't paid them. For all we know, maybe they think that already. On that subject, by the way, the police in Dunning, Connecticut tried to get your Velma and Veli at that insane asylum. Guess who they found there instead."

"U.S. Senator Whitlock of Connecticut."

"How'd you know that? He was the guy they talked to. He told them your Velma and Veli weren't there."

"Didn't the police search the place? Or did Whitlock smile and charm them out of it?"

Dahlmann wasn't smiling at all today, but he said, "He's so slick, they just slid out of there on the grease. Heatley, in case you didn't happen to notice it, I did you a big favor today. Those FBI guys were going to lock you up for a few nights, and just in case you think you have some human rights, you ought to know a couple of them already had some experience at Guantanamo."

"Hey," Joe said with wonder and some hope in his face as he looked at Dahlmann. "You don't think I'm lying."

War and pestilence and earthquakes and immorality and, yes, falsity, Dahlmann thought, and this wicked Procida Society too. He realized that Joe must think he was turning soft. He didn't want that, didn't Joe to get comfortable. Since he couldn't dismiss the FBI's suspicions, he chose to bully Joe some more: "What makes you think I believe you? Don't count on it. Don't get the idea I'm a friend of yours. You haven't taken a lie detector test yet. This business with you and Herman and Nora's murder doesn't make sense at all. Do yourself a favor, don't leave town."

After Joe left the captain thought, sundidos — what a good idea. God's inspiration is so wonderful, and Nora Heatley must have been inspired, to invent something as wonderful as sundidos. On the other hand Herman had predicted they would bring about "heaven on earth." It's just an expression, I know, but people shouldn't talk like that. The idea is blasphemy. God made heaven and the earth. Since men defile the earth with their selfishness, there'll be no heaven here. It isn't for everybody. Heaven's for us good ones, the ones who'll be raptured.

Joe got a ride home in a Franklin squad car. A frowning neighbor across the street was watching out of her picture window when Joe got out and a next-door neighbor just happened to choose that time to water her flowers and wrinkle her nose at Joe even though she had no water in her watering can.

He detached the bug from his car before he drove to Mrs. Baugh's home. This time when Barbara met him at the creaking front door she said, "Welcome to Morbidity Manor." She was now in tan shorts and yellow shirt but she looked unhappy this time. Mrs. Baugh was even more regal than before, in the same high-backed chair as before, in the same big room that seemed more dusty and old in the daylight. Joe told them about the FBI babe slandering Nora, about how Herman had lost his mind and was telling wild tales to the FBI and Captain Dahlmann. When Joe told her about Herman's sell-out she struck the arm of her chair like she was wielding a scepter. She said, "Oh, dear. We told you this was about to add to your burden of sorrows, and it did. And it's just as bad as I had feared. Barbara, show him that weekly newspaper."

"This is the newest issue," Barbara said, handing Joe a copy of a Franklin weekly newspaper from an end table. The paper had an article by Sicinski about how Herman had sold out to Kemtrola Oil. "It tells about Herman's original big ideas about his sundidos that would make fossil fuel companies obsolete, and how he now changed his mind and won't make sundidos after all. It doesn't quote you and there's nothing in it about the Procida Society," Barbara said.

"Barbara and I know all we need to know about Kemtrola Oil's solar-cell storage batteries," Mrs. Baugh said. "They're thoroughly inferior to sundidos."

"They're designed to fail," Barbara said. "They cost more to produce electricity than fossil fuels or nuclear. They're less efficient. They're not recyclable, like sundidos are."

"It's an ancient scam, Mr. Heatley," said Mrs. Baugh.

"A wolf in sheep's clothing," Barbara said.

"A short con. Comparatively short, that is, compared to the usual longer cons of unregulated enterprise," said Mrs. Baugh.

"Perfumed feces," Barbara said. She actually said "feces." Somehow it made the image nastier than the conventional word "shit." She kept looking down instead of at Joe.

"Kemtrola Oil will have Herman manufacture their batteries, and when nobody buys them they'll announce to the world, 'We told you solar energy is a failure. You'll just have to trust us and depend on fossil fuel.'" Mrs. Baugh sighed. "Our poor sundidoless planet is truly doomed."

Barbara and Mrs. Baugh listened motionless, without saying a word, as Joe described his experiences of the day with the FBI and with Dahlmann: "I told them about the Procida Society and how Herman and I were captives there. I wish I had some nyalhis myself. I'd like to use it on them and bust up their racket."

Mrs. Baugh said to Barbara, "Nyalhis. That's the stuff we looked up on the web. We hunted for it after the other time Mr. Heatley came. It can be drunk or injected."

"Nyalhis. The antidote is mictzin. That can be drunk or injected too," Barbara said.

"Nyalhis and mictzin, yes. If I could procure you some nyalhis and some mictzin, I surely would," Mrs. Baugh said to Joe. "Your legal situation is preposterous. Be sure to keep me abreast of developments. I'll gladly get you a lawyer and all the best help possible, if it ever becomes necessary to keep you free. I'd even be indiscreet and admit our connection in a court of law if that's what it'd take to free you. Of course, Mark Twain was right, the law is an ass — "

"Charles Dickens," Barbara murmured under her breath and frowned. When Mrs. Baugh looked at her, she said out loud, "It was Charles Dickens who wrote that. Sorry I interrupted."

"Him, then. Anyway, since it's an ass, you may very well be found guilty in spite of all reason and all the evidence of your innocence. If so, I'll visit you in jail. If you're sentenced to death, I'll guarantee your burial after your execution, too. Unless you prefer to be cremated. In that event I'd see to it your ashes are disposed of however you see fit."

Barbara silently led Joe to the front door. Once outside she said, "Thanks for coming over. She needed that so much. She needed to be reassured you hadn't sold out too." That unhappy look on Barbara's face now was turned to concern. "I needed to see you too." They looked at each other with the awkwardness that had become normal for the two of them, for a moment, before Joe turned to his car.

When she returned into the dim house Mrs. Baugh said, "Did you notice that whoever it was lied when he said the law is an ass?"

Barbara: "Lied?"

Mrs. Baugh: "Yes. After all, the law is arbitrary but the ass is a good and necessary body part. What would you do without your ass?" It was a jest, but Barbara just looked down, did not smile.

Joe replaced the bug on his car as soon as he got home. Only after that did he then drive to a noisy restaurant, gobble a meat loaf supper, drive home. It was evening twilight and he was watching TV, watching the failure of the latest attempts to plug the gushing oil leaks in the North Sea, when the doorbell rang. He had been certain it would ring sometime, today, tomorrow, surely the next day — but when, exactly? He had the little buzzer in his pants pocket, the buzzer the cop Sven Dahlmann had given him after they were at the Pacific Motel when Dr. Dryden had been murdered. He remembered that Alice had said these guys had no influence yet.

Tonight there were three of them at Joe's door. He'd never seen any of them before. Except that they didn't carry bibles or leaflets, they could have been recruiting for a religion, they were so well-dressed in suits, brown, dark blue, and gray, and white shirts, and well-groomed, shaven, short-haired. "Mr. Heatley? I'm sorry to come calling so late in the day," said Blue Suit, slightly the tallest of them, who had lines on his face that implied he was also the oldest. He also had the baritone voice of the unknown character who'd phoned him twice. "We tried calling on you earlier. Were you taking a walk this afternoon?"

That question told Joe that these were the ones who had planted the bug on his car. He didn't hesitate but said, "Come on in," and held the door open for them.

Blue Suit stood, the other two went for the sofa. It faced the picture window, but the shades were drawn. Joe opened those shades for one of the few times since Nora had been murdered. Then he sat in the armless, wooden rocking chair. Blue Suit said, "Mr. Heatley, I can't say everything in a few words. Please be patient and hear me out."

"You told me on the phone that the Procida Society'd held you prisoner," Joe said. "Why?"

"The same reason they held you. It was their way of testing us for membership. In my case I was rejected. In some other cases our people rejected the Procida Society's philosophies. And like I said, a few who could afford lawsuits sued the Procida Society and lost on legal technicalities. The courts were fixed, in other words."

"That why you guys started your own club?"

"The John Wilkes Booth Brotherhood. Named after the most maligned man in history. That's not an official name, though. We're together but we're not an organization. That's so we don't leave a trail. We're scattered across the country. For instance, I'm from Minnesota, my friends here tonight are from Kansas and Florida. We stay in touch with e-mails."

"So now you want revenge?"

"It's more than revenge at stake. See, the Procida Society lied to us. In every way. Did they tell you wealth and status and education and so on didn't bar you from joining?"

"Yeah."

"That was a lie. It's a club strictly for the rich and by the rich. They may allow some members who aren't rich to join, but the ones who really run it are rich."

"That's not news," Joe said.

"The agenda of the rich is what's wrong. Because those Procida Society bastards don't care at all about America. They don't care in the least about us." He looked at Joe for a reaction. Joe didn't react. Blue Suit went on, "They're internationalists. That's why they're forcing free trade on us. They're doing it so they can make America a socialist country, all weak and helpless like Europe is. Their businesses are based in places like the United Arab Emirates and the Cayman Islands and Luxembourg, where they don't pay taxes. From there their tentacles reach all over the world — factories and offices in third world countries."

"Yeah, where they don't have to pay American wages to American workers," Joe said. This was getting interesting.

Blue Suit was getting more agitated as he talked on: "And leaving

Americans defenseless. If the UN attacks us, we're going to be helpless. They're destroying America in other ways, too. They're taking away our rights. They won't let us carry guns to protect ourselves. Or pray in public any more. They're destroying our morals. They're forcing contraception and abortions and population control on us. Their same-sex marriages are destroying marriage."

"How? They make you get divorces so gay people can get married?"

Joe's sarcasm apparently went completely over Blue Suit's head, because he said, "Yes, that's just what it's coming to, mark my words. And don't forget religious persecution against Christians and racial persecution against whites, the way the white race now has to be subservient to the other races. There are other things wrong, but those'll do for a start."

"Yeah, that'll do. What's that race and religion stuff got to do with the Procida Society?"

Blue Suit was so intense by now that he was sweating. "It weakens America. It destroys the foundation of our society, so it destroys our nation. They claim they're unacknowledged legislators with the vision to guide our destiny. When it's so obvious they're sneaky radical left-wing thugs with the power to destroy us all.

"I get it," Joe said. "Why're you here telling me this?"

"Because we want you on our side. You saw through the Procida Society. They offered you a chance to join them and you didn't."

"How do you know that?"

"We have our sources. They're very thorough and accurate. The Procida Society aren't the only efficient ones."

"What you want me to do?"

"Until now we haven't been able to be as ruthless as they are because there are too few of us. But we have to fight fire with fire. The Procida Society starts wars around the world by inciting armies and guerillas and terrorists. Nothing short of war is going to stop them."

"Nothing short of war? What do you mean?"

"I'm not going to say any more. I've told you enough already for you to decide if you're with us. Whether you and I have any more conversation is up to you."

Joe stood up, scowled at Blue Suit, said, "Come on, mister. You know I'm with you, or you wouldn't'a told me this much already. If there's a way to attack the Procida Society, I want to be in on it. So far all I've heard is words. You plan to talk them to death? Or are you actually planning to do something? If you are, what'm I gonna do in it? If we're not gonna do anything, get out of my house and stop wasting my time."

Blue Suit said, now with a smile, "All right. We're going bring it home to the Procida Society. We're going to attack them right here in America. Do you remember the Oklahoma City bomber in 1995? He made explosives out of fertilizer and blew up the federal building there. He had the right idea but he aimed for the wrong target."

"Do you make explosives too?"

"We've got some, yes. We used fertilizer too. But guns can be useful to us, too — handguns, assault weapons."

Brown Suit, on the sofa, spoke for the first time: "We've got grenades and AK-47s in our arsenal. Missiles, too."

"The missiles are to attack the capitol building and the Federal Reserve," Blue Suit said. "We'd rather attack them from the ground, but there aren't enough of us. The missiles have a quarter-mile range and they can do almost as much damage as a ground assault."

Joe was standing, hands in pockets, smiling at them. He said, "The U.S. capitol building? In D.C.? Where the senators and congressmen conspire?"

Blue Suit was delighted at Joe's choice of words: "That's exactly what they do. They conspire with the Procida Society. Even the ones who aren't members let the Procida Society lead them around by the nose."

Joe now turned and looked out the big window, his back to the three. "That's the way to do it. Get the rats in the sewer where they feed."

"And blow it up. That's why we have grenades," Blue Suit said.

"And blowing up the capitol and the Federal Reserve aren't all we're gonna do, is it?" Joe said.

"See there? He said 'we' again. He's really with us," Blue Suit said to the others. "I knew he was going to. He's too smart not to do the right thing." Blue Suit was the only one smiling, but the other two were following the conversation eagerly.

Joe turned around, faced Blue Suit again. Now he was scowling again. It was an intense look. "Are we gonna attack Procida Society headquarters or not? Are we gonna hit their insane asylum or not? Are we just going to Washington, D.C., or are we gonna blow up their places in New York and Connecticut? Blowing up congress is just fine. But the rats still breed back in their dens. So we're going after them, too, aren't we?"

"That's right!" Blue Suit said. "You've guessed it. We're going to assault all four places. We'll attack D.C. and all the rats who're left in New York and Connecticut."

Joe turned back toward the picture window again. "All right, when is all this gonna happen?" He peered through the window for a moment as if he was looking at something, then reached and closed the curtains again, quickly, as if angrily. He was scowling again as he said, "The sooner the better."

"That's right. Next Tuesday we hit the capitol and the Fed and the Procida Society headquarters and the Newjoy Mental Health Institute. It's going to be simultaneous assaults on all four places."

Joe took two steps to his left, leaned on the three-level bookcase between the window and the front door. He was silent for a moment, then, still scowling intensely, even sweating, he said, "Tuesday's just fine. Now where do I fit in? Do I get to fight in one of the four places?"

"We're only going to need two men at the capitol. We'll need more men to assault the New York headquarters than at the nut house in Connecticut. But you can take your pick — what?"

Blue Suit said that because Joe had just flung the front door open. A Franklin cop burst through the doorway with gun drawn. "Freeze!" he snapped, aiming it at each of the three in turn. Three other police officers followed him into the room, each holding a gun. One went over to the sofa, where Blue Suit's two young partners had already risen to their feet. He took guns out of the suit pockets of both and a third gun out of the pants pocket of one. Another cop relieved Blue Suit of a handgun too.

"Man, you're fast," Joe said, wiping sweat off his forehead. "I just buzzed you a couple minutes ago."

"Fast relief is our specialty. We make you feel better quicker'n beer to a starving man," a cop said as he handcuffed one of Joe's visitors.

"Besides," another said, "we've been keeping an eye on you."

"Don't get the idea you're special, Heatley." This from Dahlmann, who had just come in the door to join the official crowd. "We like to keep track of all suspicious characters."

"We're going to remember this. You're at the top of our list now," the handcuffed Blue Suit said to Joe as an officer led him out.

"Yeah, you're gonna get what the Procida Society gets," Gray Suit said as another officer led him out.

"You know who came to bail out your three John Wilkes Booth brothers?" Captain Sven Dahlman said over the telephone the next morning. "Vern Kesler, that's who. In case you wonder who Vern Kesler is, he's the lawyer who defended the Nazis who burned those synagogues in New Jersey a few weeks ago and who sued Indianapolis, Indiana to spring the Ku Klux Klan killers last summer. There's a lot more about him. He's become the favorite lawyer of all the extremists." They pit nation against nation, race against race, tribe against tribe, he thought.

"He bailed them out? Where'd they go?" Joe said. He had awakened late, was feeling especially lost and empty that morning.

"He didn't. They're still here. We found a trunkful of grenades and other illegal ammo in their car last night, and get this — they had a map of the U.S. capitol building in Washington, D.C. with their attack routes plotted on it. You were telling the truth, they really were going to do it. What's more, they're all wanted in Texas for armed robbery, conspiracy, and murder. They're in federal custody now. The judge isn't allowing bail on any of them."

"Did they tell you anything about the Procida Society?"

"They did. They accused me of being a Procida Society whore." A whore, me of all people, the cop who got into this in order to stop the whore of Babylon in all her filth. "They say I've got crooked U.S. senators pulling my strings. They blabbed about international Procida Society secret schemes, too. They were backing up those wild stories you told me."

"I was telling you the truth," Joe said, without any hope that he would be believed.

"You were telling me nothing that's any help," said Dahlmann because now he'd decided enough buddy-buddy talk to try for Joe's confidence, time to act angry again. "What do you know about Alice Kim?"

"What about her? She and me own the patent on sundidos, now. She and Nora worked together. They were students of Dr. Dryden, and the three of them invented sundidos."

Oh, yes, those sundidos. Now that Captain Sven Dahlmann's curiosity had been aroused, he wanted one, was even thinking he might ask Joe to sell him one. Except that Joe was still a suspect, at least officially. So instead the captain thought about Herman's contrary testimony. He said, "When was the last time you saw Alice Kim?"

"Saturday. She came to see me and I took her to the airport. I phoned her two days ago after you showed me the pictures of the killers. She was back in Colorado by then."

"I know she was visiting you. You told the truth about that because you know the FBI was following her, didn't you."

"Naw, I didn't know," Joe said, and since Dahlmann probably knew all about his first visit to the FBI office, he added, "They told me they were gonna stop tailing her."

"Why did you lie about phoning her two days ago?"

Joe thought fast. He remembered that he'd phoned Alice on that new cell phone Barbara had given him. If Dahlmann thought he was lying, then Barbara was right, the police were listening to his calls — but they weren't tuned to the broadcast frequency of that new phone. Joe said, "Why do you say I was lying? I called her. What's this about Alice?"

Dahlmann said, "In case you don't really know, she's missing. Been missing since yesterday morning. Her FBI tails lost her completely."

Joe was stunned. "What? Missing"

Dahlmann said, "So you didn't know that already? I don't believe you called Alice Kim two days ago at all. That's easier to check than you think. If you're lying I'll arrest you for obstructing justice. Just because we saved your hide last night, don't think you're not a suspect for those two murders. If you had anything to do with making Alice Kim disappear, we'll find that out too. Whatever you do, don't leave town."

Nevertheless Dahlmann, unlike the FBI, was thinking Joe probably didn't hire someone to kill his wife and her professor. Just the opposite, he was now convinced the Procida Society alone was surely the source of this mess. So they really rule the earth, do they? But why secretly? Why did they sneak around killing people they way they did? The problem was, how to go about confronting them? I should do something like what soldiers did during the Viet Nam war, Dahlmann thought: Go to the Procida Society place and bust everybody in sight. Then leave it to God's justice to sort out the guilty ones.

Don't leave town. No, Joe didn't want to leave town. Yes he did, he couldn't stand to stay in this town. No, all Joe wanted was to be left alone. All he wanted was some peace, to think about Nora and cry for her and who knows, maybe even be done with crying. Instead everybody, the Procida Society and the police and FBI and Herman and Mrs. Baugh and Barbara and Sicinski and now this John Wilkes Booth Brotherhood and who knows who else wouldn't leave him alone. He was even suspected of murdering his own dear Nora, and Dr. Dryden too. And now Alice Kim had disappeared too.

Thoughts like these rattled in Joe's mind while he sat on a bench in a park on the shore of Franklin's lake that afternoon. In the shade because it was another very hot day. How could Herman accuse him of murder like that? Of hiring killers to murder his own wife? How could Herman claim that Nora was having affairs with himself and Dr. Dryden? That was the lie that hurt the most, to slander poor Nora like that. Had Herman gone crazy? Had Herman been brainwashed completely by the Procida Society? He should go and confront Herman. Except that now he didn't think he could stand the sight of Herman. He wasn't even afraid he might beat Herman up. Herman had made himself too contemptible.

"Poor Nora," he found himself murmuring out loud. What would she do if she knew Herman was lying about her? Sure, she respected Herman, was glad he understood the need for sundidos, admired him for having the guts to start his company. She liked him a lot. She spent long hours every day working with him and when she wasn't with him, when she was home with Joe, she talked about him: his brilliance, his cleverness, how much she hoped for his and her success. Really, she was so devoted to Herman, how could he turn around and insult her memory by making up such a lie?

And so what if she and Herman and Dryden did have affairs, like that FBI babe said. Joe could understand why Nora might have grown tired of him. After all, she was a genius and he wasn't. Next to her he was slow, dull, colorless, selfish, moody, hot-tempered too often, boring. "A stick in the mud," she'd called him. "Sex fiend," too — "You don't know how to treat a woman," she'd said more than once. Many times Joe had felt Nora was more than he deserved. Could he forgive her if she betrayed him with another man? He hoped so. Even if he couldn't, he could understand why she'd do it. Joe's eyes were filling with tears as he thought about her again.

Poor Nora. For all her genius and her energy, at heart she might really have been just a weak person. In his own way, Joe knew, he was weak himself. And he certainly wouldn't murder the other man, or hire someone to do it.

Damn Herman. Damn Captain Dahlmann. Damn all those FBI idiots. Damn the Procida Society and those John Wilkes Booth Brotherhood fools.

And now, Joe knew, he was just waiting for the next shoe to drop: arrest for two murders. Maybe for kidnapping Alice Kim, now, too. For that matter, why not arrest him for the stock market crash or for starting the Afghanistan War? It was only a matter of time. So what if he was hung or gassed or electrocuted, whatever they did in this state? Why fight it? What was there left for him in this life?

Except. The ever-increasing pressures of the last three weeks and more were accumulating in a kind of critical mass in Joe Heatley's mind and feelings. A new realization finally broke through to him. He began to remember that there were times in life when everything went wrong, one thing after another. It's a law of nature. Things are supposed to go wrong like that often, life is losing streaks, the occasional winning streak, and mostly in-betweens. After awhile, he knew, you get so used to a losing streak that you wonder, what's going to go wrong next? With this new perspective, failures, losses, the next catastrophes then become less sources of sorrow, regret, gloom, than objects of wonder, curiosity.

It was a perspective that he'd arrived at only in recent years. His childhood had been such an unrelieved bummer that he could not have understood that law of nature, fate, destiny, until after he was old enough to have experienced some periods of good in his life, too. Thinking along those lines now led Joe to a perverse kind of satisfaction. It was even a kind of comedy: The end of the world is the last joke.

The joy of despair — it was a big change in Joe's emotions, his feelings. Smile, we survived, he remembered he used to tell Nora. He hadn't told himself that in a very long time, but now he remembered it.

He didn't smile at all, but he thought, well, those two monsters who murdered Nora were still loose. Who knows, maybe they're the ones who'd kidnapped Alice Kim — have they murdered her too, even though she's a member of the Procida Society? Or was it this John Wilkes Booth Brotherhood that kidnapped Alice? Busting them and the Procida Society might save Alice's life, and getting a confession out of them both would definitely get the police and the FBI off Joe's case. What's more, it was time to bring the Procida Society to the ground — expose it, bust them too. Should've been done centuries ago.

And the sundidos, Nora's life's work. Herman wasn't even going to manufacture them now. They were too necessary, too important to the survival of the human race to be abandoned like that. So Mrs. Baugh was going to have Barbara make sundidos and the two of them had offered him an opportunity. Joe owed it to Nora to take advantage of it, to preserve Nora's memory for all time.

I'm a punching bag, Joe thought, wiping sweat off his face, and I'm tired of it. Well, why not fight back? Will I fail, will I lose, will I die? Probably. Maybe there's a chance I'll clear myself and get sundidos made — no, not likely — more likely I'll get killed or busted myself. At least I'll make something happen myself instead of waiting for someone else to do it. Joe got up. As he was walking back to his car he thought, Maybe they can even execute me for a real crime instead of the crime Herman made up.

He drove home, took the bug off his rear bumper.

Chapter 16

"I'm afraid I have some more bad news. Is this the Alice Kim who invented sundidos along with your wife?" was what Mrs. Baugh said, half an hour later, when she handed Joe a printout from a *Denver Post* web site. It began:

> Associated Press
> Scientist Vanishes
> BOULDER, COLO.
> Alice Kim, a senior researcher and vice-president of Sonnes-trahl Systems in Boulder, disappeared from her office yester-day morning in mysterious circumstances. A noted scholar in photovoltaics research, Kim had simply left her desk without speaking to anyone. She did not appear at a meeting with her employer, T.J. Sonnestrahl, or with colleagues at a luncheon gathering.
> Boulder district FBI director Perry Liddington said, "We are treating this as a disappearance and placing it in our highest priority."

"Dahlmann told me about that," Joe said.

"This is nyalhis," Barbara said, handing Joe a tiny clear bottle with a clear liquid inside it. "It's powerful. Just two or three drops are enough to cause a person to lose all inhibitions. Then the person has to do or say whatever her impulses tell her to do or say. Or his impulses. It has to be used sparingly or else it can cause severe, permanent memory loss. And here," she said, handing Joe a bottle the size of a small aspirin bottle with powder inside, "is mictzin. It's the anti-depressant to counteract the side effects of the nyalhis. You can mix it in her drink, it dissolves."

"Where did you get this stuff?" Joe said. "Are these legal? Did you get prescriptions?"

"No. I made them," Barbara said and sat again hunched forward, hands clasped, looking serious, expectantly at Joe, then at Mrs. Baugh.

The old woman, in her high-backed chair like a queen, said, "My Barbara is a wonder. It's a sad loss to the world that she's wasted her talents on solving my trivial problems for so many years. She synthesized the nyalhis and the mictzin herself. She found the ingredients named in some obscure corners of the world wide web and bought them over the counter of a drug store." She smiled adoringly at Barbara, who gave her a brief half-smile back.

"From a grocery and a fruit stand, too," Barbara said.

"Yeah, it's true, you sure are a wonder. What's your nyalhis for? What you gonna do with it?" Joe said.

"Oh, my. Mr. Heatley, this is for you." When Joe looked pleased, Mrs. Baugh went on, "Why, only yesterday you said you wished you had nyalhis."

Barbara: "To use on the Procida Society. 'To bust up their racket' was what you wanted, wasn't it?"

"Yeah. I want it," Joe said, "and the mictzin too. Thanks."

Mrs. Baugh was still smiling. "How will you use it? You can tell me. I'm feeble and harmless and an old doddering fool, so nobody will pay any attention to anything I say about you in my dotage. In my senile ramblings. In my lunacy. In my dismembering, or rather, my malremembering."

Joe told her. Barbara listened hard, more than once shook her head yesyesyes.

"Dear, dear," Mrs. Baugh said when he was done. "That's terribly far-fetched. How unfortunate that you won't have Alice Kim to help you. Of course, everything else you've been through is terribly far-fetched, too. Your idea may well not work and you may be doomed to fail, of course. On the other hand you may have been doomed to failure even if Alice Kim had been available. If it's any consolation to you, I don't believe you can fail again any worse than you've already failed. Of course I could be wrong about that. Nevertheless your idea surely ought to be tried. I have a friend in New York who may be able to help you. She owns an abandoned farm. The most immediate problem is Sven Dahlmann and the FBI, if they've really been watching you as you say. What a disappointment that he's become an obstacle to you."

"Who's going to help you do this?" Barbara said.

Joe: "Nobody. I can't put this on somebody else."

Before Joe left Mrs. Baugh telephoned her New York friend. Then she said to Joe, "What a grand scheme you have. Whatever happens, your life is going to be permanently changed. I do hope you finally have some good luck for a change."

As usual Barbara escorted Joe back to the front door. At the steps she spoke: "I want to come along and help you. You're going to need help. Especially since you won't have Alice Kim."

The intensity of her look, her eyes, her frown, again upset Joe, broke into his preoccupation with his plans. He said, "Oh, no. I can't get you in trouble too. This isn't a grand scheme, like she said. I'm gonna take some wild chances."

It made Barbara angry. He hadn't seen her angry before. Her arms to her side, her expression still intense, she said, "Well, that's so selfish. It's just terrible. Do you think you're the only one who wants to fight for sundidos? Other people care too. Just because we didn't get kidnapped by the Procida Society, just because they didn't kill our wife, don't act like we aren't committed just as much as you. You know what you're planning to do is going to be too much for one person. If I come you won't have to do it all by yourself. Or do you want to be some kind of noble tragic idealist who dies all alone? Like Hamlet or something?"

It was so hammy and self-conscious that it had to be nothing less than a completely honest, heartfelt speech. It made him realize, to an extent that he hadn't realized before, that this thoughtful person in this ridiculous mansion was not a fragile Ulalume but actually a smart, red-blooded woman, a woman of substance with faith in sundidos. And it was true, he surely needed help. Letting her help was something he owed to her. He said, "Yeah, all right, come along. You and I can die together. Cause it's probably too much for two people, too." As he left he thought, or for more, too much for a whole bunch of people.

Nobody followed Joe home, as far as he could tell. He reattached the bug on his rear bumper. and drove downtown to run errands. Joe picked up a copy of the weekly paper at a grocery near the university. The article by Ted Sicinski was titled "The End of Sundidos." Joe read the whole thing while drinking a blueberry milk shake in a restaurant. It was all about how Herman had sold out to Kemtrola Oil. It told how Herman had started to make sundidos in opposition to oil companies and other energy-establishment outfits, included some old quotes from Herman to that effect, and maintained that the murder of Nora had put an end to the sundido dream. It went on to say that Herman's ambitions were revived by Kemtrola Oil's process of making solar cell storage batteries and how he was turning his laboratory into a Kemtrola subsidiary. And Sicinski concluded by speculating that given Kemtrola's history of militant opposition to alternate energy sources, Herman and solar cell storage batteries were doomed.

It was an angry article. Joe figured it meant the end of the friendship between Ted Sicinski and Herman Sorg. That's why he telephoned Sicinski from the restaurant parking lot, on the cell phone Mrs. Baugh had given him. He said, "Remember when you asked me if I was gonna join the Procida Society? I'm gonna do it." It took over half an hour for him to explain.

"Woah, baby. S K R A U U W J! want to help you," Sicinski said. "And between you and me and anybody else who cares, the hell with Herman Sorg. Have you told Dahlmann what you're going to do? "

"No way. He told me to not leave Franklin. He says I'm still under suspicion."

"I think you got it wrong, man," said Sicinski, "I think A W K! tain Dahlmann wants to bust up those guys as bad as you do. I think God told him to punish them."

"So he should hassle them instead of hassling me. I don't want to see him again till after we nail that society with confessions and evidence and everything."

Joe had some idea of how he hoped to assault the Procida Society. His plans didn't go very far, he didn't know enough to know how to proceed. What he hoped for now, at the worst, was to become a moving target. Brooding at his probable failure, he debated for a few minutes whether to call Sicinski back and then call Barbara, tell them he was calling off the whole project. It might save their lives. He even thought of doing nothing after all, just staying there in Franklin and absorbing whatever punishment fate threw at him.

He decided to blunder ahead. Since he'd told Barbara and Sicinski what a mess was looming and they still wanted to go with him, he figured he'd fulfilled his responsibility to them. He wished he had a will leaving everything to his sister Liz. Should he phone her, tell her his plans, such as they were? Tell her cops might call on her to ask about him? That she might hear some awful things about him but don't believe them? The last phone call he'd had with her had shown him her non-support. If he called her today she might just call the cops, for all he knew.

Even while he was thinking about Liz, she telephoned him from her Chicago-suburb home. "He broke up with me. Two dates, that's all. The jerk won't tell me why, won't talk to me. He won't answer the phone. His boss told me he wasn't at work when I called, but I know he was. He wouldn't even answer the door when I went to his house." The guy had been a devastating disappointment to her. When she finished telling about it to Joe she said, "How're you doing? You're not getting into any more trouble about Nora and sundidos, I hope."

"Not really." How much, what to tell her?

"What does that mean? You're not going to stir up more trouble with that society of bigwigs?"

Joe evaded the question: "The police're looking for who killed her and Dr. Dryden. They were asking me questions again today."

"Well, don't volunteer anything they don't ask for," Liz said. They talked some more, she did most of the talking. At the end Joe said, "Good-bye. Remember, I love you a whole lot. Always did." After they hung up it occurred to Liz that it was the first time in a long time that Joe said he loved her.

That evening Barbara drove over to Joe's home. "This is my idea, not Mrs. Baugh's," she said. "It'll be more efficient if you and I leave together in the morning."

Her appearance startled Joe out of his brooding. He looked down the street. "Okay. Put your car in my garage right now," he said. "The police watch this place, they'll see it if you leave it in my driveway."

No other cars, and certainly no police, showed up on Joe's street while he raised the garage door, she drove into Nora's old parking space, and he closed the door again. He used the wand on Barbara's car — no bug there.

He pulled the curtain over the front window so nobody could see inside. A little later Joe was surprised again by his realizing he wasn't really bothered by Barbara's coming over that evening. He didn't think it again. For two people who had heretofore always been awkward with each other, this evening was quite a reversal. He cooked some sausage for supper, they ate at the kitchen table, and he explained their schedule. She said little, nodded in agreement more often than spoke.

Then while the radio played Golden Oldies from five years ago and he washed the dishes she talked about herself. She used to be married, she and her husband had formerly taught high school in California: he chemistry, she English. They moved to Franklin because he got a job at the university, they separated just before she went to work for Mrs. Baugh: "So she gave me a place to live that didn't cost me a thing."

"You lived with her and the senator?"

Barbara: "I moved in near the end of his second term as a senator. He only served two terms. Mildred says the reason he ran for office in the first place was because a woman who was his spiritual advisor told him to. She ripped him off for over a quarter million dollars and then skipped town while he was still in the state senate. He didn't miss the money, but he missed her."

"Mrs. Baugh tell you that?"

"She did. Over time I probably heard most of their history, in bits and pieces. For one thing, have you ever heard of the Sexual Freedom League? They were both members." Oh, yeah? "It's true. That's how they met. It was at a tantric sex workshop. They manipulated each other's chakras. It was love at first dight, she said."

"She said he liked to chase women."

"In his imagination, anyway. Once he was going to run off to Mexico with a psychotherapist who was going to start a Reichian clinic down there. She was too fast for him, though. As soon as she got his money she was gone, and not to Mexico. Mildred said he didn't miss that money, either. He had a few would-be romances like that."

"Did she always take him back?"

"She sure did. They stuck together, they were used to each other. He was impulsive, she was forgiving. Each time she forgave him they'd travel someplace together. She's been up the Andes and the Himalayas and down in the Serengeti and all around the world. When they were back home here they were philanthropists. So you can see hospitals and schools all over five states with Mildred and Osbert Baugh wings or Mildred and Osbert Baugh dormitories. Throwing their money around was a full-time job. A big part of my job was to see they didn't get ripped off again."

"That old mansion of hers must be depressing."

"It's wasted. Most of those dusty dirty old rooms are never used and some of them aren't even furnished any more. It's a great place to read H.P. Lovecraft stories by the fire on long winter nights. But she's an interesting lady, she's had quite a life."

Barbara talked some more about Mrs. Baugh. As she was talking he realized that she had broken up his dark mood. He was grateful for that. When they went to the front room she picked Eric Frank Russell's *Dreadful Sanctuary* from the bookcase — Nora's book, not his — and read it. After she read awhile she said, "It's incredible how realistic this story is."

While she continued to read Russell's great novel, he read a magazine article about the supercollider in Switzerland where physicists were trying to reproduce the Big Bang. He described the article to her, said, "You know what this means."

"It means they're starting a whole new universe," she said. "I wonder if it'll grow into the same dimensions of time and space as ours. Or will it look to us like a tiny universe?"

Joe: "Quantum physicists figured out this stuff a long time ago. That there's a bunch of other universes going on right now, same time as ours. Simultaneously."

Barbara: "But that new universe in Switzerland. Will a second of our time be maybe a billion trillion years of time in that one? Or vice versa? Will the same laws of physics, gravity, motion, or duration, or chemistry apply there?"

"If they do, there's gonna be planets. Eventually. Maybe some of those planets'll eventually get water. Some'll be in just the right places, the right orbits, for amino acids to appear — "

Barbara: "Then life. And if there's intelligent life — "

"Then those physicists who started it will be gods and goddesses."

Barbara laughed out loud: "They're going to bang the big bang."

Joe: "But don't you see? Our god, Jehovah, Allah, whatever he is — "

Barbara: "Or she."

"Whoever we worship is, he's maybe just a scientist in a laboratory. Or she's."

"Then heaven is a laboratory. Or a supercollider. And maybe our universe is a tiny little thing in a great big goddess's place."

Joe: "Doesn't need to be in a lab or a supercollider. God might be keeping our universe in a little jar in his kitchen — "

Barbara: "Or hers."

Joe: "Or in the children's room. Maybe the universe is a toy for god-children to play with."

Barbara: "Those physicists, those goddesses and gods, would another universe have stars and galaxies? Can they invent their own laws of physics, their own ecologies?"

Joe: "But what could those other laws of physics be? Or will their new universe be total chaos?"

Barbara: "No way. See, those gods are only human. The human instinct is to create order out of chaos."

Joe: "Yeah, that's what evolution's all about. That's what started the balance of nature. So how many other universes're going on right now? Along with our own? Are they expanding too?"

For the rest of the evening they talked mostly about the next day's moves. Joe did most of the talking. At the same time he was conscious of her body, her closeness, her pointed nose, her pale lips, her tanned face and arms, the hair on her arms, her blue eyes behind the big glasses, her breasts inside a tan short-sleeved shirt. Her eyes were so light blue that when she took her glasses off he seemed to see inside her. Or maybe he was seeing himself in them. Or maybe she was seeing inside him.

They watched a few minutes of the evening TV news, which was about thousands of deaths in Pennsylvania and New York from groundwater contaminated by chemicals used in natural-gas fracking, and about the U.S. Supreme Court's decision that American citizens' safety is not a valid concern of the U.S. government, which has no right to protect Americans from damage caused by energy companies' negligence or irresponsibility. There was almost no preliminary awkwardness about their going to bed together, either. He thought, I'm being unfaithful to Nora, even though I'm going through all this for her memory. To get justice for her. The thought didn't bother him. They were in Joe's bed, where he and Nora used to sleep, and he and Barbara fell into each other's arms right away.

Her nose wasn't actually all that pointed, it didn't hurt his face, but they murmured "ow" and "oops" and "unh" and "sorry" a number of times as they squirmed together. He was grateful she was there, grateful to be holding her. Barbara's lips were dry, she had an athlete's body, she was more eager than Nora had been, she was strong, and in the course of their rubbing together she whispered "Ah, Eddie..." Joe thought, Eddie? Not long after they'd subsided, after he'd thought Nora surely had approved if she had been looking down on them from heaven, they were asleep, Barbara's brown-haired head on his shoulder, her breath on his chest. The truth, of course, was that Nora would have been shocked and furious that Joe's mourning was beginning to abate.

At four a.m., with the first rays of twilight, they left Joe's house in Barbara's car. They picked up Sicinski at his house, and they did not see a single police car or more than a handful of moving vehicles in Franklin at that hour, until they got into the interstate traffic. Three hours later they were in the Chicago airport parking lot and Sicinski was saying, "You should get Captain Dahlmann in on this. We need all the help we can get."

"Not him. That would be a mistake," Joe said. They boarded a plane an hour later.

Chapter 17

"Four police forces — the town, the county, the state, and a private agency that I hired — all of them keep watch on this building. You were exceptionally clever to get past the security here," said Senator Ross Glenwright. "I know a great deal about you, so I'm not surprised at your aptitude. What made you change your mind and decide to join the Procida Society after all?"

I'm not exceptionally clever, I'm exceptionally desperate, Joe thought. It was late evening, they were at Glenwright's air-conditioned, chilling manor in New Jersey, in his office. The wall panels were not mahogany, but good American oak. Glenwright, in white shirt and necktie inside a gray jacket, had the solid look, the well-fed, sculpted face and erect posture, but not quite the clothing, of a solid citizen, perhaps a robber baron, who'd just stepped out of a John Singer Sargent painting. He sat in a leather-covered chair behind his desk — that was mahogany — and Joe leaned forward to face the senator in a smaller leather-covered chair in front of it. The wall was full of framed honorary degrees, framed letters from dignitaries, many photographs of the senator with the last five U.S. presidents, some prime ministers, diplomats, in groups of people, on stages receiving awards for distinguished public service. Joe said, "Senator Whitlock talked to me at the Newjoy Institute — "

"I know all about that," Glenwright said, looking down at Joe, "and I know that Dick Hoover left the door open for you in spite of your hasty initial rejection."

"Four days wasn't hasty. The Procida Society kidnapped me and drugged me and held me in their dungeon for four days."

"Which you resented. Even after hearing the reasons why they had to interview you extensively and the reasons for the Procida Society's work. You decided not to join on the basis of emotion rather than reason. And reason, along with vision, responsibility, and intelligence, is a hallmark of the society. Procida Society members are traditionally masters of their emotions."

Not really — Joe thought of Herman's and Alice's moodiness as he was saying, "And then Herman Sorg joined. He and Alice Kim made good arguments."

"No doubt. But I can't believe their examples changed your mind. Not if you're the independent thinker you're said to be." The senator leaned back, now appeared relaxed, to invite his guest's confidence, but he was eyeing Joe the whole time. He was an experienced debater, he had Joe on the defensive.

"Yeah, well, there's more. See, I've been thinking these last two and a half weeks. I realized I've been on the wrong track. What sundidos'd do is bring sudden change to society. What's wrong with that is, fear of change is a human instinct. Gradual evolution is how humanity lives. I've been obsessed with sundidos. I let my ego run away with me. I thought that I had to save the world by making sundidos."

"The wrong track indeed. I commend your realization. Especially since you came to it independently. But is there any more to your decision than that?" He sounds too pat, he sounds like he's thinks he's psyched me out, the senator was thinking. He's up to something.

"Not all independently. Sort of, I was forced into it. Lately a cult's been hassling me. They think the Procida Society is a left-wing menace to the world. They say it's socialist, it's pushing abortion, gay rights, gun control, it's anti-white but pro-European, it's internationalist."

"The John Wilkes Booth Brotherhood," said Glenwright "They're a small group, but they're still a nuisance, mainly because of their violence combined with their narrow political focus. They can't see the forest for the trees. But they're obviously merely ignorant." He liked to leave the impression that he was several steps ahead of Joe.

"Ignorant, yeah. But they came after me with guns. Main thing that happened was, their extremism made me realize how extreme I was in the opposite direction."

Glenwright looked down, smiled at that, a secret, superior smile, as if unsophisticated Joe had just made an unconscious joke. He was pleased that Joe seemed to be uncomfortable in the cool of the air-conditioned room. But he was serious again when he spoke: "I'm glad to see you've changed your mind. The more people who agree with us, the better. You must realize, though, that changing your opinion isn't enough reason for us to take you in. There's nothing in what you just said that proves a change of heart on your part."

"I expected that. You want to initiate me. You want me to do something to prove I'm really loyal to the society."

The senator was becoming rather alarmed at how much Joe now seemed to be anticipating his own moves. He gazed into Joe's face as he said, "Yes. If you're serious, we have a task in mind for you."

Joe said, "Never mind that. I got something more important. A danger you better deal with right away. The John Wilkes Booth Brotherhood is going to assault the Procida Society and Newjoy Institute and the U.S. Congress and the Federal Reserve, all four, next Tuesday. With explosives and short-range missiles."

Glenwright frowned at that: Joe was introducing a whole new surprise element into the discussion. He just looked at Joe, thinking over what Joe just said. A hoax. He's trying to shit me, of course, Glenwright thought. Why? Suppose there's a chance he's telling the truth. Am I in danger, is the society in danger, what's this guy up to? The first thing to do, he quickly decided, was to call Joe's bluff. The senator said, looking at Joe intently, "If that's true, it's too important to keep between us. You should tell the FBI, not me."

"Then I will." Joe stood up, took the cell phone Barbara had given him out of his pants. "What's the FBI's number? Never mind, I'll call 911."

"Wait!" Glenwright said, now leaning forward, hands on desk. "You say explosives? Missiles?"

Cell phone in hand, Joe said, "Yeah. The guy who told me about it says the missiles are getting delivered to his warehouse tonight. He bought them from an arms dealer at a gun show. The explosives are already there. Homemade, like the murderers used in Oklahoma City in 1995. They're serious and they're smart."

He's shitting me. Is this really a crisis? Glenwright thought, and said, "Blowing up the U.S. congress and the Federal Reserve are bad enough. But attacking the society and our institute — that's not only terrible in itself, it'll put us in the papers and on the TV news for days and weeks, years afterward."

"And lots of in-depth stories'll follow and investigative reporters telling about what the Procida Society does, its activities and methods. Now do you see why I told you first? Instead of calling the FBI right away?"

This has to be phony, he has to be lying. Glenwright thought. "Who is your informant?"

"He's a member of the Booth Brotherhood, got pissed off at them too. He could go either way. He's willing to sell out his buddies for the right price. He's not far from here, in fact, in Yonkers, New York."

Glenwright was frowning at Joe, thinking, I don't believe a word of this. What does he want from me? But what he says is so serious, I can't tell the police or the FBI or the CIA to look into it. He said, "I don't see why I should trust your informant and I don't have time to handle this tonight anyway. I have an emergency meeting to attend in Connecticut tomorrow." But damn it, I can't afford to ignore him if there's even a small chance he's telling the truth. Glenwright thought a few moments, eyed Joe again: "All right, here's what we'll do. I'm going to Yonkers and you're going with me. We're going to need protection, then. I'm going to tell Toro Security to come with us. I'll phone them right now. You call your informant and tell him we're coming." And if you're trying to shit me, the Toro team will take care of you very well.

While Glenwright phoned Toro Security, Joe made a briefer phone call. When Glenwright ended his call he said, "He's still there in Yonkers. He's gonna wait for us."

In about five minutes later a black Lincoln pulled into Senator Glenwright's driveway. A brown-haired woman was in the driver's seat and the black-suited man who sat next to her watched grimly as the senator and Joe got in the back seat. "We're going across the river to Yonkers," Glenwright said to the driver. "Take Drexel to the parkway and turn right. Only two of you? Where are the others?"

"They're going to follow us," the driver said. "They'll be right behind us. Right now their headlights are turned off."

"I don't see them. You're new, aren't you? I haven't seen you before."

"I've been an agent for Toro for almost a year," she said, looking straight ahead and driving down Glenwright's street.

As she turned a corner the senator pulled a cell phone out of his inside coat pocket. "Stop the car!" Joe barked, grabbing for the phone.

The stop was sudden. The impact helped Joe knock the phone out of Glenwright's hand. While they grappled the black-suited Toro agent leaped out of his seat, opened the car door next to Glenwright, grabbed his other arm. The car sped off with the senator between the two men and the cell phone in Joe's hands. "He was gonna call for help," Joe explained. "He could tell you're imposters."

"We figured," Sicinski, the black-suited pseudo-agent said. To the driver he said, "Better make that call to Toro now."

Barbara, driving, called Toro Security on her own cell phone. "Cancel that limousine order for Senator Glenwright. We won't need it tonight after all. I'm sorry we bothered you," she said over the stifled groans of the senator in the back seat. He was trying to yell but Sicinski had stuffed a wool sock in his mouth and Joe was pulling a black blindfold over his eyes. Barbara said, "I was in time. Their agents hadn't driven away yet."

The cities, then towns grew smaller, thinned out as she drove away from the New Jersey suburbs, across the New York state line, through the rural countryside, up and down and around hills. Nobody outside could see through the windows of the borrowed Lincoln, see the senator between Sicinski and Joe. They had strapped his wrists together and tied the wrist strap to his belt. The sock was out of Glenwright's mouth by then, so he said, "You can't get away with this. The town police phone my home every night at ten. If I don't answer they notify the state police. They're probably searching for me across the country already."

Nobody said anything to that. Barbara drove.

After awhile Glenwright broke the silence with, "Do you know I'm a U.S. senator? Do you know how many years in jail you could get for kidnapping me? You could spend the rest of your lives there. You could go to the gas chamber if you harm me." A moment later he added, "You could be disposed of by the FBI or the CIA and nobody would ever know. Unless you let me go."

Silence. Barbara drove.

After a long time Glenwright said, "You know, I'm not just a U.S. senator. I'm the American vice-president of the Procida Society. This is a delicate time for the human race, with so many terrorists and intemperate nations armed with nuclear weapons and building more and such tensions between the United States and Asia. Mankind needs our guidance. You could be doing fatal damage to the human race by not letting me free."

Silence. Barbara drove.

After much longer, Glenwright said, "How much money do you want? A million apiece?" Silence. After awhile, "Ten million apiece for letting me go?" No response. After another while, "My god, if you want more just say so. Name your price. I can raise the money. I'm a U.S. senator, raising money's what I do."

More silence. Barbara drove.

Eventually the car came to a stop. The blindfold and wrist tie didn't come off Glenwright until he was out of the car and Joe and Sicinski had hobbled his legs and bound his upper arms to his torso. Then Glenwright could see he was in an abandoned barn. He had to take little mincing steps as they led him, using flashlights, through a door and into a dusty little room with bare, old wooden walls, old brown paper covering the little window. They turned on the only light, a bare bulb hanging from the ceiling, two cobwebs on the cord to the ceiling. The room had a dirt floor, cobwebs in corners and on the sides, including two with spiders on them, five huge milk cans, a plush plastic-covered armchair with stuffing coming out of the top and sides, a dilapidated footstool, and a rough wooden table with a picnic basket on it. Miss April and, under her, four more months of a 1993 *Playboy* calendar were on a wall.

They set Glenwright in the armchair, propped his feet on the stool. He was still wearing that elegant gray jacket. As Barbara was pouring coffee from a thermos and Sicinski was unwrapping sandwiches Joe said to Glenwright, "How do you drink coffee? Cream? Sugar? Both?"

"Black and hot," said the senator, "and how do you expect me to drink it, tied up like this?" He did not see Barbara shake drops from a tiny bottle into a cup of coffee.

"Sorry, senator, all we have today is latte," Sicinski said. Joe gave the cup of coffee to Glenwright. With his upper arms tied he had to bend forward to raise the cup to his lips.

He drank from the cup anyway, even though it was latte. When Joe reached for the cup Glenwright said, "Not so fast. Are you trying to dehydrate me?" He took two long swallows.

"How much did he drink?" Barbara said.

Joe: "About half the cupful."

Barbara: "That's probably enough for the nyalhis to affect him." All three were watching the senator, Sicinski eating a sandwich.

"Nyalhis?" Glenwright shouted and lurched. Now for the first time there was a look of fright on his face. Joe and Barbara had to catch him to keep him from tipping his chair on its side.

She said to him, "We brought a sandwich for you too if you're hungry." To Sicinski she said, "It'll take a few minutes to get to his stomach and into his bloodstream. Then we can start asking questions. Unless he had a big, full meal before we got him tonight, and his stomach still hasn't digested all of it. Then it'll take longer to take effect." She began eating her sandwich.

"What does that stuff do to him? Are there side effects?" Sicinski said.

"The guy who takes it, it leaves him helpless to say anything but the exact truth. He can't hide anything he knows or distort anything. He's got to answer your questions," Joe said.

"Nyalhis, oh, damn," the senator groaned. Looking at Sicinski, he said, "It causes amnesia. It causes brain damage. That's why it's criminal for anyone besides a licensed specialist to administer it. That's why you're going to jail. Go ahead and have your fun. I'll have you all executed for treason. And I'm not going to answer any of your questions."

"He will," Joe said. "See, that's another great thing about this stuff. The guy who takes it can't refuse to answer. Cause he can't resist the impulse to say the first thing that comes to his mind. And the first thing that comes to anyone's mind is what he thinks is the truth."

"How bad was your amnesia when his club fed it to you?" Sicinski said.

"It took a few days before I could remember everything I said while I was drugged," Joe said. "Or I think I remember everything. I heard for some people it's as permanent as an alcoholic blackout."

Barbara said, "Marijuana and beer and coffee and lots of other things cause brain damage too." To Glenwright she said, "Did you have a hearty supper already, Senator?"

"No. God damn you, you bastard cunt," the senator said calmly, then gasped in surprise at his own words.

"He's ready," Joe said.

The senator began cursing his three captors non-stop, almost without taking a breath. Barbara and Sicinski pulled milk cans close on either side of him, sat on them. She held a digital voice recorder in front of his face and Sicinski aimed a mobile phone at his face.

Joe sat on a milk can facing the senator, his back to the wooden table. As the two turned on their recorders Sicinski said, "Go ahead."

Joe: "Who killed Nora Heatley?"

Senator Glenwright: "Veli Kokola and Velma Snell killed her, those incompetent fools. You fucking pimp."

Joe: "Who killed Dr. Dryden?"

Glenwright: "The same two fools. You filthy disgusting cockroach eater."

Joe: "Where are they now?"

Glenwright: "At the Daryl Newjoy Memorial Institute for Psychiatry and Psychoanalysis in Dunning, Connecticut. Bastard. Die in misery, asshole."

Joe: "Who ordered them to kill her?"

Glenwright: "Dick Hoover. They work for him. They did it all wrong. It was supposed to look like an accident. They weren't supposed to kill her where she worked. They weren't supposed to leave any evidence that they'd been rifling Sorg's office and lab. Fuck you in the face, you rotten pukelicker."

Joe: "Who ordered Hoover to have her killed?"

Glenwright: "Whitlock. It was Senator Whitlock's decision. The candy-ass cocksucker. And you can commit suicide and die."

Joe: "Did any other Procida Society members agree with that decision to kill her?"

Glenwright: "I did. The rest of the governing board concurred with him too. You pantysniffing pervert. You demented venereal brain."

Joe: "Who ordered them to kill Dr. Dryden?"

Glenwright: "Dick Hoover. I ordered Hoover to have it done. Dryden knew too much about how to make sundidos. The rest of the governing board agreed with me. It was Hoover who put the same pair of duncebrained fools to work on Dryden again. Shrivel up and die, worm dick."

Barbara: "Did Joe Heatley have anything to do with the murder of Nora Heatley?"

Glenwright: "No, not a thing, you stupid cow."

Barbara: "So is he completely innocent of any complicity in her death?"

Glenwright: "Yes, yes, he's totally innocent. Bitch, you should die in agony too."

Barbara: "Did Joe Heatley have anything to do with the murder of Dr. Bert Dryden?"

Glenwright: "Nothing. Not a thing. Damn you to the lowest hell, you loony whore."

Joe: "Why did Whitlock order the murder of Nora Heatley?"

Glenwright: "Because she wouldn't join the Procida Society. She opposed us, you cocksucking vomitface."

Joe: "How come the Procida Society wanted her for a member at first?"

Glenwright: "Because of her solar energy research, of course, dumbass. Because she invented the sundido. If she'd only become a member, we thought we could control her. Then she would no longer be a danger. Die slowly of the clap, you repulsive degenerate."

Joe: "What was dangerous about her?"

Glenwright: "You ninny, she was going to mass produce sundidos. They're so cheap to produce that other sundido makers would have quickly proliferated around the world. Sundidos work and everybody could afford them. She talked Herman Sorg into hiring her to make sundidos instead of the man we'd sent to him, the man he was originally going to hire to produce solar-cell storage batteries. He had a process that would have made the batteries too costly to manufacture, so they'd be only a luxury item. You vile disgusting maggot, damn damn damn, oh, damn you."

Sicinski: "How come you didn't kill Herman Sorg instead of her? After all, he ran the company."

Glenwright: "No need to, dunce boy. We projected we could manipulate Sorg with the promise of power. We found we were right about that. But we also projected that if Nora Heatley lost Sorg's backing, she had the will power and ambition to find another entrepreneur to work for. Possibly someone we couldn't compromise. So she was an ongoing threat. Sorg wasn't. God damn you too. Fuck you. Shit on you. Die in excruciating pain and sorrow, you butt-ugly moron."

Sicinski: "Why don't you want everybody to have sundidos?"

Glenwright: "Because they replace internal combustion engines and nuclear energy and wind power and all the other known ways of providing energy, you stupid idiot. We own international petroleum and natural gas and utilities. Sundidos would break us. They would destroy the economies of all the OPEC countries as well as half the states in the United States. We'd lose our influence over governments around the world. World War Three would come. We'd lose trillions of dollars and we couldn't tell the U.S. president and congress what to do any more. Worst of all, we'd sink to your level, we'd become little insignificant nothing people like you, with your sordid, empty, meaningless little lives. God damn you, god damn you, god damn you, suffer and die and go to hell."

Joe: "Do members of the Procida Society run Kemtrola Oil?"

Glenwright: "Yes, you foul vacuumbrain. The officers of the company are members and the society owns the largest block of shares under various names."

Sicinski: "Why did Kemtrola Oil buy Herman Sorg's operation and hire him to run it? And give him a process for making solar-cell batteries?"

Glenwright: "So that we could control him. I told you that already, jackoff. The process Kemtrola Oil gave him was the one they invented. It's going to fail. It was invented to fail. Get that through your damaged half an insect brain, you despicable sludge."

Joe: "Where are there companies that make advanced-generation solar-cell storage batteries? Or plan to make them? Besides Herman Sorg's laboratory?"

Glenwright: "Kemtrola Oil in Arlington, Texas and Sichuan province, China. Ra Industries in Idaho. The Angotti Company in Davis, California. Sondlicht-Lieber in Heidelberg, Germany. Sonnestrahl Systems in Boulder, Colorado. A new company in Japan. Oh, you putrefying offal, you syphillis pus."

Joe: "That's seven companies and nine places, now that Kemtrola has Herman's shop. Which ones're a threat to the Procida Society?"

Glenwright: "None of them, you septic tank. We now control research and production in all of them. Suck me, booby."

Joe: "Are all of them gonna fail?"

Glenwright: "You toilet licker, yes! Yes! Yes! Yes! How often do I have to tell you? Suffer agonies and die, fuckwit turdblossom."

Joe: "Are sundidos the only solar-cell batteries that are versatile and cheap enough to become popular around the world?"

Glenwright: "Yes! Yes! God damn you loathsome sewage."

Joe: "Did the Procida Society kidnap Alice Kim three days ago?"

Glenwright: "No. Course not, you putrid fucking rat vomit. She's a member."

Sicinski: "Now that Nora Heatley is dead, who knows how to make sundidos? Who's got the process?"

Glenwright: "Alice Kim is the only one who knows how any more, you excretion. And she's one of us. But you have Nora Heatley's instructions. You can pass them along to others. Anyone can learn to use them. Cretin fucking pervert."

Sicinski: "Doesn't Herman Sorg have that information?"

Glenwright: "No more, you dumb, dumb fuckface subhuman. Not after Nora Heatley's death."

Joe: "What's the emergency meeting you're gonna attend tomorrow?"

Glenwright: "The governing board. We'll plan to negate the biggest threat to the society. You fucking bastard."

Joe: "Where's that emergency meeting gonna be?"

Glenwright: "Newjoy Institute. Dunning, Connecticut. Bastard."

Joe: "What's the biggest threat to the society?"

Glenwright: "I said. You. Bastard. You own the sundido formula. Eat shit and die. Die twice."

Joe: "How'll you handle this threat?"

Glenwright: "Kill you soon as we can. Decide how tomorrow. Fuck you. Fuck you all."

"He's too tired to talk any more," Sicinski said, turning off his mobile phone. The senator's eyes were closed, he was crying, but he was still muttering curses. "He's a tough old cockroach. He fed us enough for a whole series of expose articles. We better get to Connecticut right away."

Joe said, "Yeah. Let's go there in the morning. Suddenly we're starting to get lucky."

Joe brought a bottle of water to Glenwright. Glenwright leaned forward, chug-a-lugged half the bottle, his hands in a praying attitude around the bottle's neck. Barbara already had her digital voice recorder plugged in via a cord to her laptop computer. Joe said to her, "How long will it take to upload all that?"

"Just a minute," she said. "I'm writing an e-mail to Captain Dahlmann. I'm attaching Glenwright's confession that explains who killed your wife and Dr. Dryden. And where the killers are now and that you didn't do it, why she was killed. And the Procida Society's plots and the danger to you. I'll send Glenwright's confession as an attachment.

Joe: "Not Dahlmann. He wants to arrest me. Now I left Franklin and we're here, he's got every excuse he could want to get me. And you too, both'a you. Let's get some different cops to help."

"Who?" she said. Since neither Joe nor Sicinski answered that one right away, she said, "He knows more about the murders of your wife and Dr. Dryden than anyone else. He can clear you."

Joe: "That's a mistake. Don't do it. He's trouble."

Sicinski: "I know Dahlmann. He talks tough but once he hears Glenwright's confession, he won't bust you,. He's too honest."

"And I'm copying to Mrs. Baugh," she said.

Sicinski said, "Ask Dahlmann to copy to the FBI, too. That'll make them love him even more. I'll upload the video and e-mail it to the captain and Mrs. Baugh, too, and to some friends in network television news. And I'll get it to some blogs and YouTube. They all can make it public right away."

Joe: "Whatever you do, don't tell Dahlmann where we're going in the morning. If he finds out, he'll mess everything up."

Glenwright murmured, just loud enough for them to hear, "Do that. Put me on TV. Get yourself arrested for kidnapping." He laughed, but the little laugh made him cough. He raised the bottle, drank. "My confession is worthless. I'll deny everything. That video proves you kidnapped me. Drugged me. That's all. Nothing more." He laughed an even smaller laugh, was silent. His eyes closed again. In a minute he was snoring.

They took turns guarding him, Barbara first. In the car, Sicinski, in the back seat, said, "I didn't want to ask you in front of Senator Sweet-talk. Who is Alice Kim?"

Joe, in the front seat, said, "She and my wife and Dr. Dryden in-vented the sundido. Glenwright knows she was a co-inventor. She disappeared from her lab three days ago. He says the Procida Soci-ety didn't kidnap her, so that makes her another total mystery."

Weary as Joe was, he couldn't sleep for an hour, then dozed a bit off and on until the next hour. By then Sicinski was breathing regu-larly, apparently in a deep sleep. So Joe left him in the car, went back to the barn. As soon as he left, Sicinski was on his mobile phone, calling Captain Dahlmann at the police department and also at home. He left a message on both of Dahlmann's answering ma-chines: "I'm with Joe Heatley. We're going to Dunning, Connecti-cut in the morning, to the Newjoy Institute. We're going to nail the

Procida Society and the ones who killed his wife. We just e-mailed you a sound file with Senator Glenwright's confession. We're going to need all the help we can get. Just thought you ought to know." That should get him running, Sicinski thought.

Meanwhile Joe, in the barn, whispered to Barbara, "Your turn to sleep."

She whispered, "I found a route to Dunning, Connecticut in my road maps. It looks like about two hours or so from here."

"Water." The word was a groan from Senator Glenwright. This time Joe dissolved some of the nyalhis antidote into the water before he handed the bottle to the senator. Glenwright drank, said, "Give me some food, god damn you." Joe handed him a sandwich. The senator gobbled it quickly so Joe gave him the last sandwich in the picnic basket. He ate that one more slowly.

In awhile Glenwright began cursing Joe and trying to tip the chair over. Some tools were in a corner, so silent Joe grabbed a hay rake and began poking Glenwright, with the rake handle, in the chest until he stopped trying to tip. Once he untied the cursing senator long enough for a pee, prodding him in the back with the rake as he minced, legs hobbled, into the yard far back of the barn. Tied in the chair again, then, the senator cursed Joe non-stop until he fell asleep again.

After two hours or so of watching Glenwright, Joe was relieved by Sicinski. Back at the car Barbara seemed to be asleep in the front seat so Joe climbed in the back. In a few minutes Barbara was in back next to him. Her head on his shoulder, she said softly, "So far so good. I'm glad you thought of all these details."

He said, just as softly,"I've been thinking about those Swiss scientists again. The ones setting off another Big Bang. One of them'll be the god of that new universe."

"Scientists," she murmured. "Gods and goddesses."

He liked her hair next to his neck. He whispered, "What if that scientist is evil — immoral, brutal, a liar? Then the people in the universe'd have an evil god. What kind of morals would those people have? Would lying and killing and stealing be virtues?"

"An evil goddess," she whispered back. A moment later she said, "Goddesses and gods. They might hate each other. Like Jupiter and Juno."

"Hard to guess which one to pray to, then. What to pray for."

Although the back seat was cramped, having each other made

for enough comfort that they were soon asleep. It was bright day-light when Joe awoke, alone. He went back to the barn where Sicin-ski and Barbara were with the cursing senator. "I let you sleep," Si-cinski explained, "because Honey-Lips was fast asleep till now and I didn't want to wake him."

The three males killed time at the farm while Barbara was gone for most of an hour, gassing up the Lincoln, buying more sand-wiches and bottled water. Then as they ate in the barn Barbara read from her tablet computer: News articles and bulletins stating that Senator Glenwright was missing, that FBI officials feared the miss-ing Alice Kim was dead, that a nationwide manhunt was ongoing for Joe Heatley, who was suspected of murdering Alice Kim and two other people, that an earthquake in Arkansas, which was caused by waste-water wells from natural-gas drilling, had killed over 2,000 people, that anti-government demonstrators were rallying around the country to demand that the government plug the oil wells in the Gulf of Mexico, that an oil well had just blown up off Alaska, in the Beaufort Sea, and the oil was spreading on Arctic Ocean cur-rents, that Nice, France and neighboring cities were being evacu-ated because of radiation leakage from the devastated nuclear power plant there, that a hundred and ten miners had died in a coal mine disaster in West Virginia, that another hurricane was aiming for New Orleans, which was being evacuated again. Not a word about Glenwright's confession yet. No luck googling for it, either.

Joe said, "I'm the only person with the instructions on how to make sundidos."

Barbara came over to Joe, whispered in his ear, "You mean, you are if Alice Kim is dead."

"Yeah," Joe said out loud, "So I'm gonna put the instructions on the web so everybody can see."

"And put sundidos in the public domain?" she said.

"Yeah. I got to, in case the FBI or the Procida Society kills me. Got to get those instructions available. They're on a flash drive in my suitcase. Will you copy them to your laptop and then post them on some web sites?"

"You better not do that, you bitch, you son of a bitch," the sena-tor said. "We'll kill you. We'll kill all of you idiot bastards." He con-tinued cursing while they blindfolded him again.

Chapter 18

THE DARYL NEWJOY MEMORIAL INSTITUTE for Psychiatry and Psychoanalysis was in hilly country, set back from an old two-lane paved road behind a wide lawn and a flower garden with a gazebo. A three-story nondescript building of grey brick, oaks and maples and beeches around it, a driveway led to it, sixteen or eighteen vehicles in the parking lot. Woods on the hillside around the Institute, a couple of warblers could be heard in trees. To Captain Sven Dahlmann the place looked too small and too innocuously pleasant to be a booby hatch.

It was a very hot day, but not quite hellishly hot, Dahlmann thought. He liked to imagine that somewhere there was an entrance to hell, a hole in the ground reeking of brimstone, a deep mine, an elevator that devils and the antichrist used to come up to earth. It was strictly imaginary, he knew — still, there ought to be such a hot spot, such a convenient way for Satan and his servants, the devils, to come up to earth and distort and deceive mankind, especially now when the human race that God had created in His image had become so monstrously perverse. It would have to be a place that seemed just this innocuous and agreeable. This could be that hot spot.

The Heatley case, mainly this sinister Procida Society, was keeping Dahlmann obsessing about the end times that were happening right now. He loved the Bible's symbolism — the trumpets sounding, the great seals opening. The end times explained all the earthquakes and hurricanes and wars, all the exploding power plants and oil spills, all the famines and AIDS and flu epidemics, all the whorish behavior of our leaders and celebrities, all the loveless, vain, self-centered, greedy, lying, lustful, intoxicated, hating, violent people despoiling God's sweet earth — all the unholy, inhumane stuff that people do to the planet and each other these days — all signs that the apocalypse is approaching, the world as we know it is going to be destroyed, the rapture will happen.

It was late morning and, as a black Lincoln was driving up, a Dunning, Connecticut officer was saying to Dahlmann, "I don't like this at all. You're barking up the wrong tree. I don't care if they do put mentally sick people there. These Newjoy Institute people are good and quiet, never cause any problems. Senator Whitlock's a real good man and he vouches for the rest of them."

Dahlmann was not paying attention because he had his eyes on the black Lincoln with the New York license plates that was driving up. He would never call himself a prophet, he was not so vain and wicked that he'd honor himself that way. But he had an old-fashioned cop's sixth sense. He knew how desperate Joe Heatley had become, knew how he'd manipulated Joe. He knew from Sicinski's late-last-night phone messages that Joe was on his way there and he'd listened to Glenwright's e-mailed confession, So he now had a strong premonition that this very next car was Joe, coming to this place on this very day. With some friends, too.

Sure enough, three people from Franklin got out. He especially liked it that Joe and Barbara were surprised to see him there. As two of them helped a fourth person, a stranger who was bound and gagged, out of the car, Barbara came up to Dahlmann and the local cop. "Excuse me. We need to bring in a very sick man. He's violent and he's likely to be a danger to himself and others." She was nervous as she spoke to Dahlmann but she said, "Will you help us? Please?"

Dahlmann figured the bound stranger had to be the missing Senator Glenwright. The confused local cop only watched without intervening as Joe and Sicinski helped Glenwright, whose legs were hobbled with a rope, up the steps. He was gagged and his eyes were wide open, wild looking. The local cop said, "I'm not going in there with you. I won't have anything to do with this. I'm going to tell Senator Whitlock." Nobody was paying attention to his threat. He turned his back on the five at the Institute door, walked away toward his car.

That guy would be no help anyway, Dahlmann was glad he was gone. Joe, even more nervous than Barbara, looked helpless, kept watching Dahlmann. So he said to Joe, "Don't worry, I'm not going to bust you. You're just in time. I got that confession from Glenwright that your friends e-mailed me."

He was especially pleased at Joe's nervousness because he knew how Joe had been emotionally whipped around. If we're going to be among pros, this will be the time Joe falls apart and makes a ruinous mess of things, Dahlmann figured. He wanted to be there to add to the chaos and ruin. Best of all, he wanted a fight between the Procida Society and the sundido makers. Of course he hoped the sundido people, especially his friends Barbara and Sicinski, would survive, which would mean that God was on their side. But he had to be sure. "I have two warrants here — Velma Snell and Veli Kokola. Somehow I forgot to bring a warrant for your arrest. But the FBI is looking for you again," he told Joe.

"You'll need our help. You're going to have more than two busts. Some of their co-conspirators're meeting in there right now," Sicinski said. He was holding onto his mobile phone with one hand and Senator Glenwright with his other arm. "You know we want to get all these people arrested and we're recording their confessions."

That's exactly what I like to hear, they're even collecting evidence for me, Captain Dahlmann thought. He said, "This guy here must be your senator, then. What're you going to do with him? What are you going to do here now?"

Dahlmann's assurance hadn't calmed Joe, who was holding Glenwright from the other side. He said, "We hope we're gonna get the police here to arrest all these guys."

"You can see the local police aren't sticking around. At the moment I'm all the police left here. So you need my help, I need your help. I'm going to deputize all three of you. Barbara, come with me." Dahlmann and Barbara went over to the captain's car. "I'm lucky you arrived before I went in. These are loaded. Be careful." He handed her two handguns from the glove compartment.

Barbara was shook up. She just stood there looking at Dahlmann. She had never before touched any kind of handgun in her life, let alone a loaded one. "What do we need these for? I don't know if we should...," she started to say.

Dahlmann: "Give one to Joe before we go in. Keep one for yourself. Don't give one to Sicinski, he has his hands full already."

The captain liked it that handling a gun made Joe even more nervous: "Hey, what are we supposed to do with those things?"

Dahlmann looked fierce: "They're for self-protection. We don't know what's inside that building. Don't do anything dumb." Truth was, he hoped all of them would do very dumb things, especially Joe, since Joe was surely most volatile. Loaded guns make people feel tough, encourage their recklessness, stupidity, was his experience. Adrenalin brought out the worst in some people. By contrast Captain Dahlmann knew the adrenalin flowing in his own bloodstream today was making him more sharp-witted, observant, logical, responsive, and also more cool and calculating.

"This isn't right. Somebody could get hurt," Barbara said and Sicinski said, "Yeah, real bad. Hey, Captain." They said these to Dahlmann's back, he was walking toward the institute's front door.

He didn't reply. When he got there he looked back at them. They were just standing on the sidewalk, Joe and Sicinski holding onto Glenwright. "Well, come on," Dahlmann said angrily. "You're Franklin deputy police now. You have to help. Joe, bring your sick man here." He held the door while Joe walked the shaking senator inside the building.

Deputy police? The concept was a new one to Joe. He said to Barbara, "This might be the best thing that could happen. The captain's on our side." Neither he nor Barbara or Sicinski believed it. Things were going to happen too wildly anyway, and suddenly they were deputy police with guns too .

But Dahlmann liked to hear that, was pleased at himself that he'd spontaneously thought of calling these three amateurs "Franklin deputy police." They all went in. The interior of the Institute looked, not like a hole of hell, but like the lobby of a nursing home, a rather elegant one, Dahlmann thought: new carpets down the halls, the light-green walls had been painted recently, there were framed Monet and Renoir posters. As they crossed the lobby, the receptionist gawked at the hogtied senator. "Isn't that...?" she managed to say.

Sicinski said, "It's Senator Glenwright" and Captain Dahlmann said, "We're police. Where's the meeting?"

"It's in the conference room, to your left. But you can't...I mean, they're, there's..."

Dahlmann, leading the way ignored her, so the others did too. They stopped for a moment to get themselves collected, to go into the room together. Sicinski said, "What next? What are we supposed to do when we go in?"

Dahlmann: "Don't worry about that. Just start Glenwright talking and then do what I tell you." He opened the door, prodded the hobbled senator ahead of them.

Five people were in the conference room, seated in institutional-brown plastic-covered chairs. The captain recognized two of them immediately, from seeing them on television news. So these were the people who secretly ruled the world! He saw that one of them startled Joe. Alice Kim — now the captain remembered seeing her face on a Missing Persons e-mail — was in a chair facing four Procida Society men and she was just as startled to see Joe. She gasped and then stamped the floor as a wide, open-mouth smile broke out on her face. "What is this? Who are you?" said a tall man with grey touches in his curly hair. "Is that Glenwright?"

Dahlmann had his gun out where all five could see it. Deputy Police Officer Joe didn't know what to do with the gun Dahlmann had given him, he just held it by his side. Deputy Police Officer Barbara held her gun by her side too and was more nervous, she seemed to be highly aware she now had the power to kill a fellow human being. This time fat Senator Whitlock, still wearing a gray suit, did not have the smug smile on his face that Joe remembered — instead, he was mad. He said, "Glenwright, you utter, complete idiot, now look at what you've done. How could you be so stupid?"

Way to start, fat man, Dahlmann thought. He liked it even better that Sicinski disrespected those big-time operators. First the reporter looked at the captain for directions. Since Dahlmann only nodded meaninglessly in reply, Sicinski said to the nearest man, who happened to be Dick Hoover, "Untie this guy and take the bit out of his mouth. He wants to say charming things to you."

Yes, Dahlmann thought, let's hear these fiends talk. He said, "I have warrants for the arrest and extradition of Veli Kokola and Velma Snell. Bring them here."

The tall, curly-haired one didn't hesitate, he was all business. He picked up a house phone next to him, said, "Margaret, this is Stapleton. Send Snell and Kokola to the conference room." He looked at Dahlmann the whole time.

"Oh, I know who he is. That's Max Stapleton, who runs Nobzzyn. That's the holding company that owns electric and gas utilities in eastern states. He was in the news during the New York blackouts last month," Barbara said and asked Senator Glenwright, "Who are the others?"

Glenwright, the sock now out of his mouth, named the others, finishing with, "Secretary Wayne Belanger of the U.S. State Department, you despicable sons of bitches." The secretary of state was a tall, imposing, mustachioed specimen wearing black-rimmed glasses and sitting on a rocker. The others were on two sofas. Dahlmann did not smell any sulphur from hellfire and he thought, those old artists had it all wrong. Devils aren't red-colored and they don't have horns and tails. They have white skins and wear business suits and smell of perfume. Glenwright added, "Fuck you, Whitlock. They doped me with nyalhis."

Joe said, "Who's missing?"

"Nyalhis?" gasped Hoover. What, Captain Dahlmann thought, is nyalhis? A narcotic? Some other kind of drug?

"Three are missing. Chief Justice Asseltine of the U.S. Supreme Court," Alice Kim said, "and Bernard — "

"Shut up," snapped Whitlock at her.

"How'd they get nyalhis? It's not even sold anywhere," Stapleton said.

" — Bernard Watson of Universal Dynamics and Congressman Duncan Coates," Alice finished, brightly. She was obviously relieved and happy to see Joe, with three of his friends, yet.

Now Glenwright was untied and in the center of the room. He was still wearing that gray jacket. Whitlock said, "Do you know who brought you here? That's Joe Heatley. The sundido guy. Glenwright, all this is your fault. You blew up the entire program. It's going to take weeks, months, even years to return to normal. Hey, you can't do that."

The "hey" was because Sicinski was grabbing a cell phone out of Whitlock's hand. At the same time Joe was snatching a cell phone from Stapleton. Barbara saw them and unplugged the house phone next to Stapleton.

"Hush, Whitlock, you're blowing this out of proportion. Let this policeman gather his two prisoners and leave," said Secretary Belanger, who surrendered his cell phone to Barbara without saying anything.

Whitlock said, "Can't you see? Glenwright let them dope him to the eyeballs with nyalhis. And look, they're recording this." Sicinski now was scanning the room with his mobile phone and the digital audio recorder in Barbara's shirt, microphone pinned to her pocket, was recording. "They're recording everything we say."

And there's not a thing you devils can do about it, Dahlmann thought. It's really true, Ted Sicinski and his pals are on God's side.

"Quiet, every one of you," Belanger said. "There's no need to be upset. This minion of the law has his duty to do. Let him do it without incident and without comment and then leave with his friends. After they return our cell phones."

"What's this? Who wants us?" It was the short, long-jawed, black-eyed blonde woman — Velma Snell. She had just entered the room and was standing next to officer Dahlmann. Jackpot! he thought — he recognized her immediately from Herman's video of Nora's murder.

"Do you have another job for us already?" said Tall and Stupid — Veli Kokola — beside her. Dahlmann recognized him immediately too.

"Shut up, don't say a word," Whitlock said to them.

"Senator Glenwright, who told Velma Snell and Veli Kokola to murder Nora Heatley and Dr. Bert Dryden?" Sicinski said. That's the spirit, Dahlmann thought, praise the Lord!

"Don't answer!" Belanger shouted in Glenwright's direction.

Glenwright couldn't help himself. Facing Sicinski's mobile phone he said, "I did. Whitlock did. Belanger and Stapleton and Asseltine and Watson and Congressman Coates. We all agreed to it. God damn you rotten decaying stinking-ass wretch."

By the time Glenwright was damning Sicinski, Whitlock and Stapleton and Hoover were trying to overwhelm him in a hubbub of nos and shut ups and curses. Dahlmann couldn't help himself, he was smiling — he loved this chaos, loved see the people who ran the world acting the fool, revealing what fools they were. He had his eyes on Velma and Veli. The other Procida Society people in the room were obviously just talkers. If there was going to be any action it would start from those two assassins.

Above all the babble Sicinski, his mobile phone aimed at Glenwright, said to him, "Did the Procida Society pay Snell and Kokola to murder Nora Heatley and Dr. Bert Dryden, then?"

Now Kokola and Snell joined the noise. "Yes! We did! God damn you, bastards, bitches...," Glenwright said, right into Sicinski's mobile phone, above the din. Dahlmann, sweaty hand on his gun, thought, Come on, you people, fight each other.

Velma Snell was astonished. "What's the big deal? Of course you hired us to kill those two people in Franklin," she said to Glenwright. She had her hands in her blue jeans pockets. Probably has a gun in there, Dahlmann thought. But the tall stupid guy probably has his gun in his jockstrap.

Belanger, in a calm, stern voice, said to her, "Don't say anything. These strangers came here to arrest you and — "

Kokola, even more amazed: "Arrest us! Has Glenwright been ratting on us?"

"Now, now. He's been drugged, he couldn't help saying what he said," Belanger said. "Even if this officer does arrest you, you'll never be convicted."

"You sold us out!" Kokola said and walked over to Belanger.. "I knew this was gonna happen someday. I knew you weasels couldn't take any pressure." That's it, lose your temper, oh, yes, Dahlmann thought.

"Take it easy," Belanger said to the killer standing in front of him. "Nobody's sold anybody out. Don't say anything here. You know we've got the power to quash all charges against you."

Velma Snell had her gun out and fired first. Her shot hit Glenwright, who slumped to the floor. "Stinking weasel," Kokola said and shot Belanger, who fell backward against the sofa.

It happened too fast — just the way Dahlmann wanted. He turned around, pointed his gun at Kokola, said, "Don't move. You're under arrest — "

Kokola twisted around, started to point his gun in Dahlmann's general direction, but not fast enough. Dahlmann shot him. As he fell in front of Velma Snell Dahlmann could see her well enough to fire at her, then. His shot hit her chest. As she lurched forward her gun dropped to the floor. Barbara, terrified look on her face, pounced on it.

At the same time the shaky Joe was pointing his gun, holding Whitlock and Hoover at bay. Hoover was crying in fright, Whitlock was shuddering. Stapleton looked at them, then at the aghast Alice Kim and at Dahlmann, who was now pointing a gun at Stapleton, hoping he would make a move. "Well. That was surely dramatic," Stapleton said, sitting without moving, without even twitching. "Still, the Matrix movies were better."

Captain Sven Dahlmann was more than happy — he was triumphant. He said, "Alas, alas, that great city, that was clothed in fine linen and purple and scarlet and decked with gold and precious stones and pearls — "

"What're you talking about?" Sicinski said, not looking at him, wide-eyed, mouth open, almost in shock at the carnage he'd just seen.

" — for in one hour its great riches is come to naught. For in one hour is she made desolate." Stapleton, astonished at the incongruity of Dahlmann's words, laughed. "You're under arrest," Dahlmann said to him. "And Senator Whitlock and Dick Hoover, you're under arrest too."

Alice Kim was gawking at the bodies of Glenwright and Belanger, Joe was gawking at the bodies of his wife's murderers, the stunned Barbara was looking at the bodies and blood on the floor, Sicinski was video-recording everything with shaky hands. Stapleton said to Dahlmann, "No. The senator and Mr. Hoover and I are going to forget you said that. Belanger was right. We're not going to spend any time in jail. And if Mr. Heatley here is as smart as he's supposed to be, he should know that already."

All eyes were on Stapleton now. "Or maybe you don't realize yet what you're up against," he said, and then spoke directly to Joe: "Now I see how terribly wrong we were, to think you're responsible enough to join the society. Nevertheless, you have a choice right now. You can be a big hero, the hero who killed Velma and Veli, the assassins of Senator Glenwright and Secretary of State Belanger, before they could do any more damage. We can give you and your friends more money and power than you ever imagined." He looked toward Sicinski and Barbara, then toward Dahlmann. "What would you like? Millions of dollars? Tens of millions? Or you can continue in your futile efforts to build sundidos." Addressing Joe again: "And die in prison because of it. And because you tried to discredit the Procida Society too."

Dahlmann couldn't contain his wonder: "For by their sorceries were all men deceived. So these are the filth and abominations the great harlot uses to seduce. And that woman is the great city that rules the kings of the earth."

He might have gone on but Alice Kim suddenly spoke out: "It's too late to stop sundidos. Instructions for building them are already on a number of internet sites." Her voice was shaking, her body was shaking, she was making fists and unfisting, both hands. "Before I left home I posted them on thirty web sites myself. In seven languages. 'The Construction and Uses of Sundidos' is the title. It's only a matter of time before sundidos proliferate all around the world."

"You! My god!" said Whitlock and stared at her, horrified. Hoover stared too and bawled, "Oh, no. It's over."

Stapleton was silent for a moment before he said to her, "We made a severe mistake when we invited you and Mr. Heatley to join us. We thought you both had the vision and the insight to see the crises your sundidos are going to cause. What you did was totally irresponsible, as irresponsible as Mr. Heatley. There are more than your enterprises involved, or even the Procida Society — there's the whole human race to consider."

Dahlmann was on his own cell phone, calling the state police for help. When he finished he took Senator Whitlock's arm, said, "I'm going to handcuff this bum. Joe, Barbara, point your guns at those others and then I'll get them too. Thus shall Babylon be thrown down and shall be found no more at all. And a great voice of the people in heaven'll say hallelujah."

Chapter 19

S o   t h e   s u n d i d o   m a k e r s must be the ones doing God's work, whether they know it or not, was what Captain Sven Dahlmann concluded. In longer than four hours later, at the state police building near the county seat, he came over to Joe and said quietly, "All right, you and your friends've made your statements. Now get out of here quick. The Procida Society lawyers are going to arrive before long and you can be sure they're going to file counter-charges. The FBI's on their way too. So if you hang around here, you're likely to stay for a real long time. There's TV and radio news crews starting to arrive, but you can ditch them if you go out the back door. Don't thank me, I didn't tell you a thing." And rejoice thou heaven, for I, and Joe and his friends, too, but mainly I, a sinner, hath avenged you this day, he thought. And quickly corrected himself: Not I, since vengeance was actually the Lord's.

Dahlmann's urgency gave Joe and Alice Kim and Barbara and Ted Sicinski something to think about, to fear, besides the sudden horror of the four killings they'd seen and Stapleton's cold threats. Before they took off Joe checked the borrowed Lincoln and Alice's Toyota for bugs — nobody had planted any on either. For the next two hours Barbara, with Joe, drove the Lincoln back to Mrs. Baugh's friend's farm in rural New York, and Sicinski and Alice Kim followed in Alice's gray car. They took Stapleton's threat seriously. Keeping the Lincoln would have made them too conspicuous, they had very quickly reckoned. At first both pairs were somber, the mayhem at the Procida Society had left them mostly silent, stunned. The two cars went on state roads through towns so small there were surely no mounted surveillance cameras documenting their route.

People can't stay quiet forever. When all four were in Alice Kim's car and she was driving to the Albany airport she explained that she'd come to the Procida Society meeting to find out what they were going to do to Joe: "Oh, my god, it was such a relief to see you walk into the room." After that they couldn't stop talking about the day's monstrousness, not until she turned on her car radio to catch a seven p.m. newscast.

There was no word about Glenwright's confession or about the arrests of Whitlock, Stapleton, and Hoover. But there were plenty of words about the vicious murders of six persons, including two great Americans, and the kidnappings of Senator Glenwright and Alice Kim. A witness named Joe Heatley was wanted for questioning. There was also talk about the more than 5,000 deaths from an earthquake in Arkansas, which had been caused by the collapse of wastewater wells from natural-gas fracking, about the pre-Hurricane Yasmina evacuations of New Orleans and Mobile, Alabama, the fourth hurricane to hit New Orleans so far this year, and about lower water levels in the Great Lakes, both the result of global warming, which in turn resulted from the use of internal-combustion engines.

It was after sunset when they left Barbara at the Albany airport. "As soon as you get to Toronto let me know," Barbara said to Joe, "and I'll have Mrs. Baugh transfer the money to your account there. And good luck." Out of sight of the others, they kissed. There was some momentary comfort as they embraced each other. She said, "When you get settled, I'll try to move your books and clothes from Franklin to your new place."

Joe: "Then soon as you can, move up north and stay with me and we'll start the new sundido works."

A few minutes after they left Barbara he missed her already. They'd had so little time alone together so far and he was surprised at himself that he now felt a large emptiness without her. As frantic as the day had been, as little sleep as he'd had last night, he was not tired. None of them were hungry, they had bottled water and more sandwiches to get them through the long drive to come.

The next few hours could turn out to be the toughest yet, Joe figured. If the cops wanted him for questioning, they'd ask his sister about him. He was tempted to call Liz on his cell phone, tell her he was all right and he'd never murdered anybody. Could they trace the call if he did? Probably. Besides, she was mad at him for pursuing Nora's murderers. He didn't phone Liz, he decided to wait till he got to Canada. If he actually got there. How long would Barbara take to move to Toronto and start a sundido business with him and Alice?

Alice still couldn't stop talking: "Oh my god. How can I move to Canada? My mother and father are coming to live with me, I'll, you know, have to move them to Canada too. How can I tell them that? And you know, how can I explain everything to them? It was so awful to be in that death room and watch those people kill each other. Are the police going to come after us? The state police? The police could be worse, you know, than seeing all those people die. I mean, they could put us in jail or do anything they want. The Procida Society are going to come after us. Stapleton's insane. Oh god."

"Those Connecticut police're holding Hoover and Stapleton and Senator Whitlock," Joe said and hoped he was telling the truth. He'd been having doubts about that ever since leaving Dunning, Connecticut. His worrying had increased as they had continued to travel.

Alice: "Yes, but they probably, you know, are out on bail already. Some of the other Procida Society members are probably coming after us. Somebody else, somebody we don't even know about, might be coming after us. I mean, you know, we're across a state line now, that lets federal agents come after us. What's going to happen to us? Will they at least let us go to prison together?"

As Alice was talking she was driving north on the interstate. The goal was to drive immediately north through New York state to Montreal, Quebec, Canada, then on to Toronto, Ontario. It was a Friday night, traffic was heavy, a light rain had begun to fall. State and local police departments along the way would probably be on the lookout for them. And Alice said, "Here comes another state police car. There's a lot of them tonight. You know, my nerves are quivering awfully, you know. I get scared every time one of them passes us." As she said that, the state police car passed them. She said, "Are they setting up a roadblock up ahead there? Are they going to stop us and arrest us? Oh, god, what can I do?"

Sicinski said, "Do you have enough gas in this thing to get us to Canada?"

"This doesn't have any gas at all. It's a sundido car," Alice said. "It runs directly on a sundido battery. I fixed it, I, you know, bypassed the gas tank so it just runs on the sundido. So I won't need to stop for gas."

In his state police car that had just passed Alice, New York officer Kaiser said, "Okay, so we've got police at every gas station on the interstate and roadblocks at every exit. What makes you so sure that's going to get them?"

His partner, the driver, officer Jordan, said, "They were driving a Lincoln. Our satellite is checking out every Lincoln on this road. We're sending a drone after them, too. We've got them covered every way."

"These're American citizens, aren't they? We can't shoot down American citizens with drones, can we?"

Jordan said, "I don't know, maybe we can when they're terrorists. Like these guys."

Joe wasn't paying much attention to Alice's torrent of words. As she chattered about her fears for the future he wondered, what would Barbara do if I got a long jail sentence? Would Barbara talk Mrs. Baugh into moving to Canada with her? Would something unforeseen keep Barbara from moving to Toronto after all? Was settling in Canada really the right move? Eventually, as they rode, he said, "We can't stay in Canada. We got to find some place that doesn't have an extradition treaty with the U.S."

"What country doesn't? Where do you think we're all going to live then, you know? Do you expect me to make sundidos for you in Iran? Or North Korea?" Alice said. "We're all going to be safe in Canada. They like photovoltaics there. The Procida Society won't make the Canadian government extradite you. They know if they even try, the whole story would come out — our side of the story too. The society can't, you know, stand the publicity. They don't have any influence in Canada, so they'd be exposed for what they are — crazy people."

"Besides," Sicinski said, "once we get there, I'll post today's videos on TV and some web sites and write the story of what happened. And Barbara said she'll put me to work at the new sundido factory."

"Did you know the police and the FBI were hunting for you this week?" Joe said to Alice. "How come you left Colorado and didn't tell anybody?"

"I couldn't tell them I was, you know, going to the Procida Society, could I?" she shot back. "I had to find out what they were doing to you. I had to, you know, try to protect sundidos, don't you understand?"

As Alice drove she turned on the windshield wipers and Sicinski turned on the car radio, found another newscast. They heard, "Terrorism once again struck on American soil today. The savage murders of Secretary Of State Wayne Belanger, Senator Patrick Glenwright, and two of their security personnel, by armed terrorists, have left Washington horrified. The murders took place as they were attending a conference on mental health in Connecticut."

There was silence in the car after that line about "a conference on mental health" and then Alice chuckled a muffled chuckle. That led to Joe and Sicinski breaking into hearty whoops of laughter — the kind of helpless, long-overdue laughter that for a time at least released tension. Meanwhile, the radio was continuing: "The assassinations are believed to be tied to the disappearance of physicist Alice Kim, who was apparently kidnapped earlier this week from her workplace in Boulder, Colorado. Authorities are searching for a black Lincoln with four people, two women and two men, believed to be three terrorists and a hostage. They may attempt to leave the United States..."

The broadcast went on to quote various politicians and then the president's words on the tragic losses of two great American statesmen. He ended with a promise to pass tough new laws, put up more spy satellites and cameras in public places, order more restrictions, and otherwise increase vigilance and limitations in order to preserve liberty. Other news included reports of 10,000 so-far known deaths in the Arkansas earthquake, of the governor of Tennessee ordering the evacuation of Chattanooga because of a nuclear power plant explosion, and a talk-radio host's remarks: "What's a few dead whales and fish? Why do unpatriotic bleeding hearts berate us about the death of the Atlantic Ocean, when our country desperately needs to drill for more oil?" There was no more news about Glenwright's confession or the hunt for the terrorists, so Sicinski turned down the car radio. By that time they were already back to feeling somber and Joe was trying to imagine where Barbara was right then. Alice said, "You guys, I'm scared. They're, you know, going to catch me before I get to the border."

Joe said, "Lookit, you don't have to risk your neck for us. They think you're our hostage, not some terrorist. Leave us off at the next exit. Ted and I'll find another way to get to Canada."

"Oh my god, Joe, I can't do that. I have to stay with you so I can make sundidos. I mean, you know, can't you see what a fix I'm in? Because after today the Procida Society's after me too. I don't have anyplace else to go to, don't you understand?"

Joe didn't have an answer to that. The rain was coming down harder now, Alice made the windshield wipers go faster. After awhile, to take their minds off their problems, he said to Sicinski, "Something I wonder about. How come you're coming with us? How come you didn't go back to Franklin with Barbara?"

"She's not going to stay in Franklin very long. Mrs. Baugh' s getting a new secretary to take her place." Joe knew that, Barbara had told him that already. "There's nothing left for me there, either. I believe in sundidos too much to go back and listen to Herman's garbage, and anyway he's going to leave there too. Two nights ago after you called I had a long talk with Val. She's going to move up to Toronto as soon as she hears from me."

Joe: "Val? The one with you and Herman in that commune?"

Alice: "I'm really frightened. I wish I had some coffee to calm my nerves."

Sicinski: "Yeah, the same Val. We got together again. Only I can't go back to Franklin if I'm wanted there. I don't know how what we're going to do about the birds."

Joe: "Birds?"

"Yeah, we have two parakeets and two cockatoos." That explained the hideous screeches Joe had heard over Sicinski's telephone. Up to now Joe had thought that phone simply had some kind of strange feedback. "I don't know if it's even legal to bring them into Canada. If it is, how's she going to bring them? How's she going to bring the cages up? They're too big for her car. If she can't bring the birds, can she sell them? But that's the only thing we have to worry about. Because she knows the truth — that spiritual possessions are what's valuable and material possessions are insignificant. You know?"

The farther north Alice drove on the New York interstate, the more traffic thinned out. Twilight had blackened into night, the steady rain was continuing, Joe was thinking about Barbara's gentle face, her alert blue eyes, her perfect (he now decided) nose, when Alice said, "The state police are going to catch us. My Colorado plates stand out around here. I'm seriously scared, guys. I don't know what to do when that happens. I mean, this is terrible."

Joe said, "That's a risk we got to take. Look at that fool passing us like a bat out of hell."

It was true, her little car shuddered in the tailwind and the splashed water from the blue car that just passed them. Sicinski said, "He's probably a state cop in an unmarked car."

She said, "Oh my god, I'm so afraid. I've been chased by cars, you know, so much, I think I'm going to freak out if another one comes after me."

Joe: "It was the FBI chasing you that night in Franklin. I think tonight we might get more to look out for than just state police."

In their blue car the bootylicious Jane Edgar Hooters said, "You just passed a car with Colorado plates. The Kim woman is from Colorado. That might be her car, they might be holding her hostage. Let's stop them."

The male model FBI agent, driving, said, "Let's wait till we get to the border. Then we'll have reinforcements. I want to smash that smart-aleck son of a bitch Heatley's teeth down his throat."

His remark reminded her that a concerned, caring young woman like herself would surely not waterboard Joe or throw acid on his face. Not while anyone was watching, at least.

Sicinski interrupted Joe's meditation on Barbara, said to him, "I heard about that night some guys tried to recruit you to fight the Procida Society. Not the FBI but, what was that gang?"

Alice quickly answered, "That was, you know, this bunch who're just as insane. They're all Procida Society rejects. They call themselves the John Wilkes Booth Brotherhood. They want to start a revolution. I mean, not like, you know, the sundido revolution, but a political one, a violent one. "

Joe: "They told me they were gonna blow up the U.S. capitol building and the Federal Reserve and the Procida Society buildings in New York and Connecticut on Tuesday."

Alice: "What they told you, oh god, things could be so much worse right now. Wow."

She said "wow" because she had to swerve right to get out of the way of two cars that were bearing down on them at a ferocious speed. After they both passed in a blur of splashed water Sicinski said, "That was close. The crazies are sure joy-riding tonight. Why'd this John Wilkes Booth Brotherhood pick on you?"

Alice said, "I can't take this any more. I'm losing my mind. I'm going to freak out. I wish I'd never invented sundidos."

Joe described his experience with the John Wilkes Booth Brotherhood.

In the first of the two cars the driver, Gray Suit, said, "The hell of it is, Heatley and his mob did us a big service when they killed those Procida Society bigwigs. This time he acted like he's on our side."

"But he's not," said Blue Suit. "Remember what he did to us back in Franklin — pretended to agree, when all the time he was summoning the police."

"A double-crossing traitor. No principles," said Brown Suit. "The big question about him is, who did he sell out to? The FBI? The United Nations?"

"Or even worse," said Blue Suit, "the European Economic Community. His sundidos are ideal for their purposes. They'll not only weaken America. They'll force us to use sundidos. That means they'll be taking away our freedom of energy choice. It's another government takeover. Socialism. We have to stop him."

While Joe was thinking about Barbara's idea of the universe, or universes, and wondering if she was thinking about him on her journey, Sicinski said, "Look, right here we're just a few miles west of Vermont. Let's drive over there where we won't be so exposed and cross the border from there."

"Oh, no, Ted, didn't you look at any maps before we started?" Alice said. "Don't you know, you know, Lake Champlain is between us and Vermont? We'd have to take a ferry to get across."

Sicinski: "A ferry'd make us a pretty slow-moving target. I guess we're better off staying on this road. But these drivers tonight are just nuts. It's like all the water and air pollution finally got Americans so scared that they're trying to beat us to the Canadian border."

Alice: "I'm beginning to realize what a big mistake I'm making, everything I've done today and seeing those people kill each other and die and now driving us all to Canada. I never should have done this. I mean, I should have stayed in Boulder, Colorado. I've never met your Mrs. Baugh and now I have to teach you how to make sundidos — "

Joe: "You said you posted how-to instructions on thirty web sites."

"Yes, but I still have to show you how to mass-produce them. I'll have to teach you that in Canada. And you know I've never lived anywhere except in America and you know I'll have to move my parents to live with me and I'll have to buy a new violin and find a new psychiatrist and the one I had there in Boulder didn't understand me anyway and now I don't have anyone to turn to, you know, do you understand? nobody at all — "

Sicinski: "Will you look how fast that van is coming up behind us. Like they're trying to escape the Procida Society too."

As the rented black van splashed water all over Alice's car, Senator Whitlock, inside, said, "But how can we be sure Heatley's taking this road? There are other routes to Canada."

Max Stapleton said, "He knows we know he and his pals left Connecticut in a black Lincoln. The satellite's checked out the few Lincolns on the road and they're not in any of them. So he's probably switched cars. Right now they must be in Alice Kim's car, so the satellite is checking out all the cars on the road with Colorado plates. They have to drive to Canada, to get a plane to Cuba. And we can't ask Canada to stop them, we don't have any clout there. His gang won't be fugitives from American justice there."

Dick Hoover said, "And he'll carry out his program of mass destruction. But Senator, this is the most direct road for them to take to Canada. And they're in a hurry. In fact, they're probably not very far behind us."

Stapleton: "We've got to confiscate those digital recordings before they post them on the web. We've got to destroy them. The society's whole future depends on it."

Hoover: "Fortunately, the state police are sending a drone after them. I hope it'll destroy their car and their recordings."

Sourpuss, the driver, didn't say anything, just ate his doughnut and stepped on the gas.

A few minutes after they passed the Plattsburgh exit Sicinski said, "Those bright lights ahead. That must be the border. And none too soon."

"Not yet," Alice said. "It's a roadblock. I told you there were going to be roadblocks. I can't take this, not any more. I'm going to stop right there. I'm just going to tell the whole truth, everything, and throw myself on their mercy. I can't go on like this, I'm completely freaked out, I'm going to break down. I'm too afraid, look at me shake, my nerves are screaming. What's going to happen to me if I keep on like this? Oh my god." She was already slowing down. Almost surrounded by woods, headlights and spotlights from a swarm of state police cars were making the roadblocked area of the highway as bright as Times Square. The pavement was a huge puddle, the rain was coming down hard. Just ahead of them the t-shirt-clad driver of an 18-wheeler was getting out of his cab and jawing at a trio of yellow-raincoated state police. The F B I car, the John Wilkes Booth Brotherhood cars, and the Procida Society van were already well past the roadblock.

One of the state cops checking out the line of cars one by one finally splashed over to Alice's car. He said, "How many of you are in the car?"

"Three," she said. "What's the matter, what's going on?"

"Just three," the cop said to another cop who had arrived on the passenger side and was peering in at Sicinski and Joe, who were peering out.

"We're supposed to watch for a car with four," the other cop said.

"So you're from Colorado," the first cop said to Alice. "Taking a vacation in the East?"

"Oh, yes," Alice said and smiled. "Our first time here. Nice vacation."

"Well, be careful and don't pick up anybody. There's some dangerous characters on the road tonight. Have a good night." Both state police stepped aside and Alice drove on.

Once they were back at full speed and the roadblock was growing small in the rear-view mirror Joe broke the silence with, "That had me shook up. Alice, you handled that real good, you were cool."

"Cool! Who's cool?" Alice yelled it so loud that Joe's and Sicinski's ears rang. "Look at me, how I'm shaking. Oh god. That cop didn't act belligerent, you know. That's such a relief. I can't take another stop like that, I mean, I'll freak out completely."

"I hope it's no worse than that when we get to the border," Sicinski said when his ears were back to normal.. "One thing about our Captain Dahlmann — "

"Yeah, I know. We couldn't'a busted up the Procida Society without him. But don't say he's ours, we don't want him, not after we saw how crazy he is today," Joe said, and Alice said, "Oh, no, oh, god,

Dahlmann killing that man and that woman, those horrible..."

Sicinski: "At least he took our side today. He made things right for us with the cops back there in Connecticut. We probably won't have any trouble crossing the border because of him."

I've been so wrong, so wrong, Franklin police captain Sven Dahlmann told himself as he drove up the interstate highway in the downpour, at 110 miles per hour, siren wailing, red Mars light blinking, while a Christian rock station blared on his car radio. I thought the Procida Society were the agents of the devil. And I thought Herman had sold his soul to them. Instead, all this time they were on God's side, opposing the real devils. Like the devils in that John Wilkes Booth Brotherhood. Like the sundido gang.

He stopped at the roadblock just long enough to show his badge to a state cop, then sped ahead. The real devils, he thought, were the ones who pretended to be my friends — Sicinski, Barbara, Joe Heatley. I've even known what sundidos are, so how could I ignore the danger until now? They're the ones who want to bring sundidos down on all of us. I've got to stop them, got to beat them to the border, or else they'll end pollution, end wars, end nations rising against nations, and who knows what else? If they succeed, that means these won't be the end times. There'll be no apocalypse, no armageddon. And then (and the very thought made a wave of fear pass through his body) I won't be raptured into heaven. No rapture! The urgency of that last thought led him to mash down even harder on the accelerator as he splashed past a gray hybrid car that was observing the speed limit, drenching it with water.

In the unchanging dark, in a downpour that seemed to increase in intensity every few miles, without scenery that they could see, the drive seemed to go on forever, uphill, downhill, long, exhausting, Alice at the wheel the whole time. Twice an hour the lead news on the car radio was about the manhunt for Joe Heatley and his gang of terrorists and how their capture was imminent.

Joe and Alice and Ted Sicinski discussed what they would say in a little while to the customs agents at the Canadian border. Although they were quiet, they weren't tired. Alertness, coiled energy was coursing through all three bodies and Joe was thinking, Barbara's plane must be landed and she must be on that long drive from the Chicago airport back to Franklin by now, I hope she's not too tired to drive. He'd hardly thought about Nora at all those last two days. Eventually Sicinski broke a spell of silence with, "At last. We're almost in Canada. It's going to be such a relief to not have to worry about the Procida Society and all those others chasing after Joe."

"Yeah," Joe said. "It's like the CIA is the only bunch who doesn't want a piece of us."

"I'm sure the reason the CIA isn't after me is, you know, only because it's illegal for them to operate on American soil," Alice pointed out.

Crouched behind a concrete barrier on the American side of the border with Canada, sweating in the rain under a heavy raincoat, CIA agent Morris said excitedly, "Here comes the Heatley gang, here they come. Blue car with three people inside. The very next car on the highway."

Crouched next to him CIA agent Benzelock, water running down his face, cell phone to his ear, gasped in horror: "Oh, no! That's not the Heatley gang. It's even worse. It's the FBI." He was the one who fired first.

It was about the middle of the sodden night by the time Alice and her passengers crossed the border. The downpour had made a pool of the roadway there too. On the American side shatters of gunfire (FBI, Dahlmann, state police) and grenades (CIA) and semi-automatic weapons (Procida Society, John Wilkes Booth Brotherhood) were exploding and echoing and making lightning bursts in the darkness. "Are you crazy?" asked a black-booted, yellow-raincoated Canadian customs officer as he checked the trio's passports. "You could've got yourselves killed, crossing like that. Didn't you see those smugglers're shooting at your police?"

"Smugglers? Is that what they are?" Alice said, and Sicinski said, "You mean drugs?" as they heard more furious volleys of firearms (CIA, Procidas). Some of it could have been mistaken for thunder, except for the accompanying screams of agony.

"That's right, drugs. They catch smugglers all the time over on your side. But it's never been anything like tonight," said the officer. "Those characters better not aim this way, or they'll get one hell of an international incident."

"What're these fuses?" said a second customs officer. He was inspecting Alice's car, pawing with wet hands through the backpacks on the back seat.

"They're sundidos," Sicinski said. "It's a new kind of solar-cell battery. It's going to make the internal combustion engine obsolete." Gunfire echoed in the background (FBI, state police, Dahlmann, Booths).

"Ha. It was obsolete long, long ago," the second customs guy remarked. "What do you plug them into?" Water dripped from his raincoat onto the car seat and packs.

"You plug them into fuse boxes, circuit breakers, and the ones that look like little converters, just plug them into fuse sockets," Joe said. "They disable outside lines and they make electricity for your whole building. They're gonna get sold in drugstores and supermarkets and hardwares before long. Those cube ones, see under there, the bigger ones, just plug in your appliances, TV, whatever, instead of a wall outlet. The long things're adapters, you can put them in your stove, use them instead of gas burners. We got some big ones in the trunk. They're car batteries, except they're solar-cell batteries — sundidos for short. These're all sundidos." As he said it there was a burst of weapons fire (Booths, Procidas, CIA).

"You've got it all figured out," the second customs officer said."All right, someday I'll buy some, then." More shooting, screams, yells in the background.

"Then you're here on business," the first customs guy said, handing the passports back to Alice. "What company are you with?"

"I'm working for me," she said. "So are they." When the customs men asked where they would stay, Joe gave the address of a friend of Mrs. Baugh's in Toronto.

A third customs officer, an unsmiling, motherly looking woman, was looking at some papers. "Just a minute," she said. "I want to make sure your batteries are allowed in Canada."

"You've got to be joking," the second customs officer said to her. To Alice he said, "They're going to love you guys in Ontario. They've got whole cities running on solar power there."

The third customs officer shook her head, folded her papers, looked disgustedly at her partners, said to Alice, "They're okay," and to her fellow officers, "Now check the trunk." All three of them went back to the car trunk. Joe thought, They're hunting for drugs. He and Alice and Sicinski said nothing while the pair searched the trunk and, across the border, the FBI, CIA, state police, Procida Society, Booth Brotherhood, and Captain Dahlmann fired at each other.

In a few minutes the customs officers were going back to their station. The second officer stopped at Alice's open window long enough to say, "Okay, we're done. You're sure lucky you didn't get caught up in all that gunfire. Enjoy your stay in Canada, folks"

"I'm sure we will," Alice said. As she drove her sundido-powered car north toward Montreal, leaving a wake in the water behind her, they saw more flashes from weapons-lightning, heard huge thunderclaps of firearms and more horrible screams of dying people, all on the American side. The din was topped by a huge explosion that lit the entire sky. About a mile from the border the state police drone had found a black Lincoln in a tavern parking lot. The drone had fired at the car, blowing up the tavern and the eleven innocent women and men who were inside.

Back in Franklin Herman Sorg was pleased with his successes. He had spent the day directing workers as they had dismantled his shop and his office. It was all going to be packed and moved to Texas. That's where Herman himself was moving, to be vice-president of Kemtrola Oil Company, in charge of the creation of energy from sunlight, a very important job, he believed, since he wasn't yet aware of his impending figurehead status. Best of all he was going to apply his creative talents to finding a way to reduce the preposterous population of our overburdened planet.

War? Famine? Plague? Herman decided that war and famine were too cruel and, in the uncivilized parts of the world, might cause repercussions against America. Then what plague could the Procida Society start that could be limited to the benighted Old World continents of Europe, Africa, and Asia? Wasn't starting a plague to kill billions of people an immoral act? No, for the alternative was a world so overpopulated that everyone, even Americans, would eventually starve or die of dehydration.

Still, a plague was so terribly cruel, too. After all, we enlightened ones have a responsibility to be compassionate toward the dumb human race whose inferior affairs we direct. Wasn't there some compassionate way to sterilize the ignorant populations of the other continents before they used up all the water and resources? The model of success was the chemical weed killer that had wiped out almost all of the frogs and toads in America.

Perhaps Herman could lead the Procida Society by inventing a sterilization epidemic. A sterilization virus that would only sterilize people with certain kinds of DNA? Or maybe a climate-specific sterilization virus, since overpopulation got worse in the hotter places on Earth? Why do those billions of fools, in impoverished parts of the world, like to copulate on such sweaty hot humid summer days anyway? Why, it's because they're so poor that mating is their only affordable entertainment, of course. Raising their standards of living might lead them to other interests but if they had more money then they would only use more of the earth's scarce resources. How about a topography-specific sterilization virus for coastal regions and plains, since the human population tended to be thicker there and thinner in mountains and deserts and rocky places?

Maybe the most compassionate way to handle the problem was to mass produce the gay bomb that the U.S. Air Force wanted to drop on the Iraq army during the first Iraq war. Then the Procida Society could drop it in places where only men congregate. The gay bomb consisted of a powerful aphrodisiac combined with female sex pheromones that men would breathe in or drink or otherwise ingest. The combination of aphrodisiac and pheromones would make them eager to have sex with each other instead of with women. As a result humans in sex-bombed places would not reproduce. What were other possibilities? The problem of ending the population explosion called for the finest thought and probably the most delicate planning. It was a problem worthy of him, he decided.